D0593648

EDGARTOWN
Free Public Library

A GREAT BOOK should leave you with many experiences, and slightly exhausted. You should live several lives while reading it.
— William Styron

Presented by

DISCARD

26 West Tisbury Road
Edgartown, Mass. 02539

ANYTHING
But OKAY

Also by Sarah Darer Littman

In Case You Missed It
Backlash
Want to Go Private?
Life, After
Purge

ANYTHING But OKAY

SARAH DARER LITTMAN

Scholastic Press / New York

Copyright © 2018 by Sarah Darer Littman

All rights reserved. Published by Scholastic Press, an imprint of Scholastic Inc., Publishers since 1920. SCHOLASTIC, SCHOLASTIC PRESS, and associated logos are trademarks and/or registered trademarks of Scholastic Inc.

The publisher does not have any control over and does not assume any responsibility for author or third-party websites or their content.

No part of this publication may be reproduced, stored in a retrieval system, or transmitted in any form or by any means, electronic, mechanical, photocopying, recording, or otherwise, without written permission of the publisher. For information regarding permission, write to Scholastic Inc., Attention: Permissions Department, 557 Broadway, New York, NY 10012.

This book is a work of fiction. Names, characters, places, and incidents are either the product of the author's imagination or are used fictitiously, and any resemblance to actual persons, living or dead, business establishments, events, or locales is entirely coincidental.

Library of Congress Control Number: 2018009413

ISBN 978-1-338-17748-0

10 9 8 7 6 5 4 3 2 1   18 19 20 21 22

Printed in the U.S.A.   23

First edition, October 2018

Book design by Nina Goffi

To Rob Jordan, aka "Robbie Rocker," CMSgt, USAF (retired),
who got me started asking questions and continues to inspire by
how he meets life with humor

CHAPTER ONE

"Life seems so much better in black-and-white."

I draw this conclusion as the end credits to *Casablanca* roll.

"I mean, even *war* looks better," I continue, picking through the remnants of the popcorn bowl. My favorites are the cracked but not fully popped kernels. "Not to mention so much more romantic."

"Romantic?" my best friend, Farida, says with one graceful eyebrow raised. I wish I could do that. "What's romantic about Rick and Ilsa not being together in the end? It's so sad. I mean, I'd rather it be like *Mockingjay*. You know, like it's not all rainbows and butterflies and happily ever after because they're both affected by the war they lived through, but they're *together* and they're finding whatever happiness they can."

It's true, the two main characters in the film who are sooooo in love go off in different directions at the end. I guess I can see the argument for that not being romantic. But still . . . I was definitely shipping Ilsa and Rick.

Farida got pretty into the movie, especially during the scene where the refugees in Rick's café started singing *La Marseillaise*, the French national anthem, as an act of resistance to drown out Nazi officers singing some German song. Farida's parents came to

America as refugees from Iraq after the Gulf War, or as we call it in my house, *the war where Mom and Dad met*, so I totally get why that's a powerful moment in the movie.

I have to admit to swallowing a lump in my throat once or twice. Even our other best friend Ken brushed his sleeve across his eyes, but he swore it was just allergies. It was all so brave and patriotic.

"Sure they're not together, but they'll *always have Paris!*" Ken says, quoting one of the most famous lines from the film and clutching his heart dramatically. I swear, Ken should be on stage. I tell him that all the time. He says he prefers to remain behind the scenes.

"But that's just memories," Farida says. "They're never going to see each other again."

"Yeah, well, Rick's going off to fight. He might die," I point out. "But at least now he's going to die knowing that she loved him, I guess."

"Die!" Farida exclaims. "Stella, come on. The ending was tragic enough. Do you have to make it worse by making me think about Rick *dying*?"

Ken gives me a *Why did you have to go there?* look and I reply with a *What?* look.

I feel bad, but in wartime, dying is always a possibility. I'm from a military family, so I know that all too well. My brother, Rob, left the marines for civilian life a month and a half ago after serving two tours in Afghanistan. During both of Rob's deployments, the fear of him not coming home was constantly at the back of my mind—and often front and center.

Now that he's home . . . well, I'm here with my friends trying really hard not to think about that. Thinking about Rob is a major downer these days.

"Sorry, Farida," I say. "But that's kind of what happens in war." I bite my lip, remembering about all the times I've freaked out about my brother dying.

"I know, Stella. But he's home now," she says, getting what I'm not saying. "You don't have to worry anymore."

That's what you think.

I don't tell anyone, even my best friends, that although my brother is back in our house physically, he's not back. Not really. At least, not the same brother he was before this last deployment. It was bad enough after the first deployment. He'd joined the combat club. My parents were already members. They both served in the Gulf War, Dad in the 3d Marines and Mom as a navy surgeon. That makes me the odd one out in the Walker family—the only one who hasn't served our country.

It's even worse now, though. This time he's so different from the brother who left it's like he was possessed by an alien from one of his favorite sci-fi movies while he was over there. But I came here to forget about that for a while, which I'm obviously not doing very well.

"Yeah," I say, shrugging. "So on a scale of one to ten, how do you rate *Casablanca* for the Keeping It Reel rankings?"

"I'm thinking a nine," Ken says. "It's got meme-worthy lines, great acting, and I'm officially in love with Ingrid Bergman, even though she died before I was born. Does that make me weird?"

"It's okay, we already know you're weird," I tell him. "It's part of your charm."

"Gee, thanks," Ken says, tossing a pillow at me. "You guys are the best."

I laugh and catch the pillow, then ask Farida, "So what's your rating?"

"I don't know," she says slowly. "I loved it for all the reasons Ken said but . . ." She fiddles with the corner of the pillow she's holding on her lap.

"But what?" Ken asks.

"Well, it's supposed to be Casablanca. In Morocco. Which is in North Africa," Farida says. "But everyone in the film is white—except for Sam, the piano player."

Ken gives me a quick glance from the corner of his eye.

I wonder if he noticed. I didn't. And that makes me feel like a bad friend.

"Well, it was filmed in Hollywood in 1942," Ken says. "I looked up all this stuff about it before we watched. You know the scene where they sang *La Marseillaise* and people were crying? A lot of the actors were actual refugees from Nazi Germany, so they weren't pretending to cry."

"Okay fine, but . . . are you telling me that they could only find one person of color in all of 1942 Hollywood?" Farida asks. "Just one?"

"Well yeah, that does seem kind of ridiculous when you think about it," I admit. "I feel terrible that I watched the whole movie without even noticing that."

"That's because white's your default," Farida says. "So it's not going to seem out of the ordinary for you the way it does for me."

I wonder how many other things are "default" for me, but Ken is still arguing the race issue.

"Yeah, but this movie was filmed before civil rights and all that," Ken says. "It's a film of its time. We have to judge it in its historical context."

"If you're telling me that its 'historical context'"—Farida does air quotes with her fingers—"means that it was whitewashed, then okay, fine."

"You're right," I say. "I guess I was too caught up in the story to notice. I'm sorry."

"It's not like I want to be your travel agent for an extended white guilt trip," Farida says, flopping back on the couch. "It *is* a great story. But . . . I can't turn off noticing when something's not the way it's supposed to be like you can. Just like I can't turn off having brown skin and dark hair and eyes."

"And like I was born wearing white girl goggles," I admit.

"Look, I get what you're saying," Ken says. "And I get that it's wrong. But what are we supposed to do about it?" He sounds annoyed and defensive. "This movie was made before we were born," he continues. "Before our parents were born. I'm not even sure if my *grandparents* were born yet."

I hope this doesn't turn into an argument, like it often does when Farida points out something to do with racism that the two of us have both completely missed.

If I'm honest, I have to confess that the first time it happened, I was pretty defensive, too. I took it personally, because I felt like my best friend was calling me a racist.

It was in fifth grade, before we started hanging out with Ken. We were having a sleepover at Farida's house and flipping through channels to see what was on TV. *Aladdin* the cartoon movie was on the Disney Channel.

"Oh, let's watch that!" I said.

"Ugh, no way," Farida said, skipping past it. "It's racist."

I stared at her, openmouthed. "What's racist about *Aladdin*?"

"Well, they sing about the Middle East: 'It's barbaric, but hey, it's home,'" Farida said. "How would you like if they sang that about America in a Disney movie?"

"That's different," I said without a second thought.

Farida stared at me, hurt evident in her brown eyes. "Different? How?" she asked me. "Do you think *I'm* barbaric? And my parents?"

"No, I—"

"What about Yusef? He's only seven but is *he* barbaric?"

I was taken aback by how angry and upset she was. I was too clueless to understand both what was wrong with *Aladdin* and why what I'd said was hurtful. I mean, I'm still clueless sometimes, obviously, but I'm trying to be better.

What I felt back then was defensive. Like my best friend suddenly thought I was a terrible person.

"Wait, so you think I'm horrible?"

"I didn't before," she said. "But right now you sound it."

I was so upset I almost called my parents to pick me up to take me home. It was Mrs. El-Rahim who talked us through it. She came in to bring us some baklava and saw that Farida and I were sitting on opposite sides of the room, not talking to each other and looking miserable. Mrs. El-Rahim helped me understand where Farida was coming from. She explained to me that Farida didn't bring up these things because she thought I was a horrible person, but so that I could understand her better. She was trying to help open my eyes to things that I might not notice because I'm from the dominant culture. It was *because* we were friends that Farida felt that she could talk to me about such difficult things, so we could be better friends, even closer.

Then Farida said how hurtful it was when I said, "That's different," and I started feeling defensive again, but Mrs. El-Rahim talked us both through that, too.

I'm not saying it's easy to have these conversations, or that my first reaction isn't always to be on the defensive and try to argue it like Ken is doing now.

Ken wants to work in TV or movies someday, and he's really into the history of film. He has an almost encyclopedic memory of old movies, which he supplements with rapid use of IMDb and Google to launch into the historical context defense whenever Farida makes any comment about lack of genuine representation.

It's true there's historical context. But one thing I've learned from being friends with Farida is that still doesn't make it any better.

Farida has gone silent. Ken and I might feel uncomfortable when we're called on having white as our default, but Farida has to live with that being the way things are in pretty much every movie she sees and every book she reads. And in her everyday life, which is way worse.

"I just want you to *notice*," she says finally, sitting up. "That's all. I'm not an idiot. I know you can't go back and change what's wrong with a classic movie—well, unless Dr. Who left the TARDIS in Argleton somewhere. But you *can* change whether you notice it or not. And you can recognize that Hollywood is still making the same mistakes today. For every Black Panther movie, there's, like, ten white Spider-Man movies."

There's an uncomfortable silence and I'm holding my breath, hoping that Ken doesn't keep trying to persuade her with "historical context" and just hears her.

"Oh," he says. "Fair enough."

I exhale a sigh of relief.

"And not just with movies," Farida adds.

"Got it," Ken says.

"And even . . ." Farida hesitates.

"And even what?" I ask.

"Well, like, being more aware of stuff that's happening at school. You don't seem to have noticed that there's more than the usual level of *we don't like brown people* crap going on since school started this year."

I glance over at Ken to see if he knows what Farida means, but he looks just as clueless as I feel. We've only been back at school for, like, a week. What could we have missed?

"Like . . . what?" he asks.

"Well, did you hear that yesterday, when Dev Iyer showed Isaac Taylor the schematic for his latest robotics project, Scooter Douglas reported him to the school resource officer for building a bomb?"

"What?" I exclaim. "That's ridiculous. Between Dev Iyer and Jenny Moss, our school has won practically every robotics prize going for the last two years!"

"You know that. I know that. Anyone who knows Dev or reads the school newspaper beyond the sports section knows that," Farida says. "But there are a lot of people at school who aren't in either category. Do you think Scooter would have reported Jenny Moss for building a bomb?"

"Not likely," Ken says. "And that's wrong."

"Knowing Scooter, he'd probably make some stupid crack about how girls aren't capable of building bombs," I say. "Or robots, for that matter. Even though he can't do either himself."

"Scooter ended up getting himself a two-day suspension," Farida says.

"Serves him right," I say.

"That's not all. Some of Chris Abbott's friends are taking his dad's anti-immigrant stuff to heart," Farida says. "Wade Boles and Jed Landon told Yonas Ambaye he should go back to his country the other day. Yonas said Chris was right there with them. He might not have said the actual words, but he didn't do anything to stop them."

Chris's dad is the mayor of our town, and Chris is my greatest rival at debate club. His dad is running for governor of our state on a campaign that appears to consist of telling us that the state's economy is a mess and he's the only one who can fix it, and that immigrants and refugees are to blame. Chris and I don't agree on very much. But Chris is smart, which is more than I can say for some of the guys he hangs around with.

"No way!" I exclaim.

"Yes way," she says. "Like, what, brown people can't be born in the US? Yonas was born here in Virginia."

"I haven't heard anything like that," Ken says.

Farida doesn't say anything, but her silence speaks volumes.

"Wait . . . is this another thing I'm not noticing?" he asks.

"Well, it's not like they're going to say any of that stuff *to you*," Farida says. "But if they say it in *front* of you, I hope you *will* notice."

"Of course I'd notice," Ken says. He sounds really offended.

"But will you *say* something?" Farida asks.

"Of course we will," I assure her. "You're our friend. We've got your back."

"Not just if it's me," she says. "If it's anyone."

"Well . . . yeah," he says slowly. "Anyone."

"Wrong is wrong," I say.

Farida leans back against the sofa cushions and smiles. "It's good to hear you say that," she says.

I keep thinking about Chris and his friends telling Yonas to go back to his country when his country is *this* country. Where do they get off? I want to talk to Mom and Dad about it when I get home, but as soon as I walk in the front door, I can tell something's wrong.

Clue #1: Our dog, Peggy, doesn't greet me like she usually would. Clue #2: Mom and Dad are sitting close together at the kitchen table, speaking in low, clipped voices.

The tension is suffocating. I want to turn and go back Farida's, but she's working a shift at her family's restaurant, Tigris, this evening. So I force myself to walk into the kitchen.

"Hey, I'm home," I say in a tentative bid for my parents' attention.

"Hi, Stella," Mom says. "Dinner will be ready at six thirty. Why don't you go do your homework?"

In other words, *get lost and let me finish talking to Dad.* I'm about to do what she tells me to, even though it's Saturday and my homework's done, when I notice Dad's icing his hand.

"What happened? Did you hurt yourself?"

Dad doesn't answer. If anything, his lips compress into an even thinner line, as if I'm some kind of enemy interrogator instead of his kid just wanting to know what's going on.

"Can someone tell me what's up?" I say. "Because it's pretty obvious something's not right around here."

The seconds of silence before Mom finally opens her mouth to speak feel like an eternity.

"Your brother has been having a difficult time since he got back," she says.

"Yeah. Tell me something I don't know."

"I really don't need snark on top of everything else right now, Stella," Mom snaps.

"Sorry," I mumble, but that's a lie. I'm annoyed, not sorry. "So what's his problem?"

"We don't know exactly," Mom says. "And until we can get him to admit he's got a problem, we're struggling to figure out how to get him the help he obviously needs."

"So you're telling me I just have to suffer until he figures it out?" I say.

"Stella, the world doesn't revolve around you," Dad says. "It's something we all have to learn sooner or later. You might as well learn right now."

My parents have no clue. They just don't.

"Dad, I already know that. In this family, the world revolves around Rob."

With that, I storm out of the room and head upstairs. I get better answers from stupid Siri than my parents these days.

Hey, Jason—

How's reentry to the real world treating you?

I know it's only been a few months, but it hasn't exactly been a breeze here in the land of Rob Walker.

My mom wanted to throw me a big welcome home party, and she got all hurt and upset when I said no. She's a Desert Storm vet herself, but she didn't seem to understand why I would rather get a filling without Novocain than be around a lot of people asking me what it was like over there. Even Dad didn't understand. I don't know, maybe their war was different? Dad came home an injured hero. He's got a Purple Heart and a huge ugly scar to show for his wartime service.

Sometimes I almost think I'd rather be in a firefight than back here having to make small talk about stupid crap—except for the part where one of my buddies doesn't make it.

Pretty messed up, huh?

When I was over there, all I could think about was being back here, and now that I'm back here . . . I feel like a Star Wars fan at a Star Trek convention.

Like I don't have any idea how to "Live long and prosper."

Yeah, I know. I can hear you laughing right now and saying "There's a reason we called you ThunderGeek, Rob. Emphasis on geek."

To top it all off I saw Sandra last week. Remember that girl I thought I was going to come back to? She was at church with her fiancé, Scott. Yeah, she's gonna marry the guy who stole her heart while I was over there dodging bullets and IEDs. Isn't that special?

Sandra told me I looked well and said she was happy I was back safely. No thanks to you, I was thinking the whole time, remembering how messed up I was the day I got her Dear John letter.

Scotty boy and I shook hands, and it was all very civilized 'cause we were at church, even though I wanted to punch him for taking away the imagined future that had helped keep me going.

Well, enough of me complaining. What have I got to complain about? I'm not still stuck in Walter Reed like Travis, learning how to walk again on prosthetic legs.

Or dead like Reyes.

Anyway, how are you doing?

Hope it's smoother sailing at your end.

ThunderGeek out.

CHAPTER TWO

It turns out I get a chance to test my courage sooner than I think. On Wednesday in AP Government, during our discussion of current affairs, Chris is doing exactly what Farida warned us he was doing.

"We need to restrict the flow of refugees," Chris is arguing. "They say they're just innocent people fleeing from a war zone, but how do we know?"

"We know because they have to go through a stringent vetting process," Farida says. "Trust me, I should know."

You'd think Chris might pick up on a few cues here. Not just that Farida knows because her parents were refugees from a war zone, but that what he's saying is hurtful to her.

Nope. He just carries on spouting his dad's verbal vomit, like a Mayor Abbott Mini-Me.

"But what if the bad apples slip through the cracks?" Chris asks. "We can't afford to take that risk."

I roll my eyes. I bet anything he literally took that straight from one of his dad's speeches.

I'm not at all scared to confront him on this, I realize. It's just like a debate, but this time it's not hypothetical. This time it matters more than just wanting to beat him. I'm annoyed because he's hurt my friend—and his dad is hurting so many other people by saying the same stuff in his campaign.

I raise my hand high so Mr. Walsh calls on me.

"Chris, I don't understand. Why aren't you worried about American bad apples?" I ask. "White dude terrorists have killed more people in this country than refugees."

"No, they haven't," Chris says. "That's just not true."

"If you look at the facts, you'll find it is," I tell him.

"Stella's right," comes a voice from two seats behind me. "The statistics back her up."

I turn around when I hear "Stella's right," and I'm surprised that it's Adam Swann. He's doesn't usually speak in class unless Mr. Walsh asks him a question. Adam's an outdoorsy type who wears lots of plaid shirts and hiking boots and either cargo shorts or jeans. Everyone says his dad is one of those doomsday preppers who thinks there's going to be a massive failure of systems and government, and he's taught Adam survivalist techniques so they can live off the grid. Rumor has it his dad stockpiles food, weapons, and ammo at their place in the woods on the outskirts of Argleton. Rumor also has it that his dad wasn't nearly as out there before Adam's mom died in a car crash on her way home from work when we were in fifth grade.

I smile at Adam for backing me up. He flushes and looks down at his desk.

"Instead of arguing, let's fact-check," Mr. Walsh says. He asks us for which search terms we think he should use, and then, once the results are projected on the board, he asks which links look like legitimate sources. Mr. Walsh is really big on what he calls media literacy. He says we need to use critical-thinking skills to evaluate the information that's out there in order to be good students—and just as important, informed citizens when we're old enough to vote.

Farida winks at me, because she knows I'm right.

After checking a few different websites, Mr. Walsh says, "It looks like the facts are on Ms. Walker's side, Mr. Abbott."

In debate, Chris sticks to the facts, but today he's ignoring them. I guess he doesn't want to go down without a fight, because he keeps arguing.

"Why should we put any American lives at risk?" he asks. "We need to put a pause on letting these people in."

My fingers clench the edge of the desk. Haven't American lives been put at risk for over a decade? Or do those not matter to Chris because they're military lives?

At least my brother came back alive. Thousands of soldiers didn't. And at least Rob has all his limbs, unlike his friend Travis, who had to have both his legs amputated above the knee when he stepped on an IED.

"So you're saying your life is worth more than saving the lives of my parents, just because they happened to be born in Iraq?" Farida asks.

"Yeah, what does it say on the Statue of Liberty again?" I add.

"'Give me your tired, your poor, your huddled masses yearning to breathe free,'" Adam calls out. I never really noticed before, because he's normally so quiet in class, but he's got a great voice, low and rumbling.

"All I'm saying is that those of us who were born in this country have a constitutional right to pursue life, liberty, and happiness without having to worry about being blown up by terrorists," Chris says.

Did Chris forget that once upon a time, the Abbott family came here from somewhere else, too?

But before I can say that, Mr. Walsh says, "Okay, folks, let's show some respect for one another, please. Everyone in my class-room is entitled to that. Just as we would like to see respectful dialogue around these issues in political discourse, but sadly, we all too often don't."

Farida raises her hand. "Mr. Walsh, it's hard to show respect and be civil when someone"—she glances briefly at Chris—"has been implying that you're a terrorist just because of your religion. When that *someone* is going around school telling people who are Americans but happen to have a different skin color to 'go back to your country.'"

The shock on Mr. Walsh's face would be hilarious if we weren't talking about something so messed up. When you're a little kid, teachers seem like they have eyes in the back of their heads, but now it's apparent that so much goes on within the walls of this school that passes below their radar.

"If that's true, I would hope the student to whom it was said would report it," he says. "It's against our Code of Conduct."

Mr. Walsh gives Chris a pointed look. "It's also not showing basic decency to your fellow students. If you haven't learned how to do that by the time you've graduated, then I don't care if you get into the best Ivy League college, you haven't learned the most important lesson in life."

He pauses to let that sink in. "Current events discussion time's over. Time to turn our focus back to the Constitution."

As Mr. Walsh starts going through the finer points of the Fourth Amendment, Debbie Charles, who sits behind me, taps me on the shoulder and hands me a note.

It's from Adam Swann.

If you let Abbott get to you, he wins, it says.

I know Adam's right, but it's hard not to let what he says get to me. How can it not? Chris and I are both Americans. So how did we end up with such different views of our country?

I ask my friends this at lunch, because I'm still so riled up.

"Seriously, I don't get it. It's like he's forgotten the history of the United States. We've always had waves of immigrants."

"I hate to break it to you, Stella, but you've forgotten the history, too," Ken says. "Remember, we've had people like Chris and his dad spreading the hate with every wave of immigrants. You've seen pictures in our history book of all those 'No Irish need apply' signs?"

"Yeah, and the Chinese Exclusion Act. Or what about what we did to Japanese Americans during World War Two?" Farida says. "George Takei was in an internment camp when he was a kid. And if America can put *Star Trek's* original Mr. Sulu in an internment camp, I might as well start packing my suitcase."

"It was before he was Mr. Sulu," Ken reminds her.

"Yeah, but that's not the point," I say. "You're right. I did forget that part. Which is really awful, because we're supposed to learn from history instead of repeating it."

"At least that's the theory," Ken says. "But when has it ever actually happened? Seems like we never manage to do that. We're always dumb enough to think, 'This time it'll all be different!'"

"Is it that or because first everyone has to *remember* the history?" Farida says. "All of it, including bad things like the Trail of Tears and slavery and the Jim Crow laws. Not just the good parts."

She's right. Maybe it's not just that I've forgotten history. Maybe it's also what parts of history we're taught. And maybe it's because I still want to believe in the ideal America, and it turns out the reality of my country is much more complicated.

"Hey, Stella," Haley Morani says, stopping by our table. "Are you going to debate later?"

"Of course. Like I would miss the chance to debate 'This House believes reality television does more harm than good.'"

She laughs. "Can't wait to see you and Chris face off on that one." Her smile fades. "By the way . . . is Rob okay? I saw him at the convenience store last week and . . ."

She hesitates, and I'm afraid of what's coming.

"And?" I ask.

"Jed Landon and Mike Carlson were messing around by the cooler and one of them slammed the door," Haley explains. "I was in the same aisle as Rob and he just hit the floor. At first I was afraid he'd fainted, but he got up. And when I asked if he was okay, he acted like we'd never met and walked straight out the door."

Haley and I have known each other since kindergarten. Her family goes to our church. Rob definitely knows her.

Another drop in the my-brother's-been-behaving-strangely bucket.

Do my parents know about this? I doubt Rob told them. He's not exactly being Mr. Talkative at the moment.

"I'm sorry he was rude," I tell Hayley, wondering how long I'm going to have to keep apologizing for my brother's behavior.

"That's okay." Haley shrugs. "It was just kind of weird."

She leaves and Farida asks, "What's all that about? Is Rob okay?"

There's so much about Rob that's weird at the moment. But I'm not ready to share any of it with my friends. Not yet. Not until I have some kind of clue about what's going on myself.

"Yeah. He's fine," I lie. Desperate to change the subject, I ask, "So what movie should we review next? *Gaslight* or *The Birds*?"

As I predicted, Farida and Ken disagree, so they're distracted from what Haley said about Rob.

I couldn't understand why Rob decided to enlist right out of high school, even though we come from a military family. I just didn't get why he would sign up voluntarily when there was a war going on.

"I want to make a difference," he said. "And I can get a full ride for college."

"But you have to come back first," I pointed out.

"Stella!" Mom exclaimed, giving me a horrified look and then picking up the salt, spilling some in her hand, and throwing it over her shoulder.

Dad laughed. "My wife, a woman of science, believes in silly superstitions."

Mom looked sheepish, but she was completely unapologetic. "When it comes to protecting my family, I cover all the bases."

It worked, I guess. Between his military training, the prayers, and the salt, Rob came back to us.

At least on the outside. On the inside, I'm not so sure.

"Did you hear who is running for class president?" Farida asks before school the following week.

"Who?" Haley asks.

"Imagine the worst possibility," Farida says as she opens her locker.

"Scooter Douglas?"

"Okay, maybe not that bad, but close," she says.

From the worried look on her face, that can only mean one person.

"Chris?" I ask, tugging on the string of my gray-and-white-striped hoodie.

She nods and tosses some books in her locker before grabbing different ones. "I heard him telling Mike Carlson in the hall. Ugh. I can't stand the thought of him being class president."

Chris can be annoying, but it's just class president. It's basically a popularity contest for people who want something impressive on their college applications.

"Like, I get that Chris can be a jerk sometimes, but it's not the end of the world." Haley says what I'm thinking. "It's not like the class president has any real power. All they do is plan dances and fund raise and stuff."

"That's not true," Farida says. "They get asked by the local paper to speak on behalf of students about issues that happen here at school. Do you want Chris to be the one who speaks for us?"

It's a good point since reporters from the local paper interview the presidents of each class to get the "student opinion," as if the person who wins the popularity contest for class government really represents the opinion of everyone in the entire school.

"No one else is running?" I ask.

"Amy Sarducci is, but her campaign is a complete joke," Farida says, slamming her locker shut. "Her platform consists of campaigning for softer toilet paper and ice cream at lunch on Fridays."

"Like *that's* ever going to happen when the school board barely even funds new books for the library," Haley says. "Mrs. Conway told me she goes to tag sales on weekends, buying books with her own money so there are things we actually want to read."

"Mr. Kostek had to set up a DonorsChoose to get math supplies like protractors and meter sticks," Farida adds.

"I don't know—Amy will probably win with her ice cream slash soft toilet paper platform, even though it has zero chance of ever happening," Haley points out.

"Yeah, she's pretty popular across a wide range of friend groups," I say.

"So is Chris," Farida says.

"True," I agree. "But why don't you run?"

"I wanted to," she says. "But I'm not."

"Why not?" I ask. "You'd be awesome."

"I talked it over with my parents. They're worried about me doing it with everything that's going on. You know, with Mayor Abbott and all of the hateful stuff he's saying."

"But that's out in the real world," Haley says. "We're talking high school elections."

Farida gives her some serious side-eye. "Haley, for some of us, Argleton High *is* the real world," she says. "We can't separate the two like you can."

"But . . . that seems like all the more reason that you *should* run," I tell Farida. "People need to hear that."

"Can you imagine how it would be for me to run against Chris right now?" she says. "While his dad is on TV and the radio and in the newspapers and on social media every single day talking about the danger to America from people who look just like me?" She shakes her head slowly. "My parents are worried about me being subjected to too much . . . *unpleasantness* is the word they used. Or that it might make people boycott Tigris."

"I get their concern, I really do," I say. "But isn't that just letting them win?"

"My parents said they have two kids to look after," Farida says. "One of them is me. And that's why they said that while they are really proud of me for wanting to run, right now I have to do what's best for the entire family."

"Doesn't that make you angry?" I ask her. "It seems so unfair."

She fiddles with the end of her backpack strap. "Angry? Yeah. They said I can run next year for senior class president 'if Mayor Abbott loses, because hopefully the atmosphere will be less *fraught*.'"

Farida looks at Haley and then at me.

"Can't one of you run?"

Haley laughs. "I'd love to help, but running for class president isn't my thing. Not at all." She and Farida both look at me, then Haley says, "Now, Stella—it's got her name written all over it."

I'm reading the poster for the Future Business Leaders of America Club even though I have no intention of joining. Anything to avoid eye contact with Farida, because while I want to be a good friend, I don't think I want to run for class president.

"Stella, you know how to debate Chris and win," Farida says, and I'm forced to stop pretending and meet her gaze. "You could beat him."

"If people voted because of logic and persuasive arguments, maybe," I admit. "I beat him about sixty-five percent of the time in debates. But this is a class election. I'm not going to beat him because I've backed up my arguments with facts."

"No one is going to beat him unless someone runs," Farida points out.

She's right. I don't want Chris to be president, and someone should definitely run. I just don't know if that someone has to be me. But I don't have the courage to look her in the eye and say no right at this very minute.

"I'll think about it" is what I say instead.

Luckily for me, that seems to make Farida happy for now, and I ask her about Lucy and the Legends, this new band she's really into. Hopefully, someone else will step up before I have to tell her that there's enough going on at home right now without running for office, too.

I'd planned to talk to my parents about whether I should run for class president tonight, but as usual, whenever I need to talk to them they're too busy dealing with the latest drama involving Rob. He's started taking a few classes at the local community college. The idea is that he'll start there and then transfer to a state university after his sophomore year, once he's back in the school routine. It's also cheaper that way.

I didn't realize that it's also because my parents are worried about him living on his own until I overhear them talking when I come downstairs to ask their advice. I sit on the bottom step outside the door, eavesdropping as Mom tells Dad that she thought she'd be able to stop worrying about him getting hurt once he got back, but now she's just exchanged it for a different kind of worry.

I rest my chin on my knees and study the chipping lavender nail polish on my toes. Dad tells her that everything will turn out okay in the end. After all, it did for him, and pretty much all the guys down at the American Legion, which is where a lot of the local veterans hang out.

"In the end," Mom says. "But what about Frank? He put Angelica and the kids through some rough years after Vietnam before it turned out okay. And . . . what about your father?"

Frank Meyers is a friend of Dad's from the Argleton Legion post. My paternal grandfather, who also fought in Vietnam, died of non-Hodgkin lymphoma when I was little. I don't remember that much about him other than him being really sick, so I'm not sure what Mom means.

"Vietnam was different," Dad says. "Those vets had a hard time when they got back. They didn't get much of a welcome. In fact, a lot of people were downright hostile."

"I know but—"

"Besides, Frank told me he'd grown to question the war himself. He got tired of watching so many good men die when there didn't seem be any overall strategy. It messed him up."

"Bill, kids are coming back from *this* war devastated, too. Haven't you been paying attention?"

"Of course I have, Val. I had to fight Rob to confiscate his sidearm the other day," Dad said. "I'm glad it's in the gun safe, and I changed the combination. But we still don't know exactly what's going on with Rob."

I guess that explains Dad icing his hand on Saturday when I came home from Farida's house. I'd never know anything about what's going on in this family if I didn't sleuth it out myself.

"Perhaps you forgot that I'm a doctor, dear?" Mom says. Usually, when she says *dear* it's a term of affection, but it doesn't sound much like one right now.

"No, darlin'," Dad says in a soothing voice, clearly getting the message. "But you're not a psychiatrist. And besides that, he's your son."

Or maybe my dad's not getting the message. *Oh, Dad . . .* I cringe from my listening post beyond the doorway.

"I'm aware of that, Bill. I was there when he was born."

I stand up, thinking maybe it's time to head upstairs, because it sounds like my parents, who rarely fight, are about to have a doozy.

But Dad's back to smoothing things over. "What I mean is, it's hard for a doctor to treat their own child."

"Bill, if anyone knows a child, it's his mother. And I'm telling you, our son needs help, and he needs it soon. He's too proud to ask for it, because he's afraid you'll think he's weak. That he can't hack it the way you did."

"I would never think that. I'm so proud of that boy and it's breaking my heart to see him suffer this way," Dad says. "But can't you understand why he wouldn't want that on his record? Like it or not, there's still a stigma about going to see a shrink. It could come back to bite him later in life."

"So it's more important to keep mental health treatment off his record than to go get treatment so he doesn't kill himself?" Mom's voice is rising and the anxiety that this conversation causes has made me not want to talk to my parents anyway, and I tiptoe back upstairs. Luckily, I hear music coming out of Rob's room, so I don't have to worry about him overhearing the discussion downstairs. I won't bother telling him to turn it down so I can get to sleep, because I know sleep won't be coming easy for me tonight.

My brother is shutting everyone out, my dad was worried enough to take away his gun, and my mom knows that isn't the only answer to keeping Rob safe.

But nobody in my family has bothered to actually talk to me about any of this. I just have to live with the symptoms and piece it together by luck or accident, with whatever information I can get.

I lie in bed, staring into the darkness that's broken only by the glow of my devices. As I turn toward the wall, trying to find a magical sleep-inducing position, I can't help thinking Mom's right about one thing—what's the point of having a clean medical record if you're dead?

Hey, ThunderGeek—

You heard me all right, Rob. Thanks for the laugh. I needed it.

Not exactly smooth sailing here, either.

Speaking of seeing ex-girlfriends, I saw mine. You know, Kayla, who sent me my Dear John letter while we were over there?

She just got married.

Didn't waste any time moving on, huh?

Me, I'm stuck. Can't sleep. Afraid to close my eyes because I keep dreaming about what happened with Reyes. Sometimes I see it happening again in slow motion, and I'm trying to stop it, and I wake myself up because I'm shouting.

Other times, I see him as he was after it happened, but he talks to me and asks me why I didn't stop it.

"If you weren't so busy whining about that stupid letter from your stupid girlfriend who dumped your stupid butt," he tells me, "maybe I'd still be alive instead of being a stupid ghost in your stupid dreams."

If it were me, I'd be swearing, but Reyes was a good church-going boy. He never did like how much we all cursed, did he? Was in the wrong squad if he wanted clean talking. Poor guy was in the wrong war.

I hope all that praying and church going means he's somewhere better now, 'cause it sure didn't stop him from getting killed.

Stupid guy. Wish he'd stop haunting this messed-up marine.

As if that's not enough, my family is on my case all the time.

"Are you okay, Jason?"

"Eating enough, Jason?"

"Drinking too much, Jason?"

Nag, nag, nag, all the freaking time.

Tried ignoring their calls and texts.

Yeah, good luck with that.

My sister showed up pounding on my door at six in the morning because Mom was convinced I'd died. She said the next time Mom's going to call the police. I said if she calls the police, I'm never going to talk to either of them again.

She called me something that would have made Reyes blush and told me I was going to give Mom a heart attack from worry.

It's like she could handle the idea of me in Afghanistan better than she can handle the real me being home.

Not that I blame her.

Hey, <u>Blackhawk Down</u> is on—gonna go watch it.

Keep dodging them bullets, bro.

Roadrunner out.

CHAPTER THREE

Since my parents are too busy dealing with my brother and whatever he brought back with him, I decide to ask Mr. Walsh his advice about the class president thing. Pros: He's not just my AP Gov teacher, he's also my debate coach. Cons: He's Chris's teacher and coach, too. But despite that, I feel like I can trust him to give me an honest opinion, and right now that's what I need.

As soon as I get to school, I go to his classroom, even though I know he's usually tied up doing prep work for the day. But Farida's going to ask me for a decision when I see her, and I need to talk it through with someone who knows a thing or two before I make it.

Mr. Walsh is at his desk with a big travel mug of coffee, getting ready for class.

"Morning, Stella," he says, looking up from his work. "What can I do for you?"

"Hi. Um . . . I know you're busy and this probably isn't a good time, but can I run something by you?"

"Shoot," he says, and then takes a sip of coffee.

"Farida thinks I should run for class president," I tell him. "And . . . I'm not sure if I should do it."

"Okay," he says, leaning back in his chair. "So . . . what are some of the factors in your thinking either for or against?"

"Well, mostly I've thought of the reasons against," I admit. "And those are things like that I'm probably going to lose because I'm not nearly as popular as Chris or Amy. Class elections aren't about the best candidate, really, are they?"

"I'm not going to lie and say popularity has nothing to do with it," Mr. Walsh says, rubbing his chin. "But it's not everything. Running a good campaign could potentially overcome any perceived popularity deficit."

"Except I don't know the first thing about running a campaign, so I'm not going to be any good at it," I say.

"How can you know if you'll be any good if you don't even try running?" Mr. Walsh asks.

I don't really have a good answer for that, so I move on to the other major reason not to run.

"To be honest, Mr. Walsh, there's something else. Something I haven't even told my best friends. It's . . . about my brother, Rob."

"Oh? How is Rob? He went into the marines, yes? Was in Afghanistan?"

I nod. "Two tours. It wasn't so bad after the first one, but since he's come back this time . . . well . . . things can get . . . stressful at home."

"When you say *stressful*, do you ever feel like you're in danger?" he asks.

The question takes me by surprise.

"Danger? Why would I be . . ." Then I realize he's worried my brother might go all crazy on us and remember that teachers have a responsibility to report a student at risk of being hurt at home to child protection agencies. "Oh, no, nothing like that!" I assure him. "It's more . . . he's just not himself. He used to be funny. Totally geeky, but he was hilarious. He was in your class, do you remember?"

"Oh, I remember," Mr. Walsh says. "Quite the wit, your brother."

"But he's not like that anymore," I say. "He's moody. Angry. Unpredictable. Like I never know when I open the door after school what version of my brother I'm going to get."

"Being in combat can do that to a person," Mr. Walsh says. "My father fought in Vietnam. It— Well, let's just say things weren't always so easy around our house growing up."

I wonder how bad things were, and there's so much I want to ask him, but a quick glance at the clock tells me there's not much time before the bell rings and I still haven't made a decision.

"So you understand there's a lot to deal with at home, then. That's one of the main reasons I'm not sure if I should run."

Mr. Walsh leans forward and looks at me intently.

"Stella, the decision to run is one only you can make. But I just want to give you two things to consider, okay?"

I nod.

"The first is that one of the main reasons I turned into such a political junkie was because of what happened to my dad. I wanted to understand the decisions that sent him to Vietnam and the climate that led to him facing protests when he got back instead of being thanked for doing his duty. My dad, and so many like him, fought because they were drafted."

"Okay . . . I can understand that," I say, although I'm not entirely sure what it has to do with my dilemma.

"The second thing is a question I'd like you to ask yourself: What's the point of being the ace debater on our team if you're not willing to put any of those great skills into practice?" he says.

The pride I feel when he calls me the team's ace debater is quickly followed by the realization that while he's not coming out directly and telling me to do it, Mr. Walsh thinks I should run against Chris and Amy for class president.

"I'll think about that," I tell him. "Well, I better get to class. Thanks for the advice."

"Anytime," he says, going back to his papers.

I wait to tell Farida about my decision as we walk into AP Gov. "I knew you wouldn't let me down!" she says, putting her arm around me and giving me a quick hug.

"So you really think you can beat me?" says Chris from behind us. I turn and he's flipping his hair back with his hand in that annoying way he does.

I don't, but if he thinks I'm going to admit that, he's dreaming.

"Eavesdrop much?" I say. "But why shouldn't I be able to beat you?"

He doesn't bother to answer.

He just laughs.

In my face.

I try to play it nonchalant, but the fact that I feel my cheeks warming as I sit down at my desk means Chris must be able to see that telltale flush of anger.

"Of course she can beat you."

Adam Swann, who heard this as he's walking to his desk, sounds way more confident about the probability of my victory than I feel. I flash him a grateful smile.

Chris looks from me to Adam. "Since when have you two been dating?" he asks.

Seriously?

"What makes you think this is about dating?" I say.

"I just happen to think Stella will be a better candidate than you are," Adam says.

"No doubt about *that*," Farida agrees.

"O-kay. Sure." Chris smirks and then turns his back and sits down at his desk.

As I mouth, "Thanks," at Adam, I can't help noticing that his cheeks are starting to flush. Or that when they do, it makes his hazel eyes stand out even more.

But Chris is still so wrong.

Farida noticed our exchange, though, and she calls me on it when I'm talking about the election with my friends at lunch.

"So what's up with you and Mountain Man?" she asks.

"Mountain Man? What are you talking about?"

"Adam Swann. There was some interesting blushing going on there."

"What?" I protest. "No!"

If she raises that one perfect eyebrow any more, it'll disappear into her hairline.

"Are you quite sure about that?"

Ugh. I can feel myself blushing again, which probably just confirms her suspicions. Why does my face always have to give me away like this?

"Yes . . . sure I'm sure," I say. "I mean, I guess he *is* kind of cute, but that's it. End of story."

"Ladies, can we focus?" Ken complains. "We have an election to win."

"I'm totally focused," I say, glad to change the subject. "Laser-sharp focus."

"You're going to need a campaign manager," Ken says. "So I'm pleased to offer you my services. I'm can edit a mean video and I'm great at research. Who knows what dirt I'll be able to dig up on your opponents."

"Dirt? What?"

Farida stills. "Wait—I thought *I* was going to be your campaign manager!"

Awesome. I only decided to run this morning and I already have conflict in my campaign.

"Don't worry," Haley says, seeing the look on my face. "I don't want to be campaign manager."

I burst out laughing at that. "I didn't even know I *needed* a campaign manager to run for class president, that's how clueless about this I am," I say.

"That's why you need one," Ken says.

I look from Farida—without her I wouldn't be running in the first place—to Ken, who seems to know a little about this election business and does have great research skills, it's true.

"What would you guys think about being co-campaign managers?" I hold my breath as my friends eye each other's reaction.

"It could work," Ken says.

"It could," Farida agrees.

"So . . . ?" I ask. "What's the verdict?"

Farida smiles and sticks out her fist. "Let's do it!"

Kenny bumps it. "Here's to co-managing the winning campaign," he says.

I wish I shared that confidence, but I'm glad to change the subject.

"So I guess it's time to brainstorm actual campaign ideas."

"What about a kindness campaign?" Farida says. "Respecting others. We could make that part of your platform and then even do things as part of the campaign."

"I like that," I say. "We could stick Post-its on people's lockers with compliments."

"As long as people don't think you're just sucking up to them to get their vote," Hayley says.

"That's what you'd think if you got a compliment on your locker?" I ask, worried.

"Maybe," she says. "If I knew it was from someone who was running for class president."

"You're so cynical," Farida sighs. "But fair point. Okay, the election is on October sixteenth," she says. "We need to come up with a good slogan so we can make campaign posters."

"That's right," Ken says. "We want to get those up quickly. Get your name out there."

What everyone isn't saying is: *Because you aren't as popular as Chris and Amy.*

"How about something like *Vote Stella: Because She Cares*?" I suggest.

My idea is met with a resounding *meh*.

"Maybe *Stella Walker: The Responsible Choice*," Farida says.

"That makes me sound boring," I say. "Especially compared to free ice cream."

"How about *We All Win with Walker*?" Ken suggests.

"Better," Farida says. "Inclusive."

"I like the alliteration," I say.

"Ugh, this is an election, not English class," Haley says. "What about *Stella Walker: The Smart Solution*? I mean, the whole point is that you're smart and can do the job well instead of making stupid promises that are never going to happen, right?"

There's a few seconds of stunned silence as Ken looks at me and I look at Farida and then we all look at Hayley.

"That's a great idea," Ken says.

"You don't have to sound so surprised," she says. "I have them, too."

"It's perfect, Haley," I say, trying to smooth things over. "It's says what we want to say, and it has alliteration."

"Why are you so obsessed with that?" she asks.

"Because it's catchy," I tell her. "I always remember alliterative things more."

"As long as it's not just because you're being a word nerd," Haley says. "Because that's not going to win you any elections at *this* school."

Is it nerdy or just being observant? Whatever.

"Okay, so now we've got the slogan. What's next, campaign managers?"

"We'll start making posters," Farida says. "You need to start working on your platform."

"Yeah," Ken says. "You need some good ideas."

Ken's right. I need some really good ideas if I'm going to win this election. But to do that I need to figure out what I stand for beyond just a catchy campaign slogan.

ROB: Hey, Roadrunner. Checking in. Worried after getting your email. You okay?

JASON: Define okay.

ROB: Eating? Sleeping? Not going to do anything stupid?

JASON: Heh. You know me. I'm always doing stupid.

ROB: LOL, true. Seriously though.

JASON: Seriously? Don't know. Can't sleep. Still seeing Reyes when I try.

ROB: It's not your fault.

JASON: Last night we were in a firefight and I shot Reyes instead of the enemy.

JASON: And then we were trying to save him, and we took off his helmet, and it was me.

ROB: Wow. That's messed up. No wonder you can't sleep.

JASON: TBH, it makes more sense than anything when I'm awake. I don't know who the enemy is anymore.

JASON: Most of the time, I think it's me.

ROB: Dude. You need to get help. Now. Go to the ER. Do not pass go. Do not collect $200. Just go there now. Do it. Please?

JASON: I don't know.

ROB: I do. Trust me. Go now. Your family loves you. Heck, even I love you. Just go to the ER, okay?

JASON: Heh.

ROB: Go. NOW.

JASON: Yeah, okay.

ROB: I'm gonna check in on you tomorrow, okay?

JASON: Okay. Thanks, bro.

ROB: Hey, Roadrunner, me again. Checking in.

ROB: Jay, you okay?

ROB: Jason, call me.

ROB: Come on, Jay.

ROB: Don't do this to me, bro.

ROB: DON'T MAKE ME CALL YOU, dude.

ROB: CALLING NOW, YOU BETTER PICK UP.

CHAPTER FOUR

Coming home after school used to be fun. On the days when I didn't have debate and Farida didn't have to work at Tigris, my friends would come with and we'd do homework together and watch old movies. I don't invite them here anymore, because I'd rather be somewhere else. Anywhere else.

Before, when my parents got home, they'd pay attention to me. We talked about things. School, movies, the latest news, funny jokes. I mean, it's not like it was rainbows and unicorns all the time, and there was always the underlying worry about Rob being in Afghanistan, but compared to now, those days seem like nirvana.

I feel guilty for even thinking that, because the only reason I can think of those days as so great is because Rob came home. I wouldn't want my life to have stayed easy because he didn't.

But now he's back, and he's changed, and so has home. These days, I start feeling butterflies in my stomach as soon as I get off the bus. The anxiety intensifies the closer I get to our front door. By the time I turn the key in the lock to let myself in, I'm waiting for it to hit me—that suffocating tension that's been a permanent resident ever since Rob got back.

I open the front door. Peggy usually greets me, tail wagging and ready to lick. Today the front hall is empty and strangely silent. I figure maybe Rob's napping with his door shut.

I head to the kitchen to make myself a snack before I get started on my homework. I've just taken a yogurt out of the fridge when I hear a crash from upstairs, and Peggy starts barking, high-pitched and stressed. I take the stairs two at a time, hearing more crashes as I do.

"Rob!" I shout. "Are you okay?"

It's a stupid question, because I know my brother is anything *but* okay.

He doesn't answer, but I hear him cursing and there's another loud noise, this time of breaking glass.

I wish my parents were home. I wish Farida hadn't had to work this afternoon. I wish I'd gone over to Ken's house. I wish I had debate today. Anything so I didn't have to deal with this.

Because I have no idea what to do.

I send a quick text to my parents: Rob's gone off the deep end, come home now!

Then, bunching my trembling fingers into a fist, I knock on my brother's door.

"Rob, it's Stella. Can I come in?"

He doesn't answer, but there's no more crashing and smashing. Just the sound of him breathing heavily inside his room. Then I hear Peggy whining and scratching on the other side of the door.

"Rob, open the door, please! Peggy's upset. I need to see you're okay."

Peggy barks, three short, high-pitched barks.

"Ro-ob!" My voice cracks. I'm spiraling into full-on panic mode now.

And then I hear his voice, barely. "It's unlocked."

I turn the handle, my mouth dry, and open the door slowly, trying not to make any sudden movements.

Rob is standing near the broken window, blood streaming from his fisted hand. Shards of glass litter the floor. He's punched a hole through the plaster in the wall, too, and toppled his bookshelf over onto his bed. Luckily, it hasn't broken the frame, but there are books all over the bed and the floor, and the mattress is sagging under the weight. The room looks like it's been hit by a tornado, except the tornado is my brother and whatever tipped him over the edge.

Rob looks in my direction, but I don't even think he sees me. He's got that far-off look like Peggy gets when a thunderstorm hits and she can't settle and she paces around like she wants to crawl out of her own skin.

Slowly, quietly, I bend down and pick up a T-shirt from off the floor. It's not clean, but it's better than nothing for cleaning his hand until he calms down.

"It looks like you cut your hand. Can you show me?" I ask in a voice that is deceptively calm.

He holds it out in front of him, watching as blood drips onto the floorboards.

Doesn't it hurt?

Why is he so still? Why are his eyes vacant? What's wrong with him?

"So, uh, what happened?" I ask, but he doesn't answer.

He just keeps watching the blood as it drips.

Peggy has been sitting at his feet, staring up at him, but she starts licking the blood that's pooling on the floor.

"Ugh! Stop that, you gross dog," I shout, forgetting to be calm and soothing. "Stop!"

Rob doesn't care about me wanting to help him with his bleed-ing hand, but he *does* care about me shouting at the dog. He drops to his knees and puts his arms around Peggy's neck, apparently unconcerned that she's still being Dracula Dog with his blood.

"It's her instinct. Don't shout at the poor girl."

"Okay, *okay*—sorry, Peggy," I say, wondering why my brother cares more about the dog's feelings than mine. "But can I look at your hand, Rob?"

He buries his face in Peg's neck and sticks his bleeding hand in my direction.

It's a mess.

"Maybe we should go to the hospital," I suggest.

"No." Even muffled by Peg's fur, his response is clear.

I curse my brother's pigheadedness and wrap the T-shirt of dubious cleanliness around his hand as a temporary measure.

"I'm going to try to find the first aid kit," I tell him. "Stay here, and don't destroy anything else, okay?"

Rob lifts his head and looks at me—actually looks at me with the faintest hint of a smile.

"I'll try to restrain myself," he says.

I survey the wreckage of his room. I figure it can't get much worse, so I head to the kitchen to find the first aid kit.

When I'm down there, I text Mom and Dad again.

ME: Rob's had a total freak-out in his room. He broke his window and punched a hole through the wall.

ME: But he seems to have calmed down now. I think.

ME: WHAT IS THE MATTER WITH HIM?

MOM: OMG, is he okay? Are you okay?

ME: His hand is bleeding. I think there might be some glass fragments in it. I don't know if he needs stitches, but he's refusing to go to the ER.

MOM: Send me a picture. The first aid kit is in the cupboard above the microwave.

DAD: What set him off?

ME: How am I supposed to know?!???

When I get back to Rob's room with the first aid kit, my brother is sitting on the floor, Peggy curled up next to him with her head in his lap. He's stroking her fur and staring down at the blood-stained T-shirt wrapped around his hand.

I kneel down next to him.

"I'm going to take this off and check for glass fragments," I tell him.

"Knock yourself out," he says.

Rob destroyed his room, scared us all half to death, and all he says is "Knock yourself out" like it's no biggie? Seriously?

I unwrap the T-shirt, look at the mess he's made of his hand, then take my phone and snap a picture, which I immediately start to text to Mom.

Rob grabs my phone away with his uninjured hand.

"Are you posting this on Instagram or Snapchatting it to your friends? That's so messed up, Stella!"

I'm messed up? I look around his disaster of a room. "Believe it or not, not everything's about you, Rob," I say, even though in our house, it seems like everything is. "I'm texting the picture to Mom so she can decide if you need to go to the emergency room."

"Great," he says. "Why did you have to call her? I already said I'm not going. I'm an adult. I make my own medical decisions."

"You just trashed your room. You're not about to win any awards for adulting here."

Rob's shoulders slump and he lowers his head. Peggy lifts her head from his lap and sits up, looking from him to me with anxious brown eyes, upset by the weirdness between us.

"Of course I had to tell Mom and Dad what was going on," I continue. "Now, give me my phone back so I can finish texting Mom the picture."

I hold out my hand and wait.

He puts the phone in my hand without saying another word.

I type a quick text to Mom and press SEND.

Then I grab Rob's hand and pick up the tweezers.

"You put your hand through the window. You punched a hole in the wall. What's going on, Rob?"

He won't look me in the eye. With a frustrated sigh, I look over his hand, and, spotting a tiny sliver of glass, I start trying to grab it with the tweezers.

"He checked out," Rob finally manages as I pull the fragment from his skin and drop it into the garbage can.

At first I think he's talking about someone checking out of a hotel and I wonder why that would make him Hulk out on his room.

"Who checked out?" I ask, pouring hydrogen peroxide onto a gauze pad and trying to dab some of the blood away so I can see if there's any more glass.

"Jason."

I freeze, his hand still in mine. "Jason from your squad?"

Rob nods his head.

"Wait . . . when you say *checked out*, do you mean . . ."

I'm afraid to even say the word.

"He's gone. He killed himself last night."

I can't get my mind around it. I never met Jason, except through my brother's stories, but I feel like I know him.

"Oh, Rob . . ."

I lean over and hug him. He's unyielding at first, as if he's afraid to show anything that could be interpreted as weakness. But it's too late. His physical strength has already left signs of that all over his room.

Still, at least now my brother's behavior is more understandable. It doesn't make it right, but at least I kind of get where it's coming from.

"I knew he was having a tough time since he separated from the marines, so I was checking in with him," Rob says, his voice barely above a whisper. "He's been sounding more and more down. I could tell . . . he was turning on himself. And then today . . ."

His Adam's apple rises and falls visibly.

"Today he didn't answer back. I kept texting, hoping maybe he didn't have cell service. Figured maybe he'd decided to go on a hike to clear his head or something. But then, when he still didn't respond, I called." My brother laughs bitterly. "His sister picked up. She wasn't in good shape. Turns out he'd decided he'd had enough. He's gone. Jason's dead."

My heart feels like it skips a beat. They keep talking about the high rate of veteran suicides on the news. It's why Mom is almost as scared with Rob home as she was when he was serving overseas.

"Promise me you won't do that. You have to swear to me," I beg him. "I couldn't stand it. And Mom and Dad . . . it would destroy them. It's bad enough—"

I stop, not wanting to make him feel worse than he clearly already feels.

"It's bad enough that I'm punching holes in the wall and putting my fist through the window?"

"Yeah."

There's no point in lying. Mom and Dad are going to freak when they get home, and not just because of the damage he's caused in his room. We've all being tiptoeing around Rob, painfully worried but afraid to push too much, to nag too much, to be too much anything in case it was the wrong thing for him.

Jason decided to end it all because he didn't get the right help. My heart breaks for his family—and for his friends. For my brother, who is falling apart because of this news.

I get a text from Mom.

"Mom says I should drive you to the ER. If I miss any glass and you get an infection, it's not good, and you don't want to mess with your hands. She'll meet us there."

"It's fine, Stella, I don't need to go."

"Rob, Mom's a doctor. Do you want me to text her back and say you disagree with her?" I ask him. "Because that's not going to go down very well."

He rubs his head with his good hand.

"Okay, I'll go," he grumbles. "It's not like I've got a lot of choice with all this emotional blackmail going on."

As I wait for him in the car a few minutes later, I wonder if it's really emotional blackmail like Rob says, or if it's just being family. Whatever it is, I hope the ER doctors can do more than just stitch up my brother's hand. I hope they can help him find a way back to how he was before—a way back to us.

After Mom gets to the ER, she tells me to go home and help Dad clean up the mess Rob made. Like that's fair. Like I don't have homework to do. Like I'm not supposed to be coming up with ideas for my campaign platform by tomorrow.

But after I help Dad lift the bookshelf off the bed, and we start stacking books back onto the shelves, I find a picture on the floor. It's of Rob's squad from when they were deployed. They all look so young and healthy. So alive.

No wonder Rob's mad. Jason's death isn't fair, either.

"Did you ever do anything like this when you got back from Iraq?" I ask Dad.

Dad finishes organizing the books on the shelf by height order before he answers. My father is very particular about organization. He says it's because in combat, if you're not properly prepared, it can make the difference between life and death.

"Can't say I did," he says. "And that makes it hard for me to understand. There's a part of me that wonders if Rob's just shirking because he doesn't want to grow up and face the responsibilities of life."

I feel like that sometimes when Rob just sits and plays video games for hours on end and doesn't bother to unload the dishwasher, or help with the groceries, even though Mom and Dad are working and I have school.

"Now, Frank Meyers . . . he had some real anger issues when

he came back from Vietnam, from what I've heard. He's tried talking to your brother," Dad says. "But I don't know if Rob's ready to listen."

"How come some people come back and are fine and others aren't?"

"If I could answer that question, the Departments of Defense and Veterans Affairs would give me a lucrative contract," Dad says. "But I can't, and I'm not sure if they can, either."

It seems strange that after all the wars we've had and all the billions of dollars we've spent fighting them, no one has been able to figure that out. Or if they have, they haven't worked out how to prevent whatever it is going on with Rob and how to ease the pain that made Jason decide to end his life.

But there's so much about the world that doesn't make sense to me, and it just gets more confusing every year I spend in it.

When Mom and Rob get home from the hospital, my brother's hand is bandaged, and he's quiet and subdued, in contrast to Peggy, who is jumping around him, barking and whining like he's been gone for a century instead of six hours.

"Stella and I cleaned up your room as best we could," Dad tells him. "I've put some cardboard over the window and I've got the glass people coming out tomorrow. Why don't you go rest while I put dinner on the table?"

"It's okay," Rob says, heading straight up to his room. "I'm not hungry."

Mom tells Dad and me that the doctor gave Rob some anti-anxiety medication, and when she told him about some of Rob's symptoms, like sleep patrolling, he strongly suggested Rob make an appointment at the nearest Veterans Affairs hospital as soon as possible for a psych evaluation.

"What do you mean 'sleep patrolling'?" I ask.

Dad and Mom exchange a glance, like it's some big secret that I'm too young to know, and that annoys me.

"I live in this house with him, too, you know. I had to deal with whatever you call today all by myself. Don't you think it's time you tell me the truth about what's going on?"

Mom puts on her doctor-explaining-things-to-a-patient voice. "Well, a few nights ago, we heard a noise outside. Someone was prowling around in the yard. We thought we were being robbed."

"I got the shotgun," Dad says.

"And I went to wake up Rob," Mom said, "but his bed was empty."

"What? Where was he?" I ask.

"Out in the yard, patrolling the perimeter," Dad says.

"We had to convince him that his shift was over and it was time to hit the rack," Mom says.

"And then we sat watch over him all night," Dad says. "And do you know what's even stranger than seeing Rob doing night watch in the yard?"

I'm afraid to ask. "What?"

"He had absolutely no recollection of it when he woke up," Dad says.

"None at all?" I ask.

"None," Mom says. "He denied he did it until Dad told him to look at his feet, which were all dirty. You should have seen the look on his face. But he still refused to go to the VA. It's only Jason's death that's put a crack in the armor. Now I just hope we can get him an appointment, and soon."

But it turns out Rob's just one of many veterans who've come back from the war not the same as they were before. Mom says that in all the planning for the endless streams of operations we've been running since 2001—Operation Enduring Freedom, Operation Iraqi Freedom, and all the others—they didn't plan for Operation Look After the Warriors Who Come Home with Problems. Or maybe they just didn't plan for as many of them. Is there such a rush to get into the fight that no one thinks about what will happen afterward?

Whatever the answer, the wait just for a mental health assessment appointment is eight to ten weeks, which is just plain wrong. It's taken so long to get Rob to agree to go I'm afraid by the time his appointment rolls around he'll have changed his mind.

Mom says there's not a lot we can do in the meantime except wait, and give him our love and support.

But isn't that what we've been doing all along? And at the risk of sounding like a complete brat, where am *I* supposed to get love and support if everyone's so focused on Rob? I mean, when I finally got a chance to tell my parents I was running for class president, they were, like, "Oh, that's great Stella, we're so proud of you, when's the election?" for literally three and a half minutes, which I know because the clock on the microwave was behind Dad's head so I timed it, before it was all Rob, Rob, Rob again.

Rob's not the only one who needs the VA to get its act together.

Roadrunner, why aren't you here, buddy? You thought I was just checking in on you, but I needed you just as much as you needed me. Look at me, I'm writing to a dead person at four in the morning. If that's not a sign that I'm cracking up, what is? But I have to tell you this, because I know you'll understand. Also, I know you won't tell anyone, because you're not going to read this. You're dead.

Well, it's official. I'm crazy. Well, half official. It was "strongly recommended" by the ER doctor that I go to the VA for a psychiatric evaluation. Apparently, I might have some form of combat PTSD. Did you know there's more than one kind? I didn't.

You learn something new every freaking day.

What was I doing in the ER, you might be asking yourself?

Well, that's where you come in. When you didn't answer my texts yesterday, I got that spidey sense that something was wrong. So I called you, and your sister picked up and told me.

I wish you'd just have come out here and punched me in the stomach. Just beat the crap out of me. That might have made you feel better, and it sure would have been easier for me than hearing those words from your sister's mouth.

It took me longer than it should have to be able to tell your sister how sorry I was. How much I was going to miss you.

When she thanked me for checking in on you, I could feel myself starting to cry. So I said, tell me if there's anything I can do, and then said I had to go.

And I hung up.

Then I punched a hole in the bedroom wall. Pushed over my bookshelf, too. And then punched out my bedroom window, which was why I was in the ER. Stitches.

So while I was there, the doc asked what had "precipitated" my wall- and window-punching activities.

I might have gotten away with it when I told him about you. I mean, it's not every day you lose a friend to suicide, right? It's a pretty good reason to want to punch a wall or a window, or even both. Maybe not the most appropriate way of dealing with feelings, but people get it.

But Mom was there, and she told the doc about the other stuff. Moodiness. Anger. Anxiety. The clincher was the sleep patrolling.

Do you know what it's like to be betrayed by your own feet?

Mom had that look on her face like when she's going to defend the position no matter what the cost. I think I'm tough, but there's not a guy in our platoon who's got anything on my mom when she's got that look.

"You need help, Rob. I know you think you can tough this out alone, but you can't. There's no shame in asking for help."

Easy for her to say. Mom's a superwoman.

My family tells me they love me and says all the right things.

But this is what I hear the voice in my head telling me: Man up!

It's what I hear even now, every time I look in the mirror.

A lot of times even when I don't.

ThunderGeek out.

60

CHAPTER FIVE

"How does Chris have so many campaign posters already?" I ask Farida as we walk to AP Gov the Tuesday after Rob's ER visit. "They're *everywhere*."

There are three alone on the wall in front of us. *A is for Articulate, Active, Athletic, Amusing, Attractive, Adventurous, Amazing, Admirable! Make Argleton High Awesome! Vote Chris Abbott!* is one.

"Points for alliteration," I say.

"Someone definitely Googled 'positive adjectives beginning with A,'" Farida says.

Another one is a picture of Chris surrounded by images of the school mascot, the Argleton Astro, at football games. The tagline reads: *Astro says, "Vote Abbott to Make Argleton High Awesome!"*

"What does that even *mean*?" I say. "Random mascot imagery, school colors, and *Make Argleton High Awesome!*"

"It's not exactly subtle, is it?" Farida says.

"Awesome as in people who look and think and act just like Chris?"

"And she scores!" Farida says, kicking an imaginary goal.

I notice a poster on the opposite wall. "Wow, this one really takes the cake. How can Principal Hart let him get away with it?"

There's a picture of Chris surrounded by girls from our school wearing bikinis, and it says: *Victoria's REAL secret: We're all voting for Chris Abbott!*

"I just threw up in my mouth," Farida says.

"Right? Especially since *we* get in trouble if we wear a tank top with spaghetti straps, or skirts or shorts that don't meet the 'fingertip test' because it's *too distracting for the boys to learn.*" I rip the poster off the wall. "I'm going to complain after class. They're being such hypocrites if they let Chris get away with this poster."

"Hey, what are you doing to Chris's poster?" Mike Carlson shouts from a few feet down the hall.

"Yeah, taking it down because you know you're gonna lose?" Wade Boles adds.

"No," I say. "Because it's sexist, and it violates the school dress code. I'm going to point that out to Principal Hart after my next class."

"Oh, *come on*," Wade says. "Are you serious?"

"Yes, I'm serious," I say. "If the administration enforces the dress code for us, because our skin makes it so hard for y'all to learn, then why are they letting Chris put up posters of girls in bikinis?"

"Because it's a joke," Mike says. "J-O-K-E. Where's your sense of humor?"

"It's alive and well but tired of double standards," I say.

"Why do you have to make a big deal out of every little thing?" Wade says.

"Yeah, a guy can't even sneeze around here without some girl complaining, 'OMG, that's so sexist!'" Mike says, in a lame falsetto imitation.

I give Farida a sidelong glance. She gives me a barely perceptible nod.

"Well, it's been nice chatting, but we can't be late for class," I say.

We turn and head down the hall.

"Going to search for your sense of humor?" Wade calls after us.

"Nope! Your brain," I call back at him.

I hear Wade and Mike making stupid comments about us down the hallway, but I don't care.

"Do you think they know what it's like to have to put up with this stuff?" I say.

"Getting all philosophical on me, I see," Farida replies with a laugh. "But don't you think it's a little ironic that you're saying that to *me*, all things considered?"

I stop in my tracks. "Ugh. Sorry."

"Yup. But they're human. And the fact remains, all humans hurt in one way or another. That's what I try to remind myself." She glances back down the hallway. "Although it's especially hard to remember that when they're acting like Neanderthals."

Wade is jumping and trying to punch a hole in the ceiling, because . . . why?

I hear Mrs. Harris come out of her classroom and threaten them with detention as we walk away, and I can't help smiling.

Later, I try to remember what Farida said about everyone hurting about something when Chris comes into Debate Club steaming mad, walks straight over to me, and starts yelling about me interfering with his campaign.

"You're pathetic, Walker! You know you can't win, so you try to sabotage *my* campaign? Is that how you want to play this?"

I take a deep breath and try to remind myself that he's human and hurting rather than just being a jerk.

"Chris, it's not about *you*. It's about *the issue*."

"What issue is that? Your losing campaign?"

"No. Dress codes and hypocrisy."

"Dress codes? They're posters!" Chris protests.

"Posters with pictures of real people who go to this school and so are subject to the dress code," I point out. "If the girls in your poster came to school wearing shorts or skirts that don't meet the fingertip rule, they'd still be wearing more clothes than they are in your poster, and they'd be sent home for being 'inappropriately dressed.'"

"Do you even hear how ridiculous you're being?" Chris asks. "You have no sense of humor."

"How does pointing out hypocritical policies aimed at girls mean that I'm ridiculous and don't have a sense of humor?" I ask, annoyed that he's not getting it.

Mr. Walsh comes in before Chris can answer.

"Principal Hart tells me there's been some controversy about campaign posters," he says, looking directly at Chris and me. "And I am in complete support of his decision to remove the posters."

"But, Mr. Walsh, what about my First Amendment right of free speech?" Chris complains. "I should call the ACLU. This is ridiculous."

"Please feel free to go ahead and call them," Mr. Walsh says. "But they'll probably advise you of *Hazelwood School District v Kuhlmeier* in which the Supreme Court held that school-sponsored speech—and class elections generally fall under this category—may be censored for 'legitimate pedagogical reasons.'"

Chris's hands clench into fists of frustration. I flash him a satisfied smile.

"My dad is going to hear about this," Chris says.

"I'm sure he will," Mr. Walsh replies. "And I won't be surprised when Principal Hart hears from Mayor Abbott and certain members of the school board. But it won't change his decision."

Chris is out of sorts for the rest of Debate Club, which makes it easier for me to beat him. Maybe it's because he's so used to having everything go his way. When your dad's been the mayor for most of your life, problems seem to go away. Like when he threw a Gatorade bottle at someone's head on the bus to DC on our eighth-grade trip. He was supposed to get a week of detention, but his dad intervened and it ended up being one day. And I'm sure there are, like, a billion other things he's gotten away with over the years.

I wonder if there's any way I can rattle him like this before the school election. Maybe then I could win.

When I get back from debate, Rob's playing video games. He's still wearing the same sweats as when I left for school this morning, and he smells pretty ripe.

"Did you go to class like that?" I ask.

"Didn't go today," he says without looking away from the screen. "Not that it's any of your business."

Mom and Dad would get a call and an email if I skipped school and I'd be grounded before I could say, "Why can't Rob take a shower?" But college doesn't do that, because my brother is a so-called adult, so he can slack off as he pleases.

Unless I tell Mom and Dad.

I should. They need to know.

I'm trying to be there for Rob, but shouldn't Rob be helping himself, too?

Instead, he seems to be trying to make everything worse for himself.

I go upstairs and text Mom and Dad.

ME: Rob skipped class today.

DAD: Is he playing video games?

ME: How did you guess?

MOM: Stella, you manage your life and let us deal with Rob, okay?

ME: Fine.

I thought I was being helpful by letting them know.

Whatever.

They can deal with him.

And I'll just live my life. Or at least try to.

Luckily, Farida and I have plans on Saturday to check out Walking on Sunshine, this new shoe store that opened downtown. It's good to get out of the house, away from the atmosphere that hangs over it like a cloud just waiting to rain.

"Look at these boots!" Farida says, showing me a pair of mocha suede ankle boots.

"Cute, but not as cool as these."

I hold up a pair of black lace-up boots that will go perfectly with jeans.

"Ooh. I love those!"

"I thought you would," I say. "And they are screaming your name. Can't you hear them calling, 'Farida! Buy me!'?"

"So that's the voice I keep hearing in my head. Come to me, pretty boot babies," Farida says.

When the salesperson brings us our sizes, we try them on and then walk around the store. Finally, we stand together in front of the full-length mirror.

"You *have* to get those, Farida," I say.

"So do you!"

"It's not too weird for us to have the same boots, right?" I worry suddenly.

Farida rolls her eyes at my reflection in the mirror. "Do you think guys ever think twice if it's weird that they're wearing the same brand of sneaker?"

I laugh. "Good point. I can't see Chris Abbott wasting a minute of his time thinking about it. Besides, if anyone gives us crap, we can say they're our BFF boots."

"I think you mean our lit, incredibly stylish BFF boots."

"Isn't that what I said? If it's not, it's what I totally meant to," I say.

"I vote that we wear our BFF boots to lunch, which I also vote we have right now. I'm starving."

"I'm up for lunch, especially if it's at the Jumpin' Jive Café."

"Deal," Farida says.

We pay for the boots, taking our old ones home in the store bags, and head to our favorite coffee shop to get lunch. It's warm, but not too hot to sit outside, so we grab a table on the sidewalk after we get our food.

I take a bite of my sandwich and sigh with contentment. "It feels so good to be out and not have to think about school, or running for class president. I've missed hanging out with you, you know?" Ever since Rob got home, I feel like Farida and I haven't just hung out, not like we normally do. And I miss my best friend. Miss just doing silly, fun stuff together. Like throwing dance parties in her room when a new album from one of her billion favorite artists comes out. Or this, shoe shopping. Farida has the best collection of shoes in the school.

"Yeah, I know," Farida says, tilting her head back and closing her eyes to soak up the sun. "It's good to take a break. Otherwise we'd crack up. With my eyes closed I can pretend we're in Paris or Madrid or Berlin."

"Life goals," I say.

She laughs and opens her eyes. "Or I can just enjoy the sunshine in beautiful downtown Argleton because I'm here with my bestie."

I lift my iced coffee. "Cheers! Here's to sunny days, killer footwear, and my best friend."

Ken chose the film for our next Keeping It Reel screening. It's a World War II movie that came out in 1970 called *Catch-22*. We're over at his house watching it on Sunday afternoon while making campaign posters, and I am totally confused.

"Is it just me, or does it seem like everyone in this movie is dishonest or kind of out there?" I say, tapping the cap of my Sharpie.

"It's a black comedy based on a satirical novel," Ken replies. "What do you expect?"

"Okay. But still . . ."

"I think that's the whole point, Stella," Farida says. "That the situation doesn't make sense. That's the catch-twenty-two. If you want to get out of flying the dangerous mission, you're sane, so you *can't* get out of it. But if you *want* to fly it, you're insane, but you'll still end up flying it. So there's no way out."

"So basically, even if you're a totally normal person to begin with, being in that catch-twenty-two situation all the time is enough to make you question your sanity," I say slowly, watching Captain Yossarian, the main character, pretend to lose it on screen in a way that reminds me of Rob the other night. Or is he really losing it?

Maybe losing it is the only legit response when someone is trapped in a situation that makes no sense.

I wonder if this is some kind of clue to Rob.

That thought makes my brain hurt, so I go back to working on a poster. "Do you think *Stella Walker: The Smart Solution* is enough?" I ask. "Should we come up with some funny gimmicky ones like Amy and Chris did?"

"What, you want me to round up some hunky guys in Speedos?" Ken says, grinning.

"That would be a firm no way," I say. "I'm thinking more like, *You want something done? Stella's the One,* or something like that."

"How about a picture of Marlon Brando from *A Streetcar Named Desire* shouting, STELLLLLLLAAAAAAA! *for Class President,*" Ken suggests.

"We're probably the only ones who will get it, but I love it," Farida says, grabbing a handful of popcorn.

I laugh and dial Ken's phone, because he has Marlon Brando shouting "Stella" as his ringtone for me.

We all STELLLLLLLLLLA for a few minutes, but after we settle down and Ken finds a good Brando image to print out, I say, "Chris is still super pissed that we complained about his poster. He gives Farida and me the stink-eye every time we walk into AP Gov."

"Chris's dad is the mayor," Ken says. "He's not used to having to play by the rules like the rest of us mere mortals. If he steps out of bounds, Daddy makes it better. I couldn't believe that Principal Hart actually made him take the poster down."

"Me neither," Farida says. "And that Mr. Hart stood by the decision when Mayor Abbott started up about 'political correctness' and 'safe spaces' in the press was amazing."

"Can someone explain to me why boys need safe spaces from girls wearing skirts and shorts above their fingertips, but when we complain about Chris's poster that's political correctness?" I say.

"Probably not," Ken says. "Because there's no logical explanation except for hypocrisy."

"Sometimes it feels like we live in a catch-twenty-two world, where there's no such thing as logic," I say.

"Right?" Farida says, swapping her marker for another handful of popcorn.

"That's why you're running for class president and we're supporting you," Ken says. "Wait, that gives me an idea! Picture of Mr. Spock and *Stella Walker: The Logical Choice*?"

Farida and I both laugh.

"Geeky, but funny," Farida says, putting some partly popped kernels next to my poster. I flash her a grin as I scoop them up.

"Haley won't approve," I say, "but Rob would love it."

Farida picks up her marker and taps it on the table like a gavel. "Subject change," she announces, mock-seriously.

"Hear, hear," I say, putting down my marker.

"So guess what I'm thinking of doing, if I can work it around helping out at the restaurant?"

I toss a few pieces of popcorn in my mouth to give me a few extra seconds to guess.

"Uh . . . learning karate?" Ken ventures.

"No, but that's not a bad idea," Farida says. "I can totally see myself doing some superhero moves."

"Model UN?" I guess.

"You're getting colder."

"Colder?" I say. "Uh . . . can you give us a clue?"

"Yeah, because apparently we're clueless," Ken says.

Farida strikes a pose and starts singing: "'It's time to try defying gravity . . .'"

She stops and raises an eyebrow. "Still no guesses?"

"You want to be a witch?" Ken says.

Farida throws a piece of popcorn at him. "Freezing. But if I were a witch, I'd turn you into a newt for that."

"Wait, are you going to try out for the musical?" I say.

"Yes!" she says. "Or at least I'm thinking about it—now that my parents won't let me run for class president."

"I can help you run lines if you want," I say. "But if you make me sing, you know it's not going to be pretty."

"That's an understatement," Ken mutters.

"Look who's talking!" I say. "Dogs howl along when you sing."

Farida laughs. "Let's be real—neither of you are ready for *The Voice*," she says. "But it doesn't matter when it comes to help running lines."

We sing a rousing and somewhat out of tune chorus of "Defying Gravity," then discuss potential song options for Farida's audition. Ken keeps insisting on singing his suggestions, which results in Farida and me bombarding him with popcorn because his singing *is* really that bad. It takes us a while to clean up.

By the time Farida drives me home, she's got five possible songs she's happy with, and I've got twenty new posters. I'm pretty sure there's a kernel of popcorn somewhere in my shirt and my hands are stained with Sharpie ink. Democracy really *is* a messy business.

Roadrunner—

Why, man? Why did you do it?

It's one thing to be warned about vets and suicide. It's one thing to hear about it on the news. But now it's you and it's real. I mean, real to me.

I guess it's like Spock said, "You find it easier to understand the death of one than the death of a million."

Now I'm just here at 3 a.m. again, watching the minutes go by on the clock, as slow as ketchup coming out of a brand-new bottle.

If it weren't for Peggy's soft dog snores, I'd think I was the only one alive, and I'd keep coming back to the question: Why?

Why am I still here and you aren't?

Why am I still here and Reyes isn't?

What was it all for? Did any of it change anything?

I can't see that it made a difference in the long run. Sure, we might have gained some short-term ground, but now I look at what's happening and I wonder what it was all for. Did we make things better or worse?

Here's another Spockism: "In critical moments, men sometimes see exactly what they wish to see."

So how does that work here?

What do I want to see?

I want to see that we made a difference.

But I don't.

I want to think that I deserve to be here when you and Reyes aren't.

But I don't.

I want to feel like my life is worth something, that I make my family proud.

But I don't.

So now what?

That's the problem.

I don't know.

And I don't know where to start to find out.

I guess that's why I'm doing nothing.

Because that's all I seem to be able to do right now.

ThunderGeek out.

CHAPTER SIX

I've got to get my brother out of the house before he turns into a hermit. He skipped class twice last week. He's getting lazy about showering and shaving, too. I can live with the not shaving, but the not showering? That's another story. Plus, his room is starting to smell pretty rank. I have to hold my breath on the way to the bathroom so I don't inhale Eau d'Stinky Bro.

"Can't you do something?" I complained to Mom. "It's so gross. His room smells like a cross between an armpit and a gym sock."

Mom laughed, but her sense of humor was short-lived.

"He's my son, Stella, but he's also a grown-up," she said. "I can't force him to do things the way I could when he was a little kid."

"But it's not fair," I complained. "He's not the only one who lives in this house."

"I have to pick my battles," Mom said. "And right now, I've got bigger problems to worry about."

Easy for her to say. Her bedroom isn't right across the hall and she doesn't have to share a bathroom with him.

Well, I'm picking my battles, and I'm going to get that smelly lump of a brother out of the house if it kills me. Since Jason died, the only time he's willingly gone outside is for college—when he's not skipping class, that is—or to walk Peggy. That's only because he won't let her suffer.

Too bad he doesn't seem to care about making *me* suffer. If only he cared as much about the rest of us as much as he cares about the dog.

Doesn't he see the dark circles under Mom's eyes, because she's so worried about him? Doesn't he understand how freaked out we all are? Doesn't he realize that I feel sick to my stomach every time I open the front door after school, because I'm afraid I'll find him like Jason?

Still, as angry as I am at him for putting us all through this, I keep reminding myself that he's hurting. That I need to be there for my brother.

So that's what I'm going to do. They're having a special showing of the director's cut of *Alien* at the mall. It's not really my thing, but I know it's one of Rob's favorite movies. 1979 isn't as old as I usually go for, but it still counts as a classic, and Ken said it's awesome. Best of all, for a few hours Rob will be out of the house and hopefully out of his head, too.

Going on the premise that it's better to ask for forgiveness than permission, I buy the tickets online and then go to tell Rob that he's coming.

"Hey, I got us tickets to see *Alien*. It's the director's cut. Four thirty show at the mall. C'mon, go get dressed so we don't miss the previews."

He doesn't even look up from the video game he's playing. "Did you think of asking if I wanted to go? Because the answer is no."

"The answer is always no with you these days," I say. "That's why I didn't ask. It's time to say yes for a change. The running time is one hour and fifty-seven minutes. You can handle being out of the house for that long. We'll come straight home after."

"No."

"Come *oooooooon*, Rob! You love the movie. You always tell me what a cultural heathen I am because I've never watched this movie about a gross face-hugging space monster. I'm ready and willing. Let's do it."

His mouth twitches. I've cracked the stone face. He's half smiling. *Progress!* I will wear him down. I know how to be an annoying, nagging little sister. I've had years of practice. I can do this.

"Gross face-hugging space monster?" Rob says, finally pausing his game and putting down the controller. He stretches. "That's just wrong."

"All the more reason for you to make sure I'm educated on this scary sci-fi stuff so I don't embarrass you," I say. "Or else you'll never know when I might drop that wrong phrase in front of your friends. It would be so awkward."

"*So* awkward," Rob agrees. The other side of his mouth quirks up. This is the closest he's come to a full-out grin since Jason checked out.

"Come on. Let's go see *Alien*," I beg. "It'll be fun."

The smile fades, and I'm afraid I've blown it.

"I don't know," Rob says. "I'm not up to being around people."

Like the debate queen that I am, I've already prepared for that argument.

"You don't have to be around that many people. We can get there right before the movie starts, go straight in, and come straight back after," I tell him. "It shouldn't be that crowded on a weekday."

His fingers drum his knee. He's still on the fence. I have to push him over.

"It'll be okay. I promise."

Rob runs his hands through his hair and stands up.

"Okay, little sister. Count me in."

"Yes!" I put out my fist and he gives it a half-hearted bump. I decide to push a little further. "Could you maybe . . . uh . . . change your shirt?"

"What, you don't want to be seen with me in my three-day-old green tee?" he says, lifting it over his head and giving me a gag-inducing whiff of stinky armpit.

"How about putting on some deodorant, too?" I suggest, trying not to go too Mom on him. "I mean, I have to sit next to you and all."

"Sheesh, give the girl an inch and she takes a mile," Rob complains, but he shuffles upstairs to change.

I use the opportunity to take Peggy out for a quick walk to the end of the street. While I'm doing that, I text Mom: Convinced Rob to go see Alien! 4:30 show at mall. See you later!

I'm just coming back in when she replies: Great job! Have fun. Love you xo.

Rob is downstairs, wearing a clean T-shirt and jeans and it even looks like he jumped in the shower because he smells like body wash and his hair is wet. Apparently, miracles do happen.

"Got the tickets?"

"On my phone," I say.

"Let's do this thing," he says, giving Peggy a last pat and heading for the garage.

We're halfway to the mall when he says, "You're allowed to breathe. And stop clutching the door handle."

I look down and smile sheepishly when I realize that I'm gripping the handle so hard my knuckles are white.

"You're worse than Mom when I was learning how to drive," Rob says.

"That's just cruel," I say, putting my hands in my lap.

Rob glances at me with a slight grin.

"Tell me you haven't been sitting there waiting for me to lose it."

I open my mouth to deny it, but what's the point? He'll know I'm lying. "So what if I have? Can you blame me? You haven't exactly been Mr. Normal lately."

As soon as the words leave my mouth I feel like a total jerk. I'm supposed to be supportive and compassionate and I told him he was acting crazy. *Way to empathize, Stella!*

But Rob laughs. Go figure.

"I can always trust you to tell it like it is," he says. "Everyone else tiptoes around the subject, but Stella marches right in and names it."

Ever since he got back from this latest deployment, I can count on my big brother to confuse me. Before, I could pretty much predict how he'd react in any given situation. Now I have no idea. It's exhausting.

"Don't worry," Rob says. "Sometimes it's a relief to hear it said out loud."

Sometimes?

But what about the other times? How do I know when to say it and when not to?

As we pull in the mall lot, the car in front of us stops suddenly, and my brother slams on the brakes so hard I almost hit my head against the dash, even though I'm wearing a seat belt.

"What's your problem?" Rob shouts, leaning on the horn. "No one's even in front of you, moron!"

A black-and-white dog streaks across to the other side of the road, looking even more freaked out than my brother.

"Chill, Rob!" I snap, watching the dog escape between parked cars headed for the Olive Garden trash bins. "They braked so they didn't run over a dog."

The car rolls forward and as it does, I hear what sounds like a cross between a hiccup and a burp come from Rob.

"What do you call that weird noise? A biccup?"

When he doesn't even groan at my joke, I turn to look at Rob and once again I'm confused. His face is contorted as if he's in pain.

Maybe this mall excursion was a bad idea. Maybe he's not up to this.

I'm worried that I might not be up to it, either.

"Rob, are—" *No, don't ask if he's okay, because duh, of course he's not.* "What's going on?"

He keeps driving, with slow, deliberate, careful concentration, like he's working to hold it together, until he finds an empty space not far from the mall entrance, pulls in, and turns off the engine. Then he puts his arms across the wheel, lowers his head, and breaks down, his shoulders heaving as he sobs.

Freaked out, I unbuckle my seat belt and lean across the console to put my arm around him.

"What is it?" I ask.

I wonder if I should call Mom or Dad. I wonder if I should get him into the passenger seat, turn the car around, and drive home. I wonder if I should just sit here with my arm around him until he's ready to tell me what is making him lose it.

"The d-dog," he manages to get out, but that doesn't really explain much. I know Rob loves dogs, but I can't understand why he's crying over a dog that escaped death, but he stayed dry-eyed when his friend Jason didn't.

I rummage in the glove compartment in search of tissues. Luckily, I find a few crumpled-up McDonalds napkins. I hand them to him silently.

"Thanks," he says.

After he's wiped his face and blown his nose, I finally muster the courage to ask, "So . . . what about the dog? I . . . don't understand."

Rob takes a deep, shuddering breath and grips the steering wheel.

"We had just left a village when one of the trucks in our convoy got a flat. We never liked to stop 'cause it meant we were sitting ducks, but we didn't have a choice. I was pulling security. I see this boy, must have been around ten, coming across the field from where he'd been tending his goats. He had a dog with him, this skinny, rangy-looking thing."

I'm still trying to figure out what this has to do with Mall Dog, when he continues, "The kid is smiling at me and saying something, I don't know what, 'cause he's speaking Pashto. I've still got my finger on the trigger, because you never know, but the next thing I know I'm on my back, I can't hear, and the kid is dead."

I gasp.

"He stepped on an IED. I just keep seeing it, Stella. Over and over."

Now I'm the one trying to hold it together.

"The dog wasn't dead. You could tell it wasn't going to make it, but it was still alive and suffering. My ears were messed up from the blast, but I could still hear that poor dog whining, even through the ringing."

He inhales loudly before continuing.

"So I put him out of his misery. It was the right thing to do. But later, when we got back to base, I got the letter from Mom telling me that y'all had to put down Cosmo. It felt like payback, 'cause if that truck hadn't broken down, maybe that poor kid and his dog might still be alive."

"It wasn't your fault, Rob. You were just doing your job." That's what I'm supposed to say, right? It's the truth, but will it help?

"Yeah, I was 'just obeying orders,'" he says. "Look, I know we didn't plant that IED. But maybe if I'd shouted at the kid to go away instead of smiling at him because he was a kid who could have been me if I'd been born halfway across the world, he would still be alive."

I wish I knew what else to say. I want to help Rob, but this is bigger than what I've got. Feeling helpless, I hug him and hope that's enough. "I love you, Rob. I know that you're a good person."

Rob pulls away and leans his forehead against the window with a heavy sigh.

Great job, Stella. Way to say the wrong thing.

But I don't know what else to say. If I agree with him that it's horrible, wouldn't it make him feel worse? I mean, it *is* horrible.

I look over at my brother. I don't have more to say, so I just sit there saying nothing, hating myself more for it each second the silence drags on.

Finally, Rob wipes his face with his arm, and it's as if he pulls a mask back over his face. "Let's go see this movie. That's why I bothered taking a shower and putting on clean clothes, right?"

He's acting like the crying thing never happened, so I follow his lead.

"And deodorant, I hope."

"Yeah, *Mom*, and deodorant."

I wonder if I should text Mom and Dad to tell them about this latest incident, but I don't want Rob to feel like I'm narcing on him, so I leave my phone in my pocket.

Rob tenses up as we walking into the mall. His eyes swivel from side to side, and his shoulders hunch over. His anxiety drifts over me like a cold mist, until I'm completely enveloped in it, too.

Luckily, there's no line for popcorn, and there aren't that many people in the theater.

I head toward seats in the middle, where we always sit.

"Not there," Rob says. He walks to the very back row.

"Why do we have to sit all the way back here?" I ask.

"Why not?" he says.

"Because we always sit in the middle."

"Life changes. You gotta learn to change with it," he says, his eyes darting over my shoulder.

I turn around and see an Emergency Exit sign.

Shrugging, I sit down next to him and wonder if he's given me a clue. Is whatever's going on with him about change I don't understand because I haven't changed with him?

I'm relieved when the movie starts, because it gives me a chance to escape from this mystery. I'm afraid to look at Rob, but I hope it's doing the same for him. It's not till he leans over and whispers, "This part is the *best!*" that I unclench my fingers from the armrest. I didn't even realize I was gripping it so hard.

Maybe this will work. Maybe it can be the start of something—a baby step toward bringing my brother back to us.

When the final credits roll, Rob turns to me and smiles.

"Thanks, Stella. I know you had to drag me here, but it was worth it."

"How about we celebrate by getting froyo at the food court?"

"Froyo? Nah. I want the real thing. We're getting ice cream."

"Fine," I say. "As long as it's cold and sweet."

Rob's tension seems to amp up again as we walk to the food court, and I wonder if I should have just let it go at the movie.

"Why don't we forget the ice cream?" I say, hoping he doesn't see through my obvious attempt to get him out of here. "Mom will be mad if we ruin our appetite for dinner."

"You put the idea of ice cream in my head and now you're bailing?" Rob says. "No way, wimp."

His eyes are darting one way and the other, checking out the doorway of each store. But if he's not admitting to anything bothering him, then I'll play along.

"Okay, ice cream it is."

At least the food court isn't as crowded as it would be on the weekend.

I spot Wade Boles and Jed Landon sitting at a table. With Rob acting wiggy, they're the last people I want to bump into, so I steer us around the outside of the food court toward Dreamsicle Creamsicles.

Rob orders two scoops of cookies 'n' cream with whipped cream and sprinkles; I get butter pecan with hot fudge.

I find us a table far enough from Wade and Jed so I can pretend that I don't see them.

"Man, this is the stuff," Rob says. "Mmm-hmmm."

"Yup. Hot fudge. Nectar of the gods," I agree. "So what was your favorite part of the movie?"

"Definitely the part where—"

He breaks off, eyes narrowing, his body suddenly tense and alert as he looks at something over my shoulder.

I turn around and see Wade and Jed standing by a kid who is cleaning and wiping down tables. He also happens to be Sikh, which I know because his hair is up in a topknot covered by a piece of cloth.

"Hey, raghead," Jed says. "We don't want terrorists around here. Go back to your own country."

Wait, what? I know Jed can be a jerk, but I'm still completely surprised he'd say such an offensive thing.

Rob springs up to a standing position so quickly his chair falls over. Before I know what's happening, he's stalking toward Wade and Jed, who are jeering as the kid says, "Piss off."

My heart starts beating faster, and I curse myself for suggesting frozen yogurt in the first place, because I know right now this isn't going to end well.

TRANSCRIPT OF POLICE INTERVIEW
WITH ASHAR SINGH

DO: This is Detective Brendan Overmann speaking. It's 8 p.m. on Wednesday, September 7th. I am interviewing Ashar Singh. Ashar, will you please spell your name?

AS: A-S-H-A-R S-I-N-G-H.

DO: Thank you. Ashar is 17 years old. His date of birth is January 31st. He is employed as a janitor at the Lone Pine Mall. Ashar, what time did you arrive at Lone Pine Mall for work?

AS: My shift started at 5.

DO: Approximately what time did the incident occur?

AS: About 6:25 p.m. My mom texted me just before I got to work and that was, like, 6:10 or something.

DO: Can you tell me what happened, in as much detail as possible?

AS: Sure, I guess. I started to clear off tables in the food court. You wouldn't believe how many people don't clean up after themselves. They're, like, total pigs. They just leave their garbage without thinking about anyone else. If I did that at home, my parents would never let me hear the end of it.

DO: How did the encounter with the other young men start?

AS: I was sweeping the floor near their table, when one, I think the one named Jed or Jez or something like that, he calls out to me, "Hey, raghead, we don't want terrorists around here. Go back to your own country." Like I wasn't born right here in Virginia, and I'm not just as American as he is. Where does he get off? And "raghead"? Seriously? I wear a patka as a sign of my faith. If someone wears a cross on a chain around their neck, does that make them a terrorist? Or if a guy is wearing one of those Jewish beanies, I forget what they're called—what about then?

DO: So how did you respond?

AS: I sort of told him to get lost—more or less. That just riled the guy up more. He spit on the floor at my feet and picked some pepperoni off his pizza and threw it on top of the spit. Then he's all: "Pick it up, it's your job." It's so obvious he thought I was Muslim and I'd be offended by the pepperoni, not just because he was being an ignorant bigot. As usual, I had to explain that I was born here and, duh, I'm not a terrorist. That's when the other guy came over. He told Pepperoni Guy, "You have no right to speak to him that way. Pick that up and apologize."

DO: How did the kids who were bothering you respond to that?

AS: The one who threw the pepperoni was a total jerk. He cursed the guy out, then said, "Haven't you heard of the First Amendment?"

DO: How did Walker—the other guy—react?

AS: He was pissed. He grabbed the kid by the shirt and told him again to pick it up himself. He repeated that the dude should apologize to me.

DO: Did the boy—Wade Boles—apologize?

AS: Nope. He asked the guy—is Walker his name?

DO: Yes.

AS: He asked Walker, "Are you a terrorist lover or something?" That's when Walker seemed to lose it. His eyes changed and he punched the dude in the face. The first time there was blood. The second time I heard bone cracking. It was sick. Then this girl—I think she's Walker's sister—

DO: She is.

AS: She came running over and was screaming at him to stop. It took me, the sister, and the other kid to pull Walker off Wade Boles. By that time, mall security arrived, and they took over.

DO: So Wade Boles wasn't threatening Robert Walker?

AS: I don't know if you'd call it threatening, exactly. But he was up in Walker's face, for sure. I definitely felt like Wade Boles and his friend were threatening me, and that guy Walker came over and took my side. Not everyone will do that. Most people just walk on by, like they don't see what's happening, because it's not their problem. I mean I get it, Walker shouldn't have broken the guy's nose, but it wasn't him that started it. It was those other two guys.

TRANSCRIPT OF POLICE INTERVIEW
WITH JOHN LANDON

DY: This is Detective Alan Yerwood speaking. It is Wednesday, September 7th at 8 p.m. I am interviewing John Landon, a male age 16, DOB 11/25. Mr. Landon is currently a junior at Argleton High School.

Mr. Landon, please spell your name for the record.

JL: J-O-H-N L-A-N-D-O-N, but no one calls me John except my mom when she's mad. I go by Jed. That's J-E-D.

DY: Okay then, Jed. What time did you arrive at the Lone Pine Mall?

JL: Wade and I got there around 5. We went to Game-Stop and messed around for a while.

DY: Is that the only place you went in the mall?

JL: No. Wade's in the market for some new kicks, so we went to Foot Locker. He didn't buy anything, though. Those shoes ain't cheap. Then we went to the food court.

DY: What time did you arrive at the food court?

JL: Not sure exactly. 6 maybe?

DY: What did you do then?

JL: We each got a few slices of pizza.

DY: Tell me what led up to the encounter with Robert Walker.

JL: So we were sitting there eating pizza and this kid is cleaning tables near us. And we start joking with him. You know, just friendly-like.

DY: What kind of joking?

JL: Not threatening or anything, just messing around.

DY: But you said it was friendly?

JL: Okay. Maybe not exactly friendly.

DY: Can you tell me what you said to him, exactly?

JL: I can't remember the exact words. I might have made a joke about the rag he was wearing on his man bun. And then I told him to go back to his country because we don't want terrorists here.

DY: So that's what you call "friendly"?

JL: It was just a joke. It wasn't serious. We were just messing around. You know, having a little fun.

DY: How did the kid take it? Did he take it as a joke and a "little fun"?

JL: I don't know. He told us to piss off.

DY: What happened next?

JL: Um . . . I can't remember exactly how it went down.

DY: Did you respond?

JY: No. I think Wade said something.

DY: What was that?

JL: Uh, he threw some pepperoni on the floor and told the guy to pick it up.

DY: And did he?

JL: No. Instead he said he was American and not a terrorist.

DY: Do you believe that?

JL: That he isn't a terrorist? How am I supposed to know? You're the cop.

DY: No, that he's just as American as you are.

JL: Um . . . I don't know. I guess. Maybe.

DY: Then what happened?

JY: Then Stella's brother came over and started going crazy.

DY: What do you mean by "going crazy"?

JL: He grabbed Wade by the shirt and told him to apologize and pick the stuff up himself.

DY: He grabbed Wade before saying anything first?

JL: Yeah.

DJ: Did Wade apologize?

JL: No, he asked Walker if he was a terrorist lover. And that's when Walker decked him. There was blood everywhere. He broke his nose on the second punch. Man, the sound was awful. He would have kept punching Wade if we hadn't pulled him off.

DJ: Who is "we"?

JL: Me, Stella—that's Rob Walker's sister—and the kid.

DJ: So Walker hit Wade Boles without any provocation?

JL: That's right. Look, the guy is messed up. About a month ago, I was at the convenience store with Mike Carlson, and Mike accidentally slammed the door of a cooler. Next thing we know, Walker is down on the floor with his hands over his head. C'mon, that's not normal. So it's not like I'm a hundred percent surprised that he freaked out on Wade.

TRANSCRIPT OF POLICE INTERVIEW
WITH WADE BOLES

DY: This is Detective Alan Yerwood speaking. It's 3:30 p.m. on Thursday, September 8th. I am interviewing Wade Boles. Wade, will you please spell your name?

WB: W-A-D-E B-O-L-E-S

DY: Thank you. Wade is 17 years old. His date of birth is 12/4. He is currently a junior at Argleton High School.

DY: What time did you arrive at the Lone Pine Mall?

WB: I don't know. Around 4:30? Maybe 5?

DY: What did you do there?

WB: We went to GameStop and checked out the new games. Messed around for a while. Looked at kicks in Foot Locker.

DY: When did you get to the food court?

WB: I don't know exactly. I don't wear a watch. It was probably 6. Maybe earlier, maybe later.

DY: Can you tell me in as much detail as possible what happened once you arrived at the food court?

WB: Got a few slices of pizza and a Coke at Pizza Palace. Jed and I were minding our own business when Stella Walker's older brother comes out of nowhere and starts getting in my face because he didn't like that I told this guy who was cleaning tables to pick a piece of pepperoni off the floor. That's his job, right? Walker grabs me by the shirt and the dude gets spit on me when he tells me to pick it up myself and apologize. Apologize for what? I didn't do anything wrong!

DY: So before Walker came over, your only interaction with the kid cleaning tables was a request to pick a piece of pepperoni up from the floor?

WB: That's right.

DY: Well, that's very interesting, because your friend Jed had a slightly different recollection of the events.

WB: He did? Well, you know, sir, I'm taking pain-killers because of the broken nose that Rob Walker gave me, so maybe that's what's interfering with my memory.

DY: I understand. Well, let me ask you the question again, now that you've had a chance to refresh your memory with this new information. Before Walker came over, is it true that the only interaction between you and Ashar Singh, the young man working in the food court, was that you asked him to pick up a piece of pepperoni from the floor?

[silence]

DY: Wade?

WB: Well. . . now that I think about it, maybe there was a little more than that. I . . . think Jed might have made a joke about the thing the guy was wearing on his hair bun. You know, like those people do.

DY: Do you recall what, exactly, the joke was?

WB: Not exactly. Something about him being a terrorist and how he should go back to his country.

DY: Did Ashar find that joke funny?

WB: I don't know. I'm not a mind reader. He said he wasn't a terrorist and that he was born here.

DY: And how did things proceed from there? You started this interview saying that Walker hit you without provocation because you asked Ashar to pick up a piece of pepperoni from the floor and that's his job. But it seems there's a little more to this story. Fill me in.

WB: Well, a piece of pepperoni fell off my pizza onto the floor. So I asked that guy to pick it up, since he was standing right there and it's his job anyway.

DY: Let me make sure I understand this sequence of events correctly: Your friend calls Ashar a terrorist and tells him to go back to his country, Ashar says he isn't a terrorist, he was born here, which, for the record, would make him an American citizen, and you ask him to pick up the pepperoni because he's standing there. Do I have this right?

WB: Yes, sir.

DY: And you didn't drop it on the floor intentionally?

WB: Why would I do something like that? Waste a good piece of pepperoni?

DY: Okay. So this piece of pepperoni lands on the floor, you ask Ashar to pick it up and...

WB: Next thing I know Stella Walker's older brother comes out of nowhere and starts getting in my face for telling the guy to pick up the pepperoni, like it's any of his business.

DY: When you say "getting in your face," you mean...?

WB: He grabs me by the shirt and tells me to pick it up and apologize. Apologize for what? I didn't do anything wrong! So I told him where he could go, and then he punched me in the face. He would have kept on punching me, even though his sister was scream-ing at him to stop. As you can see, sir, he broke my nose. It took three people to pull him off me.

DY: Did you ask Walker if he was a terrorist lover?

WB: Uh . . . I might have.

DY: Were you aware that Walker is a US Marine Corps veteran who served two tours in Afghanistan?

WB: Didn't stop him from breaking my nose, did it? I tell you, sir, that guy is insane. He should be locked up before he hurts someone else. He's got some serious anger issues.

TRANSCRIPT OF POLICE INTERVIEW
WITH ROBERT WALKER

DO: This is Detective Brendan Overmann speaking. It is Wednesday, September 7th at 9:00 p.m. I am interviewing Robert Walker R-O-B-E-R-T W-A-L-K-E-R, age 21, date of birth 7/10.

DO: Mr. Walker, I'm going to read you your Miranda Rights. You have the right to remain silent. Anything you say can and will be used against you in a court of law. You have the right to an attorney. If you cannot afford an attorney, one will be provided for you. Do you understand the rights I have just read to you?

RW: Yes.

DO: With these rights in mind, do you wish to speak to me?

RW: Yes.

DO: When did you arrive at the Lone Pine Mall?

RW: I didn't even want to go to the mall in the

first place. It's hard enough to go to the mini-mart or the grocery store. Have you ever served in a war zone, Detective?

DO: I have not.

RW: Maybe you won't get it. Most people don't. One day you're in a completely different world where the rules were one way, and then you get on a plane—or maybe two, because we had to transfer from military plane to civilian flight in Germany. Then, in what seems like no time, you're back home. You go from a place where every piece of debris on the side of the road could be an IED or every obstruction a trap, from a place where stopping for any reason could be death, to here, where you're stuck in traffic behind some old geezer who is driving five miles below the speed limit because he can't see as well as he used to and people act like *you're* the crazy one because you're leaning on the horn and getting road rage.

DO: So you came to the mall at what time?

RW: I get it. Just the facts. Okay, sir. We got here right before the 16:30 show.

DO: 16:30. So that's 4:30 p.m., right?

RW: Yeah.

DO: What did you see?

RW: *Alien*. I always give my sister a hard time because she likes old movies, especially the black-and-white ones. She's not a big fan of sci-fi, even if it's old, but she thought—

[silence]

DO: What did she think, Mr. Walker?

RW: She thought it would be some harmless fun. [laughs] You know how that turned out.

DO: That's what I'm trying to establish. So you went to the movie. What happened next?

RW: Stella, that's my sister, suggested getting an ice cream. Actually, she said froyo, but I wanted ice cream. So we walked to the food court. We were sitting there eating when I noticed these two kids harassing the kid who was cleaning tables. They're calling him a terrorist and telling him to go back to his own country. Here's this kid trying to do his after-school job and these ignorant punks who think they're so tough are treating him like he's less than they are. They don't even realize that he's Sikh and not Muslim, that's how much these kids know about the real world. But they think they know everything. And still, they think it's okay to call someone a terrorist, just because of his religion.

DO: Is that when you decided to intervene?

RW: I think I stood up at that point. But what really made me decide to step in was when one of the kids spat on the floor and threw pepperoni and then told the guy to pick it up. It was so offensive that I couldn't let it pass.

DO: So that's when you walked over?

RW: Yeah. Look, we worked with Afghan translators who were risking their lives to help us. But these kids think everyone they see who doesn't look like them and speaks with an accent is a terrorist? Yeah, I went over there to set them straight.

DO: Tell me how you "set them straight"?

RW: I walked over and told the kid who dropped the thing on the floor to pick it up himself and to apologize to the kid. He responded by cursing at me and saying, "Haven't you ever heard of the First Amendment?"

Look, I get it. I shouldn't have touched him. But you gotta understand. When I was in Afghanistan, I was making decisions that could literally mean life or death. And now this snot-nosed little punk who doesn't even know the difference between Muslim and Sikh is disobeying a direct order?

DO: So how did you "touch him"?

RW: I grabbed the kid by his shirt and told him again to pick it up and apologize. He said, "What are you, some kind of terrorist lover?" and that's when I punched him.

DO: How many times did you punch him?

RW: I don't know. I went into the zone.

DO: The zone?

RW: Like in—where you get extreme focus and time acts in strange ways and you're hyperaware of some senses but not the others. So I can describe exactly the sound it made when my fist hit that kid's face and how the blood spattered on my arm and the floor and for one or two seconds I felt bad that I was making a mess that the kid was going to have to clean up but—

DO: But?

RW: But that passed through my mind as fast as a bullet train and all I could feel was my blood pumping. He was the enemy and I was teaching him a lesson, so I punched him again and I heard the crack. I think I might have broken his nose.

DO: You did.

RW: What have I done . . . ?

DO: It looks to me like you've done a Class B felony, young man.

RW: Oh no. [silence] No . . . My parents . . . my sister . . .

[silence]

RW: Jason was right.

DO: Who is Jason?

RW: [crying]

DO: Mr. Walker, who is Jason?

RW: [crying]

TRANSCRIPT OF INTERVIEW
WITH STELLA WALKER

DY: This is Detective Alan Yerwood speaking on Wednesday September 7th at 9:00 p.m. I'm interviewing Stella (S-T-E-L-L-A) Walker (W-A-L-K-E-R), age 16. DOB 4/17. Subject is currently a junior at Argleton High School

DY: What time did you arrive at the Lone Pine Mall?

SW: I think it was about 4:20 p.m. We got there in time to buy popcorn and drinks and catch the previews at the 4:30 showing of *Alien*.

DY: You stayed for the entire movie.

SW: Yeah. It was awesome. Way better than I thought it would be. I'm not really that into sci-fi. It's more Rob's thing, which is why I suggested we go. He's been pretty down since he got back from his last deployment and it's one of his favorite movies, so I thought it might cheer him up. He seemed like he was in a better mood when it was over, and I suggested we go get some frozen yogurt. He wanted ice cream, so we went to Dreamiscle Creamsicles.

DY: What time was this?

SW: I think it was around 6:30?

DY: Tell me about the encounter that led to the fight.

SW: I saw Wade Boles and Jed Landon when we got to the food court and purposely tried to avoid them.

DY: And why was it you wanted to avoid them?

SW: They aren't exactly my favorite people at school. They have some, well, narrow-minded views about things. To be honest, that's what led to the fight. They were harassing the guy who was clean-ing tables.

DY: Harassing how, exactly?

SW: I feel bad even saying it because it's so offensive, but Jed called him a "raghead" and a "terrorist." That's when Rob got up and started walking toward them.

DY: How did the kid who was cleaning tables respond?

SW: He said, "Piss off," or something like that. But they didn't back off. Then Wade spit on the floor and threw a piece of pepperoni on top of the spit and told the guy to clean it up. That's when Rob intervened. He told Wade to clean it up himself and apologize. I started walking over because I had a feeling it wasn't going to end well.

DY: How did Wade respond?

SW: He swore at Rob.

DY: How did your brother take that?

SW: Not well. He grabbed Wade by the collar and told him again that he should apologize and clean up the mess himself. And then Wade said, "What are you, some kind of terrorist lover?" That was what did it.

DY: Did what?

SW: Made Rob lose it. He punched Wade, and then he kept on punching him until we were able to pull him off.

You have to understand, Detective, Rob's a marine. He did two tours in Afghanistan. Defending people is what he does.

[silence]

Do you see what I mean? You just don't go around calling someone like my brother a terrorist lover. Especially when you don't even know the difference between Sikh and Muslim, and don't even care because you think they're all terrorists anyway.

DY: Was that when security arrived?

SW: Yeah. Someone called 911 and one of the employees at the food court called mall security. Security came first, and they took Rob into their office until the police came.

DY: Detective Overmann entered the room at 9:45 p.m.

DO: Miss Walker, do you have any idea who Jason is?

SW: Is Rob okay?

DO: Miss Walker, who is Jason?

SW: He was my brother's friend. They served together in Afghanistan. Jason shot himself two weeks ago. Seriously, Detective, is my brother okay?

HALEY: OMG did you guys hear what happened?

FARIDA: No, what?

HALEY: Stella's brother Rob got arrested!! And according to Jed Landon, Stella was at the police station, too.

KEN: WHAT? WHY?!!

FARIDA: Oh no! 🙁 What happened?

HALEY: Rob went totally out of control at the mall and punched Wade Boles. He broke Wade's nose.

FARIDA: OMG. Poor Stella.

HALEY: What about poor Wade? Rob broke his nose!

KEN: Knowing Wade, he probably did something to deserve it.

HALEY: 😁 Why are you victim blaming? That's so wrong!

FARIDA: Uh . . . maybe because Wade is a jerk to me, like 100% of the time?

HALEY: Okay, that's wrong, but he doesn't deserve to have some crazy guy break his nose.

KEN: Stella's brother isn't crazy.

FARIDA: Yeah. I know Rob. So do you, Haley. How can you say that about him?

HALEY: You weren't at the convenience store when he hit the deck for no reason. It wasn't normal.

KEN: I'm sure there's got to be more to this story. We can't just, like, jump to conclusions.

HALEY: Like you haven't already jumped to conclusions about Wade?

FARIDA: Like you haven't already jumped to conclusions about Rob? 😕

HALEY MORANI HAS LEFT THE CONVERSATION.

KEN: I wonder what really happened.

FARIDA: I'm going to text Stella.

KEN: Tell me what happens.

KEN: This isn't going to do the campaign any good.

FARIDA: KEN!

KEN: I'm just stating the obvious.

KEN: I mean Haley's a friend and she believes Wade's story.

FARIDA: Maybe she wasn't really a true friend.

KEN: But we can't just count on true friends to win an election.

KEN: We need other people.

FARIDA: I know. I guess right now I'm more worried about Stella than the election. But it's not going to do us any good, that's for sure.

KEN: And it was an uphill battle to begin with.

FARIDA: Don't give her the gloom and doom. She doesn't need that from us right now. Promise?!

KEN: Yeah. Okay. I'll try.

FARIDA: There is no try.

KEN: I've turned you into Yoda. My job here is done.

FARIDA: STELLLLLLLAAAAA! What happened?! Is it true that Rob got arrested for breaking Wade's nose at the mall?

ME: What?! How do people know already? We only just got back from the police station!!

FARIDA: I heard from Haley. Then I saw that Wade posted a picture of himself in the ER on Insta.

ME: Why would he do that? He looked awful!

FARIDA: You're asking ME to explain how Wade's mind works?

ME: Fair point.

FARIDA: How are you?

ME: Not so good.

FARIDA: So what really happened?

ME: Rob and I went to see Alien at the movies. He's been really down because one of his battle buddies died—suicide—two weeks ago.

FARIDA: What?! You never told me that.

ME: Yeah. There's a lot I haven't told you, TBH. Things have been hard at home since Rob came back.

FARIDA: What do you mean?

ME: I'm really tired and I don't want to talk about it RN. It's been a long day.

FARIDA: Okay. Get some sleep. But I'm here for you. So is Ken. I'll drive tomorrow.

ME: Thanks. See you then. 💕

CHAPTER SEVEN

I curl up on my bed, wishing that there were some way I could have a do-over. That I could come home and leave Rob alone sitting in front of the TV, playing video games. That I could go up to my room and read a book or listen to music or watch videos of cute puppies trying to climb stairs. That I could do anything except convince my brother it's a good idea for us to go see a movie and then get ice cream afterward.

One decision leads to another and another. Decisions you think are good, but end up leading the person you love—and think you're helping—to disaster instead. I keep replaying the afternoon over in my head, looking for the clues that should have showed me that it was heading in the wrong direction. The little signs I didn't see, or ignored, that could have prevented the catastrophe from happening.

Meanwhile, what I didn't tell Farida was that I think I have to quit the election now.

I just couldn't face telling her the whole story tonight, even though she's my best friend. Because I know I was born wearing white girl goggles, and inevitably I'm going to say something wrong, and normally I don't mind when she calls me on it. But everything is a mess right now and it's my fault, and I just can't face messing up in one more way.

So it feels easier not to say anything. To just add it to the growing list of things I'm not telling her.

Except that leaves me alone in my room with my racing thoughts and squirming insides, feeling like even more of a coward than ever.

My phone buzzes.

ADAM: You okay? Sounds like you had an intense afternoon.
ME: Intense doesn't even begin to describe it.
ADAM: Did you really end up at the police station?
ME: Yes.

My fingers hover over the screen.

ME: Would you hate me if I quit?
ADAM: Quit what?
ME: The election.
ADAM: What?!! Why? Let's talk first. Do you want me to come over?

I check the time. It's almost midnight.

Cons: 1. It's late. Way too late to expect Adam to drive across town to talk to me. 2. My parents would freak if he showed up here. 3. I'd have to sneak out of the house. 4. I'm so tired it feels like someone harnessed a boulder to my chest and I have to drag it around with me everywhere I go.

But on the other hand, the Pros: 1. Adam just offered to drive across town to see me. 2. I wouldn't feel like I'm so alone. 3. I'm not going to be able to sleep anyway. 4. I want to see Adam.

ME: Are you sure it's not too late? What about your dad?
ADAM: Don't worry about me. What about you? Will your parents freak out?
ME: Park at the end of the street and text me. I'll sneak out.
ADAM: Okay. Heading out now. Hang in there!

And he sends a GIF of a cute sloth hanging from a branch.

A few minutes ago, I was curled up on my bed, drained of energy. Now I feel a flutter of excitement in my stomach. It's because of the cute sloth GIF, I tell myself as I jump up and throw on one of Rob's old marines hoodies and swap my pajama bottoms for jeans.

Then I check the hallway situation. My parents' door is shut, but light shines under it, meaning at least one of them is still awake. Rob's light is off. Peggy has been sleeping with him, so as long as I'm quiet, she won't bark. I creep down the hallway and tread softly downstairs. I go through the kitchen and sneak out the back door, making sure it's unlocked so I can get back in.

There's enough of a glow from the crescent moon for me to see my way around the side of the house without having to use the light on my phone. I breathe in the cool, crisp night air and snuggle into the oversized hoodie. Despite the light on the horizon from town, I can see a few stars in the dark sky. Closing my eyes, I wish for everything to turn out okay. I can't undo what happened today, but I can wish for it to end well. If wishes on stars work, which I know they don't. But I'm sort of desperate here.

I sit on the front step and wait to hear from Adam. In the meantime, I check what's happening on social media. Sure enough, Wade Boles has posted a picture of his broken nose on Instagram—both before and after it's bandaged. Not a pretty sight either way. He's made sure to say that it's my brother who broke it in both posts, each of which have hundreds of reactions and comments.

People are already linking it to my class president slogan. *Stella Walker isn't the smart solution, she's the violent solution* is one of the nicer things that's written.

How can I stay in the race after what happened?

Now that I have a good excuse for dropping out, it's strange that I don't want to. I was just starting to feel more confident about the whole thing, like maybe I could make a difference. But it looks like I'm going to have to take myself out of the running, because of Rob.

Not just because of him. Because of me. I persuaded him to go to the movies. He didn't want to go. If it wasn't for me, he wouldn't have been at the mall. This never would have happened.

I wrap my arms around my knees and shiver, inhaling the autumnal smell of decomposing leaves. I never thought of it as sad before, but as I sit here waiting for Adam, contemplating the end of a political career that never even started, I think from now on I'll always associate this smell with a feeling of "what if?"

An incoming text pulls me out of my depressing reverie. It's Adam, telling me he's at the end of the street.

My muscles are already stiff from the chill. I rub my arms as I walk to his pickup, trying to get some circulation back.

He's got a classic rock station blasting when I get in the truck, but he turns it down right away.

"Hey. How are you holding up?" he asks, reaching out for my hand—except my hand is still inside the sleeve of my hoodie for warmth, so he can't find it.

"What happened? Did they chop off your hands?" he asks. "Have you been texting me with your nose? I didn't know that worked."

He tries it on his phone and despite myself I laugh.

"Ewww. Remind me not to touch your screen now that it might have snot germs."

Adam grins. "Snot germs. More effective deterrent than any password." His smile fades quickly, though, and he reaches into my hoodie sleeve, tugging out my chilled fingers. "Yikes, your hands are freezing! Do you want me to turn on the heat?"

"No, it's okay. Your hand is nice and warm."

And it is. Comforting, too. What I don't tell him is that holding it is sending tingles up my arm.

"So I know this is a really stupid question but . . . how are you doing?"

I don't even think about lying and saying fine.

"Terrible. Awful. The world is falling apart and it's all my fault."

"Stella, you're smart and cool as anything, but no offense, I think you're overestimating your ability right now," he says. "I mean, do you seriously think that you have the power to cause *the entire world* to fall apart?"

Despite how miserable I'm feeling, I laugh again. When he puts it that way, it does seem a little, well, dramatic. But it's not what I meant.

"Okay not the *entire world*. A small portion of it that figures large in my life."

"Tell me exactly what happened, because all I know is what I've read online," Adam says. "And I'm pretty sure that's not the whole story."

And the words I couldn't bring myself to say to Farida I say to Adam. Maybe it's because he doesn't know Rob. He doesn't really know *me*. Maybe that makes it easier. I don't know. Either way, I tell him what's been going on with my brother since he got back from this last tour. I tell him how difficult things have been at home, and how Rob freaked out when Jason died. I tell him how I pressured Rob to go to the movies so he'd get out of the house. I even tell him about almost running over Mall Dog and the story Rob told me about the boy and his dog, even though I'm not sure if I should. I tell him what happened at the food court.

"Have you seen the comments on Wade's Instagram posts?

How people are already tying this to my campaign slogan? How can I stay in the race? I've got to drop out."

He doesn't say anything right away, and in the absence of words I'm acutely aware that our hands are still touching and start wondering how I can enjoy having that the point of physical contact if he doesn't understand. Except that his hand is comforting, and I don't want to let go.

"People are only saying that stuff because they haven't heard your side of the story," Adam says finally. "If you quit now, you lose the chance to tell it. You'll have let them win without a fight."

"But look at what they're writing about me already," I say. "It's so ugly. And it's not even true."

"You knew it wasn't going to be easy, right?" he says. "It's not like this was ever going to be a walkover."

"I know. But I didn't think it was going to be this hard, this big, this fast."

He pushes a stray piece of hair away from my face with the hand that's not holding mine.

"Life comes at you fast. But you can handle it, Stella. I know you can."

"I'm glad you've got so much confidence in me," I say. "Because clearly I don't."

"You should," he says softly.

I bite my lip and look down at our still interlocked fingers between us, then up at Adam. He's watching me, like he's trying to make a decision. He lets go of my hand and I'm more disappointed than I expected. (What, like I thought Adam and I were just going to hold hands forever?) But instead of saying he's got to go or something, he fists his hand around the excessive fabric of my hoodie pocket and tugs. I feel myself sliding across the truck's leather bench seat and when I collide with Adam, I giggle. A smile lights up his face and I notice the slope of his cheeks and his smooth, tanned skin and his single dimple. How does that happen? Don't people usually have them on both cheeks? Note to self: Look this up on the internet later. I reach up and touch his dimple, and his smile deepens.

He releases my hoodie and winds his hand around the back of my neck. I let my fingers slide from his dimple so I can run my thumb along his jaw. He gives me a look, like checking to make sure this is cool, and I give a small nod in return.

Then his soft lips are on mine. This intense feeling of happiness explodes in my chest, winding its way around my heart. His fingers tangle in my hair, urging us closer.

When we break apart, my heart is fluttering and my brain is buzzing.

"Have I persuaded you to stay in the race?" Adam asks, like he's just picking up our conversation right where we left off.

I raise my eyebrows. "So that's what this is all about? Using your masculine wiles to get me to stay in the running?"

"Totally," he says. "Did it work?"

I hesitate, and not because I want to keep him guessing so he'll kiss me again, although I hope he will.

"I don't know if I'm as brave as you think I am," I confess. "Sometimes I wonder if I was adopted. The courage gene seems to have skipped me."

"Being scared doesn't mean it skipped you," Adam says. "It just means you know the odds. It takes courage to keep going despite that."

I want to be as brave as Adam sees me. But right now, even in the cocoon of his truck and warmed by his kisses, I'm not sure I can I do it.

"Can I sleep on it and let you know tomorrow?" I ask.

"Sure," Adam says, squeezing my hand. "Although now I'm feeling all insecure about my masculine wiles."

I lean forward and kiss him. "Don't. They are very persuasive."

"Keep telling me that," he says.

"Speaking of sleeping on it, I better go do that," I tell him. "Tomorrow is going to be hard enough as it is."

He cups my cheek and pulls me closer for another kiss. "Good night, Stella. Don't give up."

I don't promise him anything except that I'll see him in the morning, but I watch the taillights of his truck until they disappear, before sneaking back into the house.

When I finally get to sleep, my dreams are of face-sucking aliens taking over the mall. I call out to Rob, but he's being led away in handcuffs by the police. Except the police are Wade, Jed, and Chris, and they just laugh at my despair.

I wake up at four in the morning with a start, heart thumping in my chest and sheets tangled around my legs.

While I'm relieved that it was just a dream, the real nightmare of Rob being arrested isn't, and that makes it impossible to get back to sleep.

When I tell Dad I didn't sleep well, he makes me a big travel mug of strong coffee—what he calls "battery acid" from his own marine days.

"If I'm addicted to coffee as a grown-up, I'm blaming it on you," I tell him.

"If that's the worst of your problems when you're an adult, I'll pat myself on the back for having done a good job," Dad says. "Better that than having to bail you out on an arrest charge."

I glance over at Dad, because I can't tell if he's joking or serious. There's no crinkling around his eyes, no hint of humor in his face.

"Rob didn't start it," I say. "Wade and Jed did."

"That's not the issue here, Stella."

I want to ask him what the issue is, but Farida pulls up outside and honks the horn. So instead I grab my travel mug and backpack. "Gotta go. See you later."

"Chin up, head down," Dad says.

"Yeah, okay," I say on the way out the door, although I've never understood how doing both things at the same time is possible.

Farida usually plays music in the car, but today her radio is tuned to the last thing in the world I want to hear this morning: Mayor Abbott on some talk show being interviewed about his campaign.

"Hey, Stella," she says, leaning over to accept my hug. "Did you hear this? My parents were listening at home earlier."

"Hear what?"

"Wait. It's coming up."

Mayor Abbott is blathering on about business or something, but then the host asks: "Some consider your position on immigration extreme. How would you respond to those critics?"

"How is it extreme to protect American lives from the evil forces that are trying to sneak past our borders?" Mayor Abbott says.

"But hasn't immigration been part of what has made America the great nation that it is? The fact that we're a melting pot of ideas and experiences? Isn't it exactly that diversity that's made us stronger?" the host asks.

"I'm not saying we have to permanently halt immigration," Mayor Abbott says. "I'm saying we need a pause. To think more clearly about what we're doing, and make sure that we're vetting people thoroughly and properly so that no bad apples slip through the net to cause harm to innocent Americans."

"But you've gone significantly further than that in your speeches," the host says. "We have concerned listeners calling in about the impact such talk has already had in their communities and schools."

"Let me tell you about something that happened just yesterday at the Lone Pine Mall near Argleton," Mayor Abbott says. "My son's good friend was brutally attacked by a mentally unstable male who it appears may sympathize with radical Islamic extremism. The kid had his nose broken."

"What?!" I gasp.

The host says, "But, Mayor Abbott—" before the mayor cuts him off.

"When an American teenager can't even go to the mall safely in this great country, what have we come to?" Mayor Abbott ends with a dramatic flourish.

"He's lying!" I shout at the radio. "What's he talking about? That's not how it went down! He wasn't even there! I was!"

"And your brother isn't an immigrant, so it's not like it had anything to do with the discussion anyway. He's deflecting." Farida switches it off. "So what did happen, Stella?"

I hesitate.

"Seriously?" she says. I can hear frustration in her voice. And she's right. She's my best friend and I should be able to tell her everything. But once I do, there's no escape. No place where I can be just . . . me. Not an afterthought to Rob's drama.

I take a deep breath and launch into the story. The *whole* story. The good, the bad, and the ugly. And when I'm done, we're almost at school.

"So, uh, in that radio interview, what do you think Mayor Abbott meant by 'sympathizes with radical Islamic extremism'?" Farida asks as she drives into the high school parking lot and finds an open space. She turns off the car. "I mean, where did *that* come from?"

"I . . . don't know. Um . . . Maybe because Rob served in Afghanistan?" I say.

Farida looks at me, her brown eyes narrowed. "You really think that's the whole reason?"

"What other reason could there be?" I ask.

"Come on, Stella," she says. "Don't play dumb with me."

Except I'm not playing dumb—it takes me a few seconds to figure out what she's talking about.

"Wait—you think they're making the leap from us being friends to Rob sympathizing with radical Islamic extremism?"

"Not yet, maybe, but they will."

I laugh. "Like anyone would believe that."

Farida isn't laughing. She's dead serious.

"But it's ridiculous. What do you and I have to do with Rob? And anyone who knows you—"

"But most of the people who just heard Mayor Abbott don't know me, or my family, do they? They'll just hear our foreign-sounding name and see our brown skin and my dad's beard and the fact that my mom wears the hijab. And that'll be enough to make us threatening."

I want to be able to tell her she's wrong, that we're better than that, but I know she's right, especially after what happened at the mall yesterday.

"I need to think about these things more, don't I?" I say, breaking the awkward silence.

Farida nods. "Yup. 'Fraid so." She starts tracing the word *Ford* in the middle of the steering wheel with her index finger. "For a smart person, you're really slow to pick this stuff up sometimes."

"I'm sorry," I say. "I don't mean to be a clueless idiot."

"I know you don't *mean* to be. But . . ." She hesitates and looks out the window. "It gets really old having to walk you through this stuff all the time. Sometimes I wonder if you're ever going to get it."

"I try," I tell her. "I'm not perfect."

"I know that you try. But sometimes it feels like trying just isn't enough. I want you to get it."

"I'm sorry," I say again. "I'm sorry for being continually clueless, and that you might be dragged into this mess for just being friends with me."

"I know you're sorry. And I know you didn't mean for this to happen. But it did. And like it or not, meant for it to happen or not, no matter how good your intentions, my family is going to feel the impact, trust me. We're going to be collateral damage from your drama, and you didn't even want to tell me what happened, even though we're supposed to be best friends."

I know she's right, and I understand why she's hurt. I should have told her. I'm silent, trying to figure out how to explain why I didn't.

"Stella, why didn't you tell me what was going on with Rob before this? Why didn't you tell any of us?" She asks the question softly, and that makes it hurt worse. Because she knows me so well, and it's a fair question, but it's not one I know how to answer.

"I'm not sure, exactly . . . maybe because I wanted to keep it separate from my life?" I say. "It's bad enough that it is taking over everything at home without having to talk about it with you guys, if that makes sense?"

"I guess," Farida says. "But I still think it's strange that you've been keeping it from me. It's the kind of thing we'd normally talk about. It makes me wonder what else you're not telling me."

I flush, thinking about last night—about Adam and our first kiss.

"See, you've got secret written all over your face," she says, and I can hear the sadness in her voice.

Why did I get stuck with a telltale face instead of a poker one?

"Adam and I kissed last night," I confess.

"You and Adam? Kissed? *Last night?*"

I nod sheepishly.

"But . . . *when?* You were too tired to tell me what happened, but not too tired to make out with Mountain Man?"

"I'm sorry. I just—"

I stop because I'm afraid telling the truth about why I didn't want to talk to her last night will just make things worse, especially if she's right about Mayor Abbott making the radical Islamic extremism link because of our friendship.

"I just couldn't sleep. And Adam texted me to see how I was holding up, and then he offered to drive over. Which was crazy, but I was so frustrated and upset and . . ."

"So you told him what's going on?" Farida asks, arching her eyebrow at me.

I hesitate, but that's enough.

"Really, Stella? You've apparently been hiding stuff from me for months and Adam calls you up in the middle of the night and you just tell him everything? We're supposed to be best friends!"

I cringe at her words, but she's not wrong. I squirm in my seat, not sure how to make it right. "I know! I should have told you. I'm sorry. But . . . it's just . . ." I stop, afraid to admit this because I know she wanted to run for class president in the first place, but her parents were worried about her involvement. Except now, because of Rob, they're probably going to be involved anyway.

"I didn't mean to tell Adam everything. But I was thinking about quitting the race for class president, and I was scared you'd get mad at me if I tried to talk to you about it. And then Adam was just . . . there. And it just happened."

Dead silence follows my words before Farida finally says, "Are you kidding me? Quit? You drag my family into this mess and now you're going to quit?"

I don't think I've ever seen Farida this angry.

"I didn't drag you into this mess, Mayor Abbott did," I protest.

"Way to miss the point, Stella! Did you even hear what I said, like, two minutes ago?" Farida says. "I wanted to run and my parents were worried about the fallout. But now we're going to get the fallout anyway. How can you even think of quitting?"

"Have you seen what people are saying on Wade's Instagram posts?"

"Come on, toughen up. My little brother has worse stuff said to him every day on the school bus. You still don't get it, do you?" She checks the time on her phone. "We better get in. But don't you dare quit on me, Stella Walker."

I bend down to pick up my backpack so I don't have to answer, because I still don't know what to do.

Just before she slams her door, Farida says, "And you're right: I am mad at you. So don't think this conversation is over."

I try to imagine myself as the brave Stella that Adam thinks I am. But I don't feel at all courageous as I follow Farida's stiff back into school. She's furious and I don't blame her.

Maybe I'm like the Cowardly Lion in *The Wonderful Wizard of Oz* and I have courage hidden deep inside.

Or not. I'm pretty sure I'm just completely terrified at this particular moment.

Is everyone looking at me or is it just my imagination? Are they talking about Rob and what happened at the mall?

"Stella! Farida! Wait up!"

Haley catches up to Farida and me.

"What happened at the mall?" she asks before even saying hi.

I glance around to see if anyone is looking. Strangely, it seems like everyone is purposely *not* looking, which gives me the feeling of being shunned.

"Why would Rob break Wade's nose?" Haley continues. "I mean, I know he's been acting kind of weird, but that's super messed up."

"I don't want to talk about it right now," I say. "But Rob didn't start it. Wade did."

"But Mayor Abbott said—"

"Mayor Abbott wasn't at the mall," I tell Haley. "I was."

"I know but—"

I glare at her. "Haley, are you my friend or aren't you?" I ask her. "I'm telling you, Rob didn't start it."

"I *am* your friend, Stella. I'm just saying, I was there that time at the convenience store. So was Jed."

Oh crap. Would Jed have told the police about that? Could that influence the case against my brother?

"That's got nothing to do with what happened yesterday," I insist.

"All I'm saying is that your brother was acting pretty strange that day. Maybe he's messed up from being in the marines or something."

Some way to thank my brother for his service.

"Are you trying to be a friend and make me feel better about how awful the last twenty-four hours have been?" I ask her. "Because if you are, I hope there's a plan B."

Haley pushes her straight black hair back from her face. "Fine. Sorry I said anything. See you later." She turns and walks away.

I look at Farida, who stood stone-faced throughout the conversation. "You still think I should stay in the race? Haley's my friend and she doesn't believe me."

"Maybe she wasn't really your friend," Farida says, giving me a pointed look. "Maybe you should trust the people who *are* your friends."

Even though her words hurt, I nod slowly, hating that we're at odds, and knowing that I'm going to have to find the courage to fix it.

Ken catches us in the hallway on the way to AP Gov, and he wants all the details, so I have to explain everything that went down yesterday again.

"I mean, I get it. Obviously, Rob shouldn't have broken Wade's nose. But to make out like Wade was just hanging out doing nothing?" I shake my head in frustration.

Farida touches my shoulder and I notice that she's staring at the wall where Chris's and Amy's campaign posters hang. There's an empty space where my campaign poster used to be. It's been ripped into little pieces, just like the truth of what happened at the mall, and tossed onto the floor like garbage.

"That didn't take long," I say, trying to keep my voice steady. "I knew this was going to be a disaster."

"It's not a disaster," Farida says. "We can make new posters. Right, Ken?"

"Riiiiiight," Ken says.

I think he shares my agreement that it's a disaster more than Farida's optimism.

"I should quit," I say quietly.

"No!" Farida says with such ferocity that Ken and I both stare at her.

She's grasping her books tightly to her chest like a shield. "How many times do I have to say it? You can't give up now, Stella," she says. "You can't let them beat you."

"Even if there's no chance that I'll win?"

"Even then," she says.

"But what's the point?" I ask. "Can you imagine how humiliating it's going to be when I come in third after Amy Sarducci and the soft toilet paper ticket?"

"You won't," Farida says.

I look at the shredded remains of my campaign poster on the floor and give a bitter chuckle. "Right. And you're basing this on what, exactly?"

"Because we're going to show them how wrong this is," Farida says.

"How?" Ken asks. "How are we going to do that?"

"Et tu, Kenny?" Farida says. "You promised last night you'd be positive."

"Oops. My bad," Ken says, flushing under Farida's glare. "I forgot."

"You've got the memory of a goldfish—unless it's for

something you *want* to remember," Farida says, her frustration with Ken more than evident. She turns back to me. "Don't quit, Stella. We've got the truth on our side."

"But is that enough?" I ask. "Is the truth enough? I mean, look at how Mayor Abbott just twisted the truth on the radio."

"My point exactly," Ken says.

"Honestly, how do you two survive in this life when you give up on everything so easily?" Farida says. "I can't deal with you right now."

She marches ahead of us into class, while I try to ignore the smirk on Chris's face as I pass his desk, the one that makes me decide that maybe Farida is right. I *am* giving up too easily. I shouldn't back down—because if I do, then I'll have let the liars win.

Adam catches my eye, too, as I sit down, and he gives me a half grin that makes my stomach flip. I give him a quick, secret smile, then turn around before my transparent face starts giving me away.

He catches up to me at the end of class.

"How are you doing?" he asks. "Did you get any sleep?"

"Not a lot," I confess. "Nightmares."

"Yeah, I can imagine."

"Did you hear what Mayor Abbott said this morning?"

"Yeah," Adam says. "He's bad news."

"So you don't believe my brother is some psycho terrorist lover?"

"Like I'd believe anything that Chris's dad says? Besides, I know Wade and Jed," he says.

"That's a relief," I tell him.

"I mean, even if your brother *is* a little weird, we're all entitled to a strange relative. I know all about that. Most people at this school think my dad's a tin foil hatter."

"Is he?"

"Nah. He'd never waste good tin foil on a hat when it could be used to make a solar oven in the event of the zombie apocalypse."

Adam makes me laugh out loud, something I didn't expect to do today.

"It's good to hear you laugh," he says. "Listen, I saw that some idiots have been ripping up your campaign posters. If you want help making new ones, count me in."

"Thanks," I say. "I'll definitely take you up on that. I'm going to need all the help I can get."

"Well, I'm here," he says.

I don't know if it's because of the way his eyes lock with mine or the warmth of his fingers on my arm, but I want to believe him.

I also want to kiss him again.

While I was at school, my parents and Rob met a lawyer, Ms. Tilley, who says given that Rob was acting in defense of another and considering his otherwise exemplary record, the case probably won't even go to trial—most likely they will plea bargain and he'll have to do community service and pay for Wade's medical bills.

"Unless the prosecutor decides to play hardball because he's listening to the mayor's campaign speeches," Ms. Tilley warned.

Mom was shocked. She asked if that could really happen.

Ms. Tilley reminded her that in our state, not only are prosecutors elected, but if the mayor wins election as governor, he could influence legislators in the General Assembly who elect judges. He'd remember a prosecutor he viewed as acting favorably to his interests.

"That doesn't seem right," I say when they tell me about it at dinner. "Isn't justice supposed to be blind?"

"*Supposed to be* is the key phrase there," Dad says. "Doesn't mean it is in practice, necessarily."

"Which basically means I'm screwed," Rob mutters.

"No, you aren't," Mom declares. "Because we're right here beside you."

I'm not saying that Mom's wrong or anything. But a fat lot of good that did for Rob and his problems before this happened. What makes her think it will be enough now?

Roadrunner, buddy—

You could have told me.

I had no business going out of the house. I should have stayed home.

I just wanted to believe I could hold it together for a few hours to hang with Stella like we used to.

Drive On. Charlie Mike. Continue Mission.

Fat chance.

Mission Failure.

Fun trip to the movies?

End up in handcuffs with a felony assault charge.

Conduct unbecoming.

Oh wait, I'm not an officer.

I'm just a messed-up grunt trying to make sense of the fight so I can function now that I'm home.

And not scare the crap out of my family.

Not be a burden to my family.

Not have to see that look in their eyes, wondering what happened to the son, the brother, they knew before.

I remember when I saw pride.

I want to see that again.

I need to feel that for myself.

Instead, I keep seeing the kid smiling as he came toward me, and then . . . and then the whimpering of that poor dog that I had to put out of its suffering.

Instead, I keep seeing Reyes before and after the IED.

Instead, I think about why we did what we did and if it really made a difference. I want to believe it did. I don't want to think that we fought for nothing. That we killed for nothing. That we watched our friends die for nothing.

Instead, I watch the news and think: Was there ever a real plan?

Instead, I wonder: Are we really any safer? Or did we solve one set of problems only to create new, even bigger ones?

Now the mayor of my town has decided to make the "incident" part of his campaign for governor. He's making me out to be this unhinged guy who can't hack it like a real American should and, get this, a "supporter of radical Islam."

Pretty ironic given that I spent two years risking my life to "fight them over there so we didn't have to fight them over here."

Why does the fact that I punched a white kid in the defense of a brown kid wearing a patka automatically make me a "terrorist lover"?

It doesn't make sense to anyone except the guy who wants to be our next governor—and the people who support him.

Dude who has never served in the military struts around wearing a flag pin and gives every speech surrounded by American flags like he's the World's Biggest Patriot.

What I don't get is how people believe this stuff.

I guess if you spout a big lie convincingly on TV enough times, people start believing it's true, even if there's plenty of evidence that it's crap.

How do you fight back against that, if people aren't willing to use their brains?

It's been hard enough fighting myself since I got back. Fighting things I don't want to think about but that keep pushing their way back into my head. You know how that goes.

Now I've got to fight against people in the country that sent me over there and put those images in my head, too?

Something's wrong with this picture.

But you know that. Maybe that's why you stopped fighting. I'm still furious at you for doing it, but now I'm starting to understand.

ThunderGeek out.

CHAPTER EIGHT

Mom is fierce. She served in Desert Storm. She isn't fazed by blood or broken bones. She's a good shot. She's not scared of mice or snakes or spiders. I don't think she's scared of anything, except for something bad happening to one of us.

That's why the sound of her screaming for Dad on Sunday morning wakes me from sleep instantly. I leap out of bed, my heart pounding in my chest. I can't help but assume the worst, running toward Rob's room, whispering, "No, no, no . . ." but before I get across the hall, his door opens and my brother emerges in pajama bottoms and an olive-drab T-shirt.

He's alive.

I'm so happy about that I launch myself at him and throw my arms around his neck.

He shoves me away. "What's the matter with you, Stella? Don't you hear Mom?"

He pushes past me, heading down the stairs. I can't tell him I'm relieved it wasn't about him, so I follow him instead.

Mom and Dad are on the lawn, staring at the front of our house.

Ugly words in black spray paint.

TRAITOR

TERRORIST LOVER

DIE SCUM

UN-AMERICAN

Our American flag is missing from the pole by the front door.

This is our home.

This is our state.

This is our country.

This is America.

But right now it doesn't feel that way.

How can this be our country if we can wake up and find our house vandalized with hateful words like this?

How can this be the country my parents and my brother served?

Mom comes and puts her hand on my back to comfort me.

"We'll get through this, Stella. We'll be okay," she says, but the tremor in her voice belies her words.

I don't know how we'll get through it. It was bad enough having my posters torn down, but this has used up whatever little crumbs of bravery I had left. I just want to get away from here, to someplace where people don't hate us.

The question is, where? Farida's family thought they were safe when they came to America, but they still face prejudice. I guess hatred can appear anywhere, even here in the land of the free and the home of the brave.

I think about what Farida said the other day about Ken and me giving up so easily. She has to deal with this constantly, way more than I even know, but somehow, she's still optimistic about change. I think of all the time she's spent over the years, trying to get me to understand what it's like for her, to understand what it's like for other people. It must be so frustrating, and I feel exhausted just thinking about it. How is it fair that I'm tired already?

I glance over at my brother. His hands are clenched into fists, and he's got the same look in his eyes that he had at the mall right before he beat up Wade.

Dad walks over to him and puts a hand on his shoulder. "Don't worry, Rob," he says. "We'll get this cleaned up."

"We shouldn't have to clean it up," Rob spits out through clenched teeth. "It shouldn't be here in the first place. I thought I left the enemy overseas."

"It's a blow to the core to realize we've met the enemy and it's us," Dad says. "People right here in Argleton."

Rob recoils as if Dad hit him. His face pales and I'm afraid he's going to keel over. I'm not the only one.

"What is it?" Mom rushes to Rob's side and puts her arm around him. "Rob, what's the matter?"

At first Rob says, "Nothing, I'm fine," and he tries to shake off her arm, like he's going to escape into the house.

But suddenly he turns back, bends, and lays his head on Mom's shoulder. His shoulders heave and he emits a strangled sound.

Dad is staring at them, looking stricken and confused. I don't blame him. I'm as at a loss to understand as he is.

I notice a curtain twitch from across the street—the Kirchmars' house. Do they think Rob's a traitor and a terrorist? Their daughter Jana was in the same class as Rob at Argleton High. She knows him. The Kirchmars know us. How could anyone think that?

Mom strokes Rob's hair as he clings to her like she's the rock that's keeping him from being lost at sea.

And then he gasps, "Jason . . . said . . . that."

My parents look at each other over Rob's head.

"Said what?" Mom asks, pushing his hair back from his forehead.

Rob lifts his head from Mom's shoulder. His face is pale and his eyes haunted.

"I'd been keeping in touch with him . . . I knew he was struggling. Like I am," Rob admits. "The day he . . . I told him to get help, to go to the ER. And he said . . ." Rob swallows, like he's trying to keep himself from losing it again. "He said, 'I don't know who the enemy is anymore. Most of the time, I think it's me.'"

"Oh, honey, it's not your fault," Mom says. "You did what you could, but Jason needed professional help. He needed medication, therapy, and a good support group."

I can't help thinking maybe Rob needs that, too. I don't want him to end up like Jason. Or in jail.

Dad glances around. "How about we take this inside?" he says. "I need to make some calls."

He takes one of Rob's arms and Mom takes the other, and between them they guide my distraught brother into the house, away from the scrutiny of any watching neighbors who may or may not agree with the ugly sentiments spray-painted on our house.

Once inside, Dad goes to call the police. Meanwhile, Mom and I make breakfast and Rob sits at the table, staring down into a cup of coffee like it holds the answers to the meaning of life.

Mom's gotten the eggs and bacon ready and I've made a stack of toast and am almost finished buttering it when Dad comes back into the kitchen. "Police are on their way to take a statement," he says. "Frank Meyers is going to be coming by, too, with some of the guys from the Legion. Frank had some choice words to say about what happened."

"I'll bet he did," Mom says. "Come get something in your stomach before the police get here."

When the food is on my plate, I don't feel like eating, even though it smells good. I nibble at the crust of my toast and push the eggs around my plate so it looks like I've had something.

"You're not going to let good bacon go to waste, are you, Stella?" Dad asks me as the doorbell rings.

"You can have it," I tell him. "I'll get the door."

A police officer is standing on the porch. He asks to speak to

Dad. I invite him into the kitchen, and then I go upstairs to get my phone. I need to tell my friends what's happening, because inevitably news about this will get out around school and become another subject for flame wars on the Junior Class Facebook page.

When I get outside to take pictures of the graffiti, Dad's there with the police officer, who is also taking pictures.

"Well, you know tensions are high," the policeman says. I can't tell if he's making excuses or being sympathetic.

"And Mayor Abbott is playing it for all it's worth. Listening to him, you'd never know my son is a US Marine Corps vet, would you?" Dad says. "Is it any wonder people don't trust politicians?"

I freeze as I finish taking a picture of the word *traitor*, and without saying anything, walk back inside, go up to my room, and slam the door. I know everything is all about Rob right now, but has Dad completely forgotten that I'm running for class president and that's a political position? Does he not approve of that because he thinks politicians are untrustworthy and dishonorable?

I've been raised my whole life hearing from my parents how military service upholds our democracy and the American way of life. But is that the only way to do it? It seems to me like there are many types of service, and I still don't know which is the right one for me. Can I serve my country without being in the military like my parents and my brother?

I'd like the opportunity to try—if my brother hasn't destroyed any chance of that before I've even started.

But, based on what Dad just said, I wonder if he'd ever be as proud of me as he is of my brother, if that's the path I choose?

Sighing, I text the pictures of the graffiti to my friends.

ME: Look what happened on lovely Maple Street last night.

ME: At risk of sounding like a coward again . . . Do you think I should quit?

It only takes a few seconds before I hear back.

ADAM: That's messed up. Are you okay? And no way. Don't back down!

Farida sends an angry face and a tear emoji and a firm agreement with Adam. That's so horrible. But NO WAY!!! You can't give in to the haters!!!!! We've got your back!!!!!

Ken is next with an entire row of alternating angry face and flame emojis followed by: WHO WOULD DO THAT? OH WAIT! LET ME GUESS . . .

Does he mean Chris and his friends? But . . .

ME: Chris's dad is running for governor. I don't think he'd risk this. He might be a jerk, but he's not stupid.

KEN: But his friends . . .

He's got a point. It's not enough that Rob's been arrested and faces charges. With Mayor Abbott making angry speeches about immigration and using the incident with Rob as a reason to get people riled up, I wouldn't be surprised if Wade and Jed and the rest of their crew might be inspired to do some retaliatory artwork.

Just then I hear cars pulling up on the street outside our house. I look out the window and see Frank Meyers getting out of his old woody station wagon. Three cars and four pickups pull up behind him.

Got to go, I text my friends.

When I get outside, my parents and Rob are standing on the lawn, talking to Mr. Meyers.

"As soon as I heard from you, I started calling people from the Legion," he says, gesturing to the people getting out of their vehicles armed with rags, brushes, and buckets.

One of them is Mr. Neustadt, who walks up with two big bags from Home Depot.

"I've got some special graffiti remover," he tells us. "And some paint. Don't worry. We'll have this cleaned off in no time. But I don't want to get it cleaned off too quickly, because I called the local TV station and they're coming out."

"TV?" Dad says. "Should we be—"

"Fighting fire with fire? Yes," Mr. Neustadt says.

"Thank you," Mom says, even though Dad still looks worried. "Really, we can't thank you enough." She glances over at Rob, waiting for him to say thank you, too, but my brother's arms are folded over his chest and he's staring down at his feet.

"I'll go put some more coffee on," she says, obviously trying to cover for my brother's lack of appreciation and Dad's concern. "Robert, come inside and help me."

Rob follows her inside like a huge reluctant puppy.

He's about to get himself a major dressing down. Mom has our six through thick and thin, but she's not to be messed with when it comes to bad manners.

Mr. Meyers hauls a box out of the trunk of his car. He walks up to the flagpole and pulls a flag out of the box. It's seen better days, like maybe it should be retired on the next Flag Day. As he's putting it on the flagpole, he tells Dad and me, "I brought this flag home with me from Vietnam. It's been in the attic ever since."

When it's up, he takes a few steps back. Then his bearing changes. He stands, ramrod straight, eyes ahead, and snaps a salute.

My father joins Mr. Meyers in his salute, and then the other Legionnaires come and stand next to them, saluting, too. I put my hand over my heart like I do for the Pledge. My heart beats strong and true under my hand, and I wonder if underneath the hateful graffiti, my country's heartbeat is still there, too. I always thought I knew the things we believed in our hearts held us together, but now I'm not so sure. Not after this.

But the men here fought for America, just like Rob. Not just the men. Women like Mom.

And these people are volunteering to help us clean off the hate defiling our house.

After a minute, Mr. Meyers drops his salute. "These walls aren't going to clean themselves," he says, his voice husky.

Mr. Neustadt and a few of the other Legionnaires clap him on the shoulder, and they start to get to work.

I grab a rag and Mr. Neustadt makes me put on some safety goggles and rubber gloves so I don't get any chemicals on me. Mr. Meyers sprays some of the graffiti remover on a patch of wall and I start scrubbing, channeling my feelings into it.

It's hard to get the paint to shift, but it feels good to rub the hateful words off our house, surrounded by people who care enough to help us do it. I work until my arms hurt from scrubbing, and *Die Sc* is only faintly visible.

The TV reporter from the local station arrives and starts filming an intro with the house in the background. I take a break so I don't have to be in the shot. Mom's making ice tea to take outside for the volunteers.

"Can you get those plastic glasses and a tray?" she says. "And see if we have any chips or pretzels in the cabinet. I wasn't counting on company today."

"I wasn't counting on waking up and seeing *Traitor* and *Die Scum* spray-painted on our house," I say, grabbing a bag of pretzels from the pantry. "But that happened."

Mom stops stirring the ice tea mix and turns to look at me.

"This is upsetting for everyone, Stella. But it'll be easier to get through if you could put a lid on the snark."

It would be easier to get through if you and Dad actually listened and answered my questions once in a while.

But I know better than to say that right now. I *should* stay in the race for class president, because I'm demonstrating the ability to show diplomacy under pressure.

When I've poured the pretzels into a bowl, Mom hands me the tray of ice tea and tells me to take it outside and serve people.

"I've got to hunt around to see what else we've got for snacks," she says.

I head outside and set the tray down on the front steps. Then I start pouring cups of ice tea to hand out.

"How about I pour and you hand them out?" Mr. Meyers says. "Teamwork makes the job go faster."

That means I have to be in the line of the shot, which is the last thing I want to do, but Mr. Meyers went in the line of fire. I can't be that much of a coward.

"Okay," I say, grabbing three cups and taking them to people who are busy scrubbing the front of our house.

I bring one over to Mr. Neustadt.

"Thanks, Stella," he says.

"Can I interview you about why you're here?" the reporter asks.

"Sure," Mr. Neustadt says. He gestures at the ugly black words on our house. "My father fought the Nazis over in Europe during

World War Two. I fought in Vietnam. I never thought I'd live to see the day where I'd have to scrub hateful graffiti off the home of an American veteran here in this country. It makes me sick to my stomach." He looks straight into the camera. "But one thing I can tell you for certain: The Walkers are patriots, not traitors."

"So you don't think Rob Walker was radicalized while serving overseas?" the reporter asks.

Mr. Neustadt laughs. "It's the most ridiculous thing I've ever heard," he says. "Almost as ridiculous as any politician who'd make that claim."

I've thought of my family as patriots my entire life until this thing happened. I still do. But it seems like some people view us differently now, and I don't understand why. I feel just as much an American and a patriot as I did before Rob broke Wade's nose at the mall, but thanks to Mayor Abbott and his quest to be the governor, this all blew up into a bigger thing than it might have otherwise.

So who gets to decide?

I look around at the people who have come to help us. They apparently don't think we're un-American traitors and scum. And that's when I get the idea. But I have to wait until after the reporter and cameraman leave.

Right now they're trying to get Rob on camera and he's not cooperating. Doesn't he realize that is playing straight into Mayor Abbott's portrayal of him? Dad and Mr. Meyers are huddled next to my brother, obviously trying to talk sense into his thick skull.

I wonder if I should go get Mom, since she can sometimes get through to Rob when Dad can't. But I decide to go over instead.

Giving my dad a *don't yell at me* look, I pull Rob aside.

"Listen, I know the last thing you feel like doing is talking to a reporter after that stupid interview Mayor Abbott did on the radio. But you can't just let Wade and Jed and Mayor Abbott let their side of the story be the truth. Because it's not—I know. I was there."

"It won't do any good. People have already made up their minds," Rob says.

"How can you say that when you haven't even tried to change anyone's mind yet?" I say. As I say this, I realize that he sounds like me and I sound like Mr. Walsh. Did Mr. Walsh feel this frustrated by my negativity?

"You think I've got a chance now that Mayor Abbott has painted me as a psycho radical vet?" Rob says. "Dream on."

I've always looked up to Rob, but right now I think he's being an idiot.

"Does it look like all these people helping have made up their minds you're as bad as Mayor Abbott says you are? I always thought that I was the coward of the Walker family. But I guess it was you all along."

And I walk away, ignoring his stricken face because I'm so furious with him for letting us all down.

I go back to get some more ice tea. The next thing I know, Rob is standing in front of the camera, looking uncomfortable and awkward, but answering the reporter when she asks, "How did you feel when you woke up to see these words spray-painted on your house this morning?"

"Betrayed," Rob says. "Angry. Confused. I risked my life for this country. I watched my friends die. And now I'm being called a traitor because I stood up for a guy who was being harassed while he did his job at a mall?"

"You did break someone's nose," the reporter says.

"He's not going to talk about that on the record," Mr. Neustadt intervenes. "Not with charges pending."

"What about off the record?" the reporter asks.

"I don't want to talk about it at all," Rob says. He pulls off the mic, hands it back to the reporter, and heads into the house. The camera follows him and I want to scream "Leave him alone!" except I know that will only make things worse.

"You've got your story," Mr. Neustadt tells the reporter. "If you need more, ask why a politician running for office is on the air spreading irresponsible hate speech and how that's affecting our young people. Or talk to the Department of Veterans Affairs about why it's taking so long to get appointments for young men like Robert Walker who are returning from combat in need of help."

"Both interesting angles," the reporter says. "I'll see which way my producer wants to go. Thanks for the tip."

"Anytime. You'll be covering the Veterans Day parade, right?"

"Sure thing. See you then!"

After the TV people leave, everyone gets back to cleaning. Mom and Rob come back out of the house. Mom goes around offering snacks, and Rob goes back to scrubbing graffiti. I decide it's time to put my plan in motion.

"Mr. Neustadt, can I ask you a question and record your answer? I'm doing a project for school."

It's a project that I just made up earlier, but he doesn't need to know that.

"Sure," he says. He finishes the rest of his ice tea and sets the glass down. "Fire away. If you don't mind me working on getting the rest of this garbage off your house while you do."

"No, that's fine." I start VOICE MEMO on my phone as he puts his protective goggles back on, sprays the house, and starts scrubbing the graffiti again. "This is Mr. Jack Neustadt, head of the American Legion Post in Argleton, Virginia. Mr. Neustadt, when and where did you serve? "

"I served in Vietnam, US Army, First Infantry, the Big Red One."

"Mr. Neustadt, what do you think makes someone a patriot?"

His arm stops, and he turns to look at me through his goggles like an amused insect. "I see asking easy questions runs in the family," he says, a smile quirking his lips.

"That's why I want to do this project. To tell you the truth, it's not really for school—at least, not yet," I confess. "Right now it's for me. To help me understand."

"It is getting mighty confusing," he says, nodding toward the wall of the house. "But to my mind, a patriot isn't someone who has to blather on the TV about how patriotic they are. They show you, by the way they live. By being willing to put themselves at risk to confront what's wrong instead of walking past and pretending they don't see it."

I glance up at the wall of the house. *Traitor* is starting to fade, thanks to the work of our volunteers.

"I'm talking about your brother, too," Mr. Neustadt says. "I'm not saying he had to break the kid's nose. He lost control of himself, and that was wrong. But he's not the only guy in the history of the world who came back from war with some anger issues." He shakes his head, frowning. "And we never learn."

He starts scrubbing furiously, as if he's got an anger issue himself all of a sudden.

"That answer your question?"

I press STOP.

"I think so. Thanks."

But I want to get more ideas, too. So I go around and ask other volunteers the same question. It turns out there are as many definitions of what makes someone a patriot as there are people to interview.

"Plain and simple—someone who loves their country," Mr. Lee says.

Mr. McNeill agrees. "It's about respecting our history, but not being afraid to recognize times where we got it wrong, or speak out about what's holding us back. A patriot is someone who is willing to fight for liberty and justice *for all*."

I look over at Rob, who is scrubbing *Scum* off the siding with so much ferocity I worry about both the shingle and his hand. Whatever it is that my brother is struggling with, I think he's a patriot, no matter what the graffiti says.

Hey, Roadrunner—

I wish I could have shown you a video of this morning. Maybe you would have changed your mind and decided to stick around. Maybe not. When I saw what they'd spray-painted on our house, I thought for the first time you'd made the right decision.

Because I was embarrassed.

It's one thing to mess up for myself. But this is home for Mom, Dad, and Stella. And because of me, our house, the place where my family lives and sleeps, was covered with hate.

Then Frank Meyers showed up with a contingent from the Argleton Legion.

At first that made it even worse. That all these older vets, friends of my parents, guys I've saluted at every Veterans Day parade growing up, were there to witness it all. I was so ashamed, so messed up in my own head, that I couldn't even look them in the eye and say, "Thanks for helping out."

That voice in our head is our own worst enemy. As hard to fight as snipers and IEDS, I think sometimes.

But you know that.

You listened to yours all the way to the end.

Mom took me inside and read me the riot act. She said she understood I was having readjustment issues, and she and Dad are going to kick up a stink to see what is going on with that appointment at the VA hospital, but right now I needed to get out of my own head and go help the guys who had been gracious enough to come help us, on the double.

So I quick marched myself outside and started scrubbing that crap off the house, and what do you know? Even though every time I looked at those words I felt rage, I was part of a unit again, and we were working together for a common purpose—fighting the hate.

That felt good. Until the TV reporter came. The last thing I wanted to do was get in front of a camera and talk. Dad and Mr. Meyers were trying to persuade me how it was in my best interest to do it, but I didn't want to hear it. Reporters let that jerk Abbott smear me, based on nothing—how could I possibly trust that the story wouldn't get twisted again?

Then Stella came over and told me I was a coward. Can you believe? Stella telling ME that I'M a coward.

Some kind of reverse psychology, because of course I HAD to do the interview then.

It'll probably be a long-term disaster, because the reporter started asking me about punching Wade Boles and Mr. Neustadt interrupted saying I can't talk about that because of the legal issues. I was pissed that they'd asked the question when all that hateful stuff was on the wall of our house and stormed inside. Didn't come back out until they'd left.

The strange thing is, I feel better tonight than I have for a while. Who knows if it'll last, though.

Still, those folks had my six. Just like I'd have had yours, if you'd hung around long enough to let me.

ThunderGeek out.

CHAPTER NINE

"This is ridiculous," Mom says, slamming Tuesday morning's paper down on the kitchen table. "He's just trying to make this situation even more absurd. If that windbag tries to build his political career on the back of my kid, I will . . ."

She trails off, clearly trying to think of a bad enough punishment for the windbag, who I can only imagine is Mayor Abbott.

"What now?" I ask, even though I'm not sure I want to know.

She shoves the newspaper across the table so fiercely it almost knocks over the milk.

The headline reads: "Governor Candidate Wants Prison Term for Violent Vet."

I feel breakfast coming up the back of my throat.

"Prison term? But . . ."

"Now we have to hope that the prosecutor isn't going to be influenced by politics," Mom says.

"That's all we can do? Hope?" I ask, trying to keep the tremor out of my voice.

Mom comes over and hugs me.

"Ms. Tilley is an excellent lawyer. She came highly recommended."

The ugly headline shouts out at me from the table, but then I remember Mr. Neustadt telling me, *"A patriot isn't someone who has to blather on the TV about how patriotic they are. They show you, by the way they live. By being willing to put themselves at risk to confront what's wrong instead of walking past and pretending they don't see it."*

That's when I get an idea for the campaign and how to fight. Mayor Abbott is never seen without an American flag pin on his lapel, but all of his campaigning seems to imply that if anyone doesn't look or act or think the same as he does, then they aren't "real" Americans.

But we are. All of us, even if we look different or speak differently or worship at a different place. What he doesn't understand is that's what really makes our country strong and successful, not everyone being all the same.

And isn't high school just a microcosm of life? If everyone at Argleton High had been born and raised in this town, I wouldn't have learned nearly as much about the world as I have because I know kids like Farida and Dev, whose families came here from somewhere else. Our town doesn't exist alone. Neither does our state or our country. We're all part of a bigger whole. What do we gain by pretending otherwise?

———

Luckily, when I talk the idea over with my campaign managers, they like it.

"So if we do all these interviews asking what makes you a good member of the Argleton High community, then I can make a campaign video using them and incorporate the themes into my speech. We can make it into Stella's Ten Point Plan for Unity, or something like that."

"I like it," Adam says. "Especially if we can get other groups involved in the project, because then hopefully they'll be more likely to vote for you in the election. Maybe it'll help negate Chris's and Amy's edge in popularity."

He looks at me, a horrified expression spreading across his face.

"Wait . . . I'm not saying it's like you're *unpopular* or anything—"

Ken laughs. "Awk-ward."

"I am such an idiot," Adam groans. "Open mouth, insert foot."

"It's fine," I assure him. "I know what you mean. It's hard to compete with ice cream and soft toilet paper."

"Do you think maybe you're underestimating people?" Adam says. "Like maybe they do vote on the issues and facts instead of believing in things they know can never realistically happen?"

"Nope," Ken says. "Not at all. People have the attention spans of squirrels and are too easily distracted by shiny things."

"I don't know. I think Adam's right. People want to feel like they're seen and heard," Farida says. "That has to count more than a promise of ice cream, which will never be kept."

I want to believe Farida and Adam are right. I want to believe the best about everyone. But then I see how easily some people believe whatever Mayor Abbott says about my brother, even if it isn't the truth.

"I'm going to ask the International Club if they'll help," Farida says. I smile gratefully. Things are still weird between us, but it seems she hasn't totally given up on me. It gives me hope that maybe we can fix things.

"I can ask the Amnesty International Club, too," Ken says, "since I'm involved with that."

"I'll ask the Community Service Club," Adam suggests. "And I've got some friends in the Environmental Club who might be willing to lend a hand."

"Good thinking," Farida says. "The more people we can get involved the better."

"Do you seriously think they'll want to do it?" I ask. What seemed like a good idea this morning at breakfast suddenly has me filled with paralyzing doubt.

"We'll never know if we don't ask," Farida points out matter-of-factly.

True. I hear Mr. Walsh asking, *How can you know if you'll be any good if you don't even try running?* when I doubted if I'd be any good at running for class president.

One thing I am indisputably good at is second-guessing myself.

We manage to get ten volunteers for the project from the clubs we asked, which is ten more than I thought we'd get.

Adam, who is a whiz with a spreadsheet, it turns out, divides the school into different areas and time periods, depending on everyone's schedules, and then—armed with nothing but our smartphones and the question "What makes you a good member of Argleton High?"—we set off to create a vision of our school in the words of its students.

"Don't just interview your friends," I warn everyone at our project kickoff. "Stop people randomly in the area where you've been assigned."

"Yeah, we want to make sure we get as many different viewpoints as possible," Adam says.

"What if we ask someone to answer the question and they won't answer?" asks Dante Maragos from the International Club.

"It's a free country," Adam says.

"Well, at least it's supposed to be," Farida mutters.

"People don't have to give you their opinion," Ken says. "It's optional."

"Some people don't like being on camera," I point out. Like me, for instance. Remind me again why I'm running for class president?

———————————————————

My first shift of interviews is after school in the hallway leading to the athletics wing.

I go up to three guys on the soccer team who are heading for practice.

"Hey, I know you're on the way to practice, but can I ask you a quick question for a project?"

"As long as it's quick," Rick Sperry says. "Coach makes us run wind sprints if we're late."

I turn on the video. "What do you think makes a good member of our school?"

They all look at one another, as if they think between them someone might hold the answer, but they're not sure which one of them it is.

Finally, Tom Zweibel says, "I'll tell you what doesn't—hauling off and breaking someone's nose for no reason."

It's like a punch to the gut. I want to turn off the video, but I don't, even though keeping my hand steady is a challenge. Especially when Frank Maniaci and Rick start cackling like a bunch of overgrown hyenas.

"Any other thoughts on the subject?" I ask in as calm a voice as I can manage.

Their failure to get a rise out of me apparently makes Rick decide to answer the question.

"Someone who comes out for games," he says.

"Bonus points for traveling to cheer us on at away games," Frank adds.

"Yeah, and it's a person who has good school spirit," Tom says. "Remember when Kelly Larsen dyed her hair blue and painted her face white for one of our matches?"

"That was sick," Rick says. "But we better get to practice."

I switch off the camera. "Thanks for your views." *Even if you don't know the whole story about my brother and are just willing to believe whatever Wade and Jed say.*

As they walk away, I can't help thinking that their definition is really different than mine. I think that being a good member of the community is respecting and supporting others—and working to make the school as a whole a better place, not just the one thing you care about. But I guess that's the point of doing this—to learn.

I catch Erika Jones and Felicity Rose on their way to swim practice.

"I think it's someone who gets involved in school, above and beyond just academics. It doesn't matter how. People find their own thing," Erika says.

"Yeah, you find your own place but you're, you know, part of a bigger whole that makes the school what it is," Felicity adds.

Charity Hernandez, who is on her way to basketball practice with Sierra Foster, looks straight into the camera and says, "What would make someone a good school member is if they stopped always making it about guys' sports and recognized that the girls' teams kick butt just as hard."

"Harder," Sierra agrees. "When was the last time you came to one of our games?"

"Never," I admit. "But I haven't been to that many guys' basketball games, either."

"But you've been to some, right?" Charity asks.

"Uh . . . yeah. One or two," I say.

I'm pretty sure admitting this means I'm not going to get their votes. I wonder if Chris or Amy have been to any girls' basketball games.

"See what we're saying?" Sierra says. "And we've won State more than the guys' team."

"That's awesome," I tell them, and I really mean it. "I'll come to your next home game. And bring some friends with me."

"You're not just saying that?" Charity sounds suspicious and I can't say I blame her. I *am* running for class president, after all. This could just be a campaign promise, and those end up being broken on a regular basis.

"No, I mean it."

She holds up her fist and I bump it. "We're gonna hold you to it, right, Sierra?"

"Too right," Sierra says over her shoulder as they walk away.

By the time my shift is done, the answers have just given me more questions. Is that what happens when you start looking closely at the way things are—that you end up with more questions than answers?

I wait for Farida at her locker on Friday morning, because I hate that things are still awkward between us.

"Hey," she says, giving me a brief, wary glance before fiddling with her combination.

"Hi . . . I just . . . well, I just wanted to see if we could, you know, talk about the, uh, weirdness between us."

"Weirdness? You mean like how I'm tired of always having to explain everything to you a million times and you still don't get how life is different for brown people?" Farida says, rummaging in her locker for books. "Or do mean how you told some random guy everything that's going on in your life before your best friend?"

"Both," I say. "All of it. I guess having our house vandalized was a wake-up call on the first part. And as for the second part . . ."

Farida slams the door shut and finally meets my gaze.

"Well, what about that?" she asks. "Why, Stella? That really hurt."

"I'd been holding everything in from everybody for so long. Not just you, everyone. Every time I tried to talk to my parents about stuff they'd be too busy talking about Rob, or they just wouldn't be honest with me about what was happening. And then, that night it was all too much, and the thing is . . . Adam's not some random guy. I like him. I mean, *like* like him."

"Duh," Farida says. "I kind of figured that."

"And when he offered to come over I was feeling so alone and stressed out and confused and overwhelmed and . . . I don't know. I just spilled it all to him. Seriously, it was total word vomit."

"So when did the making out happen, then?"

"After the word vomit," I say. "He's a good listener."

"Is he a good kisser?"

"*Farida!*"

"Come on, Stella, you have to spill something. You owe me!" she says with a hint of a smile.

"Yes," I mumble.

"Well, that's a relief," she says. "I'd have hated to be this mad at you and then find out he wasn't even a good kisser. That would have been the worst."

Even though she's joking, there's a slight edge to her tone that tells me she's still hurt. I know things aren't going to be smoothed away so easily.

"I'm really sorry I told him before I told you. I'm sorry for all the rest of it, too. I'm going to try harder, I promise."

"And I'm going to hold you to that promise," she says.

"Deal," I tell her. "Want me to come over after school and help you with your audition monologue?"

"Yes! I still can't decide on one," she says, and as we head down the hall, she starts listing options, with me giving a thumbs-up or thumbs-down as she goes.

The heaviness that's been following me around while Farida and I have been at odds lightens a little. It doesn't go away completely—the air still isn't fully cleared. But at least it's a start.

———————————————

Farida and I are sitting in her kitchen, going over monologues, when Yusef comes home from school.

"Hey, buddy, what's up?" I ask.

"The sky," he says with such deadpan casualness that I can't help laughing.

"Don't encourage him, he's already unbearable," Farida groans.

"What's that? You say I'm unbeatable?" Yusef says. "Definitely when it comes to winning at *Injustice Two*."

"That sounds like a challenge," I tell him. "One I just might have to take you up on sometime to see if it's true."

"Narrator voice: He's not," Farida says with a grin.

"I totally am," Yusef says. "You just don't want to admit it."

"Don't you have some homework to do?" Farida says. "We're busy here."

"Ugh, yes," Yusef says, sighing. "But first I need a snack."

He heads to the refrigerator and we go back to monologues.

"Hey, what do you think about the opening monologue from *Rebecca*?" Farida asks. She slips into her best Joan Fontaine imitation: "Last night, I dreamt I went to Manderley again. It seemed to me I stood by the iron gate leading to the drive, and for a while I could not enter for the way was barred to me. Then, like all dreamers, I was possessed of a sudden with supernatural powers and passed like a spirit through the barrier before me."

I make ghostly sound effects and Farida falls into a dramatic swoon. I catch her before she hits the floor. We burst out laughing.

"You two are *so weird*," Yusef announces from the refrigerator, where he's still looking for a snack.

"Did you say funny?" Farida says. "I'm sure I heard him say funny."

"He definitely said funny," I agree. "And that scene is a great choice. It showcases your dramatic timing."

"Great! Well, now that that's taken care of, let's celebrate by making chocolate chip cookies."

"Now you're talking," Yusef says. "I'll get the butter and eggs." He grabs them from the refrigerator and puts them on the counter.

"Are you sure you want to eat our cookies? You might catch weirdness cooties," Farida says, taking flour and sugar out of the cupboard.

"I didn't say weird. I said funny, right, Stella?" Yusef says.

"Wait, am I stuck in the middle of a sibling dispute *again*?"

Yusef raises an eyebrow, looking impressive like Farida usually does. Then I noticed Farida's eyebrow raised as well, and she's looking at me like, *Let's see you talk yourself out of this one, Walker.*

"I'm pretty sure I heard you say that we're funny in a weird but good way," I lie, for diplomacy's sake.

Yusef and Farida exchange glances and smirks.

"It's a fair cop-out," Yusef says.

"I give it a six out of ten," Farida says.

"Six? Only six?"

"At most six point five," she says.

"I need some chocolate chips to console me from your tough grading," I say. "Hand them over."

Yusef helps himself to a few and then passes me the bag. We take turns measuring ingredients and mixing the batter. Once the cookies are in the oven, Yusef grabs his backpack and says, "I'm going to make a start on my homework, but call me when they're ready."

"If you're lucky and we don't eat them all first," Farida replies.

"Stella will call me," he says, flashing me a big grin.

I roll my eyes. "Maybe."

When he's gone, Farida puts on the latest album from the Summer Transistors, *Liberty and All That*, and we dance around the kitchen until the cookies are ready. It feels great to let loose and be silly for a while—and we agree that hot-from-the-oven cookies are the best thing ever.

After a week of interviewing students all around school, we have another meeting to look through the footage we've got.

"So did you notice any common themes in your interviews?" I ask.

"For a lot of people I interviewed, attendance at school sports events seems to be the main criteria for being part of the school community," Crystal Clark, from the Environmental Club, observes. "I can play you at least ten, no wait, probably fifteen interviews that say that. It got boring after a while."

"Funnily enough, I interviewed Dev Iyer and Jenny Moss from the Robotics Club and they were complaining about that, too,"

Pete Alacantara says. "Our football team didn't even place in the top three in States. The robotics team won the state trophy but how many of us knew that?"

Only a few hands go up.

"I interviewed twenty people who were rehearsing for marching band and they said pretty much the same thing," Charlene Thomas tells us. "They think the arts should get more attention at Argleton High."

It turns out that even groups that get attention don't think they get enough, and the ones that don't get much attention can't understand why the other groups are complaining. We're just like one great big unhappy family. But the loudest message I get from this is that everyone wants to feel like they are being seen and heard. How can I work to make that happen and help to bring us all together?

"Do we have others that are more . . . positive?" I ask, wondering how any of this is going to be able to compete with soft toilet paper.

"What do you mean by positive?" Farida asks. "This is real. This is what people think."

"I know. But school isn't totally awful, and we need to show that, too," I say. "Besides, if we don't show something good, this will be such a downer."

"Especially compared to free ice cream," Ken points out.

"I think I've got something," Adam says. He fast-forwards through a few interviews, then presses PLAY on one he filmed during lunch. Keith McCray looks into the camera and says, "A good member of our school isn't a bully. A good member is an awesome friend." He turns to Malik Jenkins. "My friend Malik is a good member."

Malik high-fives Keith, and the smiles they give each other are so genuine it feels like my heart's about to explode right out of my chest.

This is better than free ice cream. At least I think so.

Malik is on the soccer team and Keith is the team water boy, and they've been friends for years. Keith also happens to have Down syndrome. Freshman year, two seniors bullied Keith something awful, and Malik and the other guys from the soccer team got involved trying to help Keith. Keith's parents actually sued the school district and it was in the papers. The guys who did it ended up getting suspended and almost weren't allowed to graduate.

"Now, *that's* what being an Argleton Astro is all about," Crystal Clark says. "Or at least what it should be. That we're not just here to get good grades and go to college or get a diploma and get a decent job. We're here to learn how to be good people, too."

"So as I see it, we want to make sure that everyone feels like their contribution to the school matters, and it's not just about prom and boys' sports. That's what we want to work toward," I say.

"And we have to show what the problems are first," Tanzie Greene says. "Otherwise what's the point of doing all these interviews?"

"Exactly," Farida says. "We're not going to pretend Argleton High is problem free."

"And that the biggest issue is raising money for prom," adds Tanzie. "Because it's not."

Some kids might think it is. And I don't know if this is going to be enough to overcome popularity, toilet paper, and ice cream. But at least I feel like now we have a plan.

Later that night, I'm upstairs in my room, looking at some video footage that Ken edited together for me when I hear shouting from downstairs.

"What now?" I groan to Peggy, who was curled up on the bed next to me but jumped off at the noise and is now slinking toward the door with her head hung low and her tail between her legs.

I follow her downstairs to the family room, where my parents and Rob are in the middle of a heated discussion.

"He's never going to get a fair trial," Mom says. "Look at the dirty tricks they're using."

"What's going on?" I ask. "What dirty tricks?"

Rob is pale and tight-lipped. He picks up the remote and rewinds the news show from a national cable channel. There's a clip of Mayor Abbott giving his usual campaign speech about immigrants and crime, and then he brings up the mall incident. The anchorman says that there's new footage from a cell camera— taken by one of the employees at Big Al's Burritos. When they roll the clip, it doesn't show Wade or Jed harassing Ashar. All viewers see is Rob grabbing Wade and punching him in the face until Jed, Ashar, and I pull him off. It makes Rob look violent . . . and seriously unhinged.

But then, to my horror, it gets even worse. They rewind the footage and focus on me. And they interview Wade, who tells them that my best friend, Farida El-Rahim, is Muslim and that her parents came from Iraq. The interviewer nods knowingly, like that means something sinister. Even worse, they bring in national security experts to discuss the danger of radical Islamic extremism, like that has anything to do with Farida and her family.

This can't be real. It can't be. But it is. It's a cable news show going out nationwide, dragging my best friend into a situation she had absolutely nothing to do with, just because she happens to be Muslim—and friends with me. This is my fault. Farida warned me this would happen and I didn't believe her—not one hundred percent. I thought she was being super paranoid, that no one would go that far.

But she was right. I still didn't get it. She kept telling me and telling me, and I didn't get it, because being white means I have the luxury of not getting it.

"How can they do that?" I whisper, shocked. "How can they make this about the El-Rahims and radical Islamic extremism when they have nothing to do with that, and Farida wasn't even there! And that video—it doesn't show the whole story. It doesn't show Wade and Jed—"

"What do they care?" Rob says. "They already have their story."

"Why didn't they interview Ashar?" I ask, furious that everyone who watches this news show is going to get such a false impression. "How can they only show Rob's reaction if they don't show what caused it? How can they just say such awful things about people who weren't even there? Why do they let Mayor Abbott spout this stuff unchecked? Aren't they supposed to fact-check him?"

"You'd think. But this makes for better ratings," Rob says. "And the guy from Big Al's Burritos probably didn't start videoing until I went over and it looked like a fight might happen. Before that, it was just two high school kids mouthing off to another kid cleaning tables. He probably sees that every day."

"What can we do?" I ask. "It's not fair."

"That's the sixty-four-thousand-dollar question," Dad says.

"It could be more than sixty-four thousand dollars if we have to go to trial," Mom says. "I should reach out to Layla. I'm worried that this could put the El-Rahims at risk. Not just the restaurant, but their safety."

Rob slumps onto the sofa and puts his face in his hands. Peggy goes to his side and rests her chin on his knee. Dad gives Mom a warning look, and she sits next to Rob and pulls his head onto her shoulder.

"Don't you worry about the money," she says. "I don't think it's going to come to a trial, and if it does, we'll figure it out."

"You shouldn't have to figure it out," Rob mutters. "If I'd held it together, you wouldn't have to. And forget about the money—the El-Rahims might be in danger because I'm such a screwup. They're our friends. People I was supposed to have been protecting with my service."

"If you'd been able to get an appointment at the VA hospital earlier, maybe you'd have been able to hold it together," Mom says in a no-nonsense tone. "We can play the blame game all day long, but that's not going to get us anywhere. We need to figure out our strategy for moving forward."

Silence, except for Rob's haggard breathing and the sound of Peggy licking his hand to comfort him.

"Wait," I say suddenly, remembering something Rob said. "You say that they already have the story—this one that makes for better ratings. Like you're this unhinged violent vet who belongs behind bars."

"Yeah," Rob says. "And now they have bystander video to 'prove' it. So?"

"Look, I know you're going to hate this idea, but we have to do more of what we did when the house got vandalized," I say. "Give them a better story. The *real* story. That Rob's a marine who did his duty, but despite that can't get an appointment with the VA, and then when he does his duty again, by standing up for someone who was being harassed because of his religion, he's disrespected by two kids, pushed to the edge . . . and . . . well, something like that."

Dad rubs his chin, considering my words, then nods his head slowly. "Guess what, Val? I think our daughter might have a future in PsyOps."

Mom smiles. "I think you might be right."

"What's PsyOps?" I ask.

"It's the branch of the military that engages in information campaigns to support our national objectives," Dad says.

"So you mean . . . like . . . *propaganda*?" I ask.

"It all depends on how you look at it, Stella. When another country does it, it's called propaganda. When our country does it, it's called PsyOps," Mom explains.

"But I just want to tell the truth about Rob and Farida, not spread propaganda," I say. "What about the graffiti on our house? How come this national cable news show didn't show any of that? They could have. But they didn't even mention that it happened."

"It wouldn't matter, Stella. Even if they showed the graffiti, I'm sure the world would think I deserved it," Rob says with a sigh.

Mom gets up and heads for the kitchen. "I'm going to call Layla. Maybe I'll suggest she ask the Argleton Police Department to send a patrol car to drive by the restaurant a few extra times, just in case."

"I'll call Jack Neustadt," Dad says, getting up and pulling out his cell. "If he doesn't have an idea of how to go about this, he'll know someone who does." He kisses me on the top of my head on his way out the door. "Did I ever tell you that you're smart?"

"Maybe. But it's worth repeating," I say.

"Don't exaggerate or Stella won't be able to get her head through the door," Rob says.

I stick my tongue out at him, proving that while I might be smart, I'm still not that mature when it comes to sibling relations.

I may have figured out something that has a chance of helping my brother, but in the meantime, my completely innocent friend has been dragged into this mess, and this isn't going to help her. I need to figure out some way to do that.

When I go back to my room, I call Farida, fingers trembling.

She doesn't pick up.

I text her.

ME: I just saw the cable news. I'm so, SO sorry. I don't know why they dragged you into this.

ME: You weren't even there.

ME: It doesn't make sense.

ME: Forget that. I mean I KNOW why. You warned me they would do it. And it sucks. I want to do something to change it.

ME: What can I do?

ME: How can I help?

ME: Call me? Please!

Sighing, I go back to edited footage of the interviews Ken sent. But now, I'm looking at it differently. What would happen if we cut some parts versus others? I know we're supposed to be editing this to present a full, honest picture, so that everyone feels heard.

But what if we don't?

We could present a totally different picture of what happened in those interviews, just by cutting them together to present a version of reality that benefits my campaign more than Chris's or Amy's. But it wouldn't be the truth. It would be selective truth.

The question I have to ask myself is: How badly do I want to win? Would it be better to create a lie in service of the greater good so I win and Chris doesn't? Or am I better off sticking to the truth and trusting that will be enough?

I don't know the answer.

I pick up the phone and call Ken to talk to him about it.

Farida still hasn't texted me back.

ARGLETON ASTROS JUNIOR CLASS
FACEBOOK PAGE

SABRINA CHAPMAN: OMG did you guys see the story on America News Channel? It had video of Stella Walker's brother breaking Wade Boles's nose. It's sick.

OSCAR DANIELSON: That guy is seriously messed up. He just hauled off and started whaling on Wade, man.

CARA DELGADO: I don't see why they had to bring Farida into it. That was just wrong. And totally racist. So what if Stella and Farida are friends? It had literally nothing to do with anything. And what was with all the "radical Islamist extremism"? That was bananas!

DAVE EBERHARDT: I mean, it's totally relevant. It shows the entire Walker family are Muslim sympathizers.

CARA DELGADO: What are you even talking about? That's ridiculous.

DAVE EBERHARDT: Wade said Stella's brother punched him because he wouldn't apologize to a Muslim kid.

CARA DELGADO: Apologize for what? I thought Wade said he didn't do anything and Stella's brother just punched him out of nowhere. See, he's such a liar he can't even keep his story straight!

SABRINA CHAPMAN: Wade's totally telling the truth! That's what happened in the video.

TANZIE GREENE: You do realize a video can be edited, right? And that video only starts right before the punch. We have no idea what was happening before that. It's Wade and Jed's word against Stella and her brother and the mall dude.

DAVE EBERTHARDT: The video evidence.

TANZIE GREENE: Uh, what part of "the video can be edited" didn't you understand, Dave? BTW, the guy is Sikh, not Muslim. Which makes it even more messed up that they brought Farida into this news report because they're not even the same religion.

SCOOTER DOUGLAS: Jed said he was wearing one of those Muslim do-rag things on his man bun.

MALIK JENKINS: Sorry to break it to you, Scooter, because I know you're just dying to hate us and defend your boy at the same time, but we don't have "do-rags" on our "man buns." I have a feeling you're talking about a Sikh guy, with a rishi knot covered by a patka. But hey, I guess to you all us brown people look the same, right?

SCOOTER DOUGLAS: Go back to where you came from, loser!

MALIK JENKINS: Where I came from? You mean Virginia Beach? That's where I was born. I know it kills you, dude, but I'm just as American as you are.

SCOOTER DOUGLAS: I don't think so. With a name like Malik?

CARA DELGADO: So Scooter is normal but Malik isn't? Do you realize that you aren't making any sense?

SCOOTER DOUGLAS: Scooter's just my nickname, idiot.

CARA DELGADO: I know. I'm just saying that I wouldn't pick a fight about people's names if I actually choose to go by Scooter.

SHANE BAIRD: Stella should be disqualified from running for class president.

MALIK JENKINS: For what, exactly?

SHANE BAIRD: While this legal stuff is going on.

MALIK JENKINS: Has Stella been charged with anything?

SHANE BAIRD: No, but it's pretty clear there's some messed-up stuff going on in that family.

TANZIE GREENE: "Pretty clear"? Nothing is clear except that you believe Wade and Jed.

SHANE BAIRD: And the video.

TANZIE GREENE: It scares me that we're graduating in two years when you don't understand logic yet.

SCOOTER DOUGLAS: Go back to Africa, Tanzie.

TANZIE GREENE: Just out of curiosity, where was your family from originally, Scooter?

SCOOTER DOUGLAS: We're American. My family has lived in Virginia for five generations.

MALIK JENKINS: So you're not Chickahominy or Mattaponi or Pamunkey in other words?

SCOOTER DOUGLAS: Obviously not.

TANZIE GREENE: So what is your family's heritage?

SCOOTER DOUGLAS: Us? We're proud Welshmen.

TANZIE GREENE: So when your family moved here, by your definition, they weren't "real" Americans, right? How many generations of being born here did it take before they were able to qualify as Americans according to the Scooter Douglas definition?

MALIK JENKINS: LOL! Yeah, please tell us the magic number, Scooter.

SCOOTER DOUGLAS: I don't have to tell you jerks anything.

TANZIE GREENE: Point made.

MALIK JENKINS: LOL.

Roadrunner, buddy—

I have to ask myself this question, because it's starting to eat away at me, like so many other things: Why is it easier for me to talk to you than it is to my own family?

I could always talk to them about stuff before.

My family is tight. Or at least we were. I'd like us to be again. But . . .

There's always a "but" . . .

I've screwed up life for everyone in my family that I can't even look at them without feeling shame. Now Stella's best friend is caught up in my mess, for absolutely no reason other than she's Stella's friend. Stella is my sister, and—oh yeah—her friend's family is Muslim. Doesn't matter that Farida wasn't there. They created this story about an unhinged vet brought up in a family of radical Muslim lovers, and they're gonna run with it.

So much for the Constitutional freedoms we thought we were protecting with our lives.

Is it any wonder I feel like a puzzle piece that doesn't fit anymore? Like a part of me broke off over there, and maybe I'll never be able to fit right again—in my family, or with anyone, anywhere.

Maybe I'm going to feel alone with this stuff in my head for the rest of my life.

Maybe they should have had an Island of Misfit Puzzle Pieces for us when we got back.

A place where we could talk about what happened and figure out how to go from 360-degree alert 24/7 to being a person with normal senses and reflexes. If that's even possible.

My parents came back and got on with their lives, which just makes me feel like more of a failure. I carry their DNA. What's the matter with me that I can't do the same?

About a few weeks after I separated from the marines, when I was feeling really down, Mr. Meyers from the Legion offered to take me fishing. I was going to say no, but there was something in his eyes, some glint of understanding, that made me say yes.

We didn't talk much about anything while we were out on the lake, but he did say "it was no picnic for anyone" when he returned from Vietnam.

I should have asked him what he meant by that, but I was afraid to.

Afraid to know how long it took for it to be a picnic again.

I was thinking about that conversation last night when I couldn't sleep. Again. That three o'clock in the morning thing. I tried to imagine a picnic, when things are good again. At first I thought about Virginia Beach, because I loved it before the war.

The sand between my toes, the sun on my skin, girls in bikinis, waves crashing against the shore. Beach volleyball. The smell of salt and seaweed, and suntan lotion warming on skin. The senses of summer that brought me joy.

But then I realized that the beach just reminds me of being over there, and that crowds mean danger coming from any possible direction when you're least expecting it.

A picnic on the beach wouldn't be much of a picnic anymore. Do you think it ever can be again?

Duh, stupid question. Of course you don't.

Not being able to do something you loved because your brain won't let you—it's enough to make you want to punch things.

But punching things is what got me into the mess I'm in now.

So what do I do with that?

If it can't go out, it goes in.

And when it goes in, you just want to numb it. But that only works for a while, until it erupts to the surface like a volcano that's been dormant.

Times like this I feel like I'm going to be alone with it forever.

Alone forever.

Alone.

ThunderGeek out.

CHAPTER TEN

Farida still hasn't called or texted me when I wake up the next morning. I try texting her again.

ME: Hey . . . are you okay? I'm so sorry.
ME: Really want to talk.

I stare at my phone, hoping to see the little speech bubble that she's texting me back, but there's nothing.

Then I get a text, but not the one I wanted.

KEN: You should probably avoid the Argleton Astros Junior Class Facebook page for a day or two.

That, of course, has the opposite effect of what he intends, because I have to know what's being said, even though I know it's going to hurt. And it does. Big time.

Now I can understand why Farida isn't calling me back. Not only has she been dragged into this mess, but she can see that people want me to pull out of the race. I've failed her before the first ballot's even been cast.

If I want to get to school on time, I need to get out of bed and start getting dressed, but I just can't do it. It's as if my body is being crushed to the mattress by an overwhelming weight of dread and despair.

Because of me, my brother is facing felony assault charges and my best friend and her family have been put at risk, even though they've done absolutely nothing wrong.

I look up the Yelp page for Tigris. Sure enough, there are hundreds of hateful reviews, calling the El-Rahims terrorists and worse. How do people even think of such messed-up stuff, let alone write them on a restaurant review site? Who are these people? They write under screen names, like anonymity makes it okay to be offensive. Do they live far away or are they our neighbors? It makes me afraid to go out of the house because I don't know if behind every supposedly "nice" neighbor's face there's someone who thinks that way.

It's the same story on the Tigris Facebook page. I report all the nasty comments, but that doesn't feel like enough. They're all time-stamped starting after last night's news broadcast, which means that it's because of me and my stupid decision to take Rob to the movies that they're there in the first place.

"Stella! What are you doing messing around on your phone?" Mom exclaims. She's standing in the doorway of my bedroom, wearing her work clothes and a frown. "Is Farida driving you? Because at this rate you're going to be late and I've got an early meeting, so I can't if she's not."

"No, Farida's not driving me. She's not even answering my

texts. Not that I blame her. Have you seen what people have been writing on the Tigris Yelp and Facebook pages since the news broadcast? It's horrible!"

Mom stills. "Like what?"

I hand her my phone, and she scans the Facebook page, her eyes widening in dismay as she reads the awful things people have posted there.

As I see the expressions crossing her face, I feel so smothered with guilt it's hard to breathe. If only I'd just let Rob be, sitting on the sofa, playing his game. What made me think that I could help him?

"I always knew there were some people who thought this way, but seeing so many of these . . . it makes me feel like I don't even know the country I served anymore," Mom says.

"It's scary," I say.

"If you're scared, just imagine how the El-Rahims must feel," Mom points out.

I've been thinking about that ever since I woke up and saw the hateful comments. It makes me feel guilty for saying what I do next.

"Mom, I can't go to school today. I need a day off."

"Stella, school is your job. You can't just decide to randomly take a day off. Do you think Farida is going to be getting a day off? I don't. If she can face it, so can you. Friends support each other, especially best friends like you and Farida. "

"Rob takes days off. He's been skipping classes a lot recently."

"We're not talking about your brother. We're talking about you."

"*Now* you want to talk about me? Whenever *I* want to talk, you and Dad are too busy talking about Rob."

"That's not fair. You know he's going through a tough time right now and—"

"And that doesn't affect me? You and Dad expect me to keep on being the perfect daughter because *Walkers don't quit*," I say, so overflowing with pent-up anger and resentment I'm not sure I could stop now if I wanted to—and I don't. It's a relief to finally say these things to my mom's face instead of just swallowing them like a foul-tasting medicine. "I'm so sick of it. Because it *does* affect me. Not as much as it does my best friend, but still. I just can't handle going to school today. The entire junior class thinks I should be disqualified from running for class president because Rob broke Wade's nose." I pause only long enough to breathe. "And you're telling me *I'm* not being fair?"

I want my mom to understand me. I want her to say, "I get it. Dad and I have been preoccupied with Rob, and I understand how that feels unfair, and we will try to give you more time because we love you, and, sure, take a mental health day, sweetie."

But that's not what happens. At first she seems to register surprise, and then something else—I'm not sure if it's hurt or anger. Finally, her face becomes a mask—calm, emotionless, businesslike. It's Valerie Jones-Walker, MD, who says, "I just told you I had an early meeting and you decide to dump this on me now?

Stella, Rob's condition, this situation, it affects all of us. I have to go to work and you have to go to school. Get up and get dressed. We'll talk about this later."

She closes my door, and I throw a pillow at it because I'm so angry. But, like a true Walker, I obey orders, getting dressed in under three minutes, throwing on the first pair of jeans I find and a super-soft purple T-shirt. I jam my feet into my boots and start stuffing books into my bag. I just might make the bus if I skip breakfast and run.

But as I come out of my bedroom, Rob's standing in his doorway, car keys in hand.

"I'll drive you."

"It's okay, I can make the bus."

"Shut up and get yourself something to eat. I'll drive you," he says, heading to the stairs.

The walls are thin, and in my anger, I wasn't exactly whispering. Guilt washes over me as I follow him downstairs and grab a granola bar, a banana, and a juice box.

Rob's already pulled the car out of the garage. Heavy metal blasts from within even though all the windows are rolled up. It assaults my eardrums when I slide into the front seat, but I don't complain. It's protection for both of us so we don't have to talk.

And we don't, till we're halfway to school and stopped at a red light. My forehead's pressed to the passenger window, trying to cool down my racing thoughts as I wonder if I should ask Mr. Walsh for his advice about staying in the race, and if Farida will talk to me, worrying about what's happening with her family, and just how awful today is going to be and—

Rob switches off the radio, and the silence hits like a club after the booming bass and shredding guitars. "I'm sorry."

I turn to him, but he's still looking straight ahead at the light. "For what?"

"For messing up your life. For messing up the family. For being a mess, period."

He's speaking in a monotone. Is this how Jason sounded? Has what I said made Rob feel so bad that he might feel like life isn't worth living?

"I was just venting this morning, Rob. I didn't say it to make you feel guilty. I know you're going through a tough time. It's just—"

"Don't make excuses. Just take the apology, Stella, all right?"

"But . . . are you okay?" I can't help asking.

He laughs. "Oh, I'm just *great.*"

His sarcasm cuts to the heart of me. The light changes and he puts his foot down on the gas a little too hard so I jerk back in my seat.

"Look, I know it was a stupid question, but are you going to kill us both to make the point?"

He doesn't apologize, but he does ease off the accelerator.

"Are you . . . ?" I can't finish the thought.

"Not planning on it today, but thanks for asking," Rob says.

"What about *tomorrow?* What about the *next day?*"

I count the seconds of his silence in anxious heartbeats. Finally, he says, "I'm not planning on doing anything, but let's just take it one day at a time, Stella. That's the only thing I can do right now."

Not very reassuring, but that's apparently all he's willing to give me, because he turns the radio back on, and we don't exchange another word until he says, "See you later," when he drops me at school.

"I'm holding you to that," I tell him.

He half smiles and drives away. But I take his "see you later" as a promise, one that he better not break. Because I have to find the courage to walk into school right now, and that's hard enough to do without worrying about my older brother.

Is this how Rob felt when he walked into a potential combat situation? I wonder as I approach the school entrance, conscious of my elevated heartbeat, dry mouth, sweaty palms, and the sense that everyone who looks in my direction might be hostile.

Turns out, my instincts weren't wrong.

Scooter Douglas hocks a loogie in my direction as I walk past. The blob just misses me and lands on the ground at my feet. I do some fancy footwork to avoid stepping in it.

"Terrorist lover," he says.

"Un-American traitor," Dave Eberhardt adds.

"Get out of the race," Scooter says. "No one's gonna vote for a traitor."

Do I ignore them or respond? *Sticks and stones will break my bones but names will never hurt me* isn't true. Being called these things hurts—a lot.

I walk on a few paces and then turn back.

"You'll just have to wait and see about that, won't you?" I tell them. "Because like it or not, that's what democracy is all about."

They keep calling out, "No traitor for class president!" and "Get out of the race!" and "Terrorist lover!" as I continue into the building.

I'd planned to find Farida to make sure she's okay and try to talk things through with her, but instead, I go straight to Mr. Walsh's room.

He looks up as soon as I walk in.

"Ah. I wondered if I'd see you this morning. How are you and Farida holding up?" he asks. "Someone forwarded me a link to the latest news story, so I've seen it."

"You and everyone else in the entire world, it seems like."

"Some of the other national cable shows picked it up this morning. If I were you and Farida, I'd take your social media accounts private for now, if you haven't already," Mr. Walsh advises me. "They'll be scouring those for anything they can find."

I hadn't even thought of that. Ugh.

"That's another strike against me in the class president campaign," I think out loud. "Since that's how we do most of the campaigning."

"True," Mr. Walsh says. "But I still think it's the prudent thing to do."

"Mr. Walsh, do you think I should pull out of the race?" I ask. "Scooter Douglas spit at me and called me a terrorist lover on the way into school this morning. He said no one would vote for a traitor."

"Oh, he did, did he?" His mouth thins to a narrow line. "Sounds like Mr. Douglas needs to take a trip to the main office. Has he said anything to Farida?"

"I don't know. I haven't seen her yet."

"I'll check in with her to see how things are going," he says. "And I'll take care of reporting Scooter Douglas. But before I do that—do *you* think you should pull out of the race?"

I should have known he'd throw the question right back at me.

"Part of me feels like I should, because I don't have a chance. I mean, even if I'm the best candidate in the world, there's all the stuff going on with my brother, and now Farida's been pulled into this disaster."

"I'm sensing there's a 'but' . . ."

"But that would be like letting the bad guys win. Because they aren't telling the truth about what happened. I don't think Chris should benefit from the lies. Or Amy, for that matter. I don't want to give up, because then it feels like they've won because of the situation."

"It sounds to me like you already have your answer," Mr. Walsh says. "You don't need my advice."

"But how do I fight back?"

"Right now, they're controlling the narrative. You've got to create a more compelling story," he says.

"You mean, like . . . *lie*?"

He chuckles. "You kids today are so literal. No, I mean tell the truth, but in a more compelling way to grab the interest of your peers," Mr. Walsh says.

"So . . . you mean, like, propaganda? Or what my parents call PsyOps?"

His eyes widen and he shakes his head. "PsyOps? Let's dial it back a bit, shall we?"

"So what *do* you mean, then?"

"I mean figure out the main theme of your campaign and create a good narrative," he explains. "After all, what's been the most effective way of transmitting information since the beginning of time?"

I know where this is going.

"Storytelling?"

"You got it. That's how you hook people. You have to be able to tell a good story."

I thank him for his advice and head off to my first class, texting Farida, begging to talk to her before AP Gov.

But I've made my decision now.

I'm not going to withdraw from the race, no matter how many people spit at me and call me names. They don't get to tell my story. Or Farida's story. We're going to tell our own.

That is, if Farida's still talking to me.

Farida finally agrees to meet me after second period, so we can talk as we walk to AP Gov. For one nanosecond, I imagine asking her to skip class so we can really talk things through, but neither of us is the class-skipping type, and besides, it's not the kind of thing a candidate for class president should do, especially when she is already at a major disadvantage in the race.

When I see her waiting outside my classroom, I want to hug her, but she's holding her books in front of her like a barrier and has her arms wrapped around them. She looks closed off, not that I can blame her after what's happened.

"Hey," she says.

"Hi," I say back. I feel awkward, not sure where to start.

Farida takes care of that for me. "So how's your morning been? I've had my parents telling me all about the crap that's been threatening the restaurant, my little brother was up with an anxiety attack half the night because he's afraid some of the crazy online threats people have made toward us and the restaurant might actually come true, and now I get to come to school worrying whether a bunch of idiots will call me a terrorist. So it's all been super fun."

I hear the frustration in her voice and I feel my heart drop.

"Has anyone?"

"No. Not yet, at least. But it's only been two periods. How much do you want to bet it happens before the end of the day?"

Since Scooter Douglas spit at me and called me a terrorist lover before school even started, that's not a bet I'm willing to take.

"I'm sorry," I say. "Poor Yusef. This is so messed up and I feel awful for you guys. I know you warned me this would happen, but I still didn't think it really would."

"Well . . . it did," she says. "My parents are coming in to meet with Principal Hart later today. They want to talk about the stuff people have been saying at school—not just to me, but to other kids."

She stops walking and fixes her gaze on me. "The only thing that surprises me is that after all these years of being my best friend, you're still surprised."

I nod in embarrassed confirmation. Farida continues down the hall, and I fall in beside her.

"See, I can explain it to you, time after time after time, but you *still* don't get it. I told you what it was like in the car that morning, when I asked why Mayor Abbott would say Rob sympathized with radical Islamist extremism. I thought maybe when you woke up to that graffiti on your house, maybe you'd finally get it," she says. "That you were beginning to know how awful it feels to be thought of as the enemy in your own country."

"I thought I got it then, too," I say.

"Yeah. But you didn't. You don't know what it's like constantly dealing with people asking, 'Where are you from?' And then when you reply Virginia, having them say, 'No, where are you *really* from?' Because what they mean is, 'Why aren't you white?' Or having them ask stuff like, 'How can you really be Muslim if you aren't wearing a hijab?' or 'How can you *live* without eating bacon? It's *so delicious!*'"

I cringe at the last question, because I'm pretty sure I've said that to her at least once, and Ken has, too. And I'm afraid to ask her the next question, because I'm going to sound stupid and insensitive, but I have to do it in order to clear the air. "So . . . what else am I missing?"

Farida laughs. "What is Stella missing? Let me count the things . . ." she deadpans in a parody of Elizabeth Barrett Browning's "Sonnet 43." "Well, first of all, how can you have been so shocked that having an Iraqi American BFF would be held against you? Where have you been since first grade? We always seem to be the bad guys, even if we're not. How many movies have we gone to see where the people who look like me are the bad guys?"

She's right. "This had nothing to do with you," I protest.

"I know that! But you're acting like facts still matter!"

I've been guilty of the same cynicism, at least when it comes to our school elections. But that's high school. I guess deep down, I still want to believe that when we leave this place, things will be different; that adults will do things better and behave more logically than we do.

Not that I've been getting a whole lot of evidence of that recently. And suddenly, the weight of this realization feels crushing, because if the people we're supposed to look up to don't have the answers, then who does?

"But . . . if facts don't still matter, then what's the point? Why did we waste all that time getting people involved and doing all those interviews? Why am I even running for class president?"

Farida lets out a bitter chuckle. "Stella, you've said a lot of stupid things to me in the time we've been best friends, but hands-down that's the dumbest one of all. *This* is why I didn't return your texts. Because I had to deal with everything that was going on at home because of the situation." She takes a deep breath and looks me straight in the eye. "Besides, I needed time to deal with my own feelings before having to listen to your cluelessness."

It's a slap in the face, and my first instinct is to want to slap back, but as I open my mouth to speak, I suddenly think back to when we were kids watching *Aladdin*, and everything Mrs. El-Rahim explained to me then. So instead of fighting back, I take a deep breath and zip my mouth shut. The best thing I can do right now is to listen. Like, actually listen this time.

"I don't have the luxury of whining, 'What's the point?' when things get hard because things are *always* hard. Sometimes they're less hard than others, but it's not like I can ever relax and say, 'Life is good, everything's cool, we're safe here, and liberty and justice for all.' Because it's not like that for us."

"I know it's hard—"

"You say that, but you don't really *know*. You don't know what it's like to have to always be on, to always be the best version of yourself because the world is always waiting for you to screw up so they can say, 'See? Muslims *are* bad.' To not be able to take a break from the scrutiny because today you don't feel like being a model minority—you just want to be you, flaws and all. No one expects you to speak for all white girls, Stella, but they sure expect me to speak for all Muslims. So no, you don't know. Otherwise you'd understand that *the point* is that you keep on fighting because you have no other choice. You have to resist the injustice or else you die inside a little bit more every single day."

We're almost at the door to Mr. Walsh's classroom.

"At least one good thing that's come out of this mess is that my parents realized that they should have just let *me* run in the first place. Everything that they were trying to prevent by telling me to keep my head down ended up happening anyway. I might as well have taken the chance and used my own voice instead of playing it safe."

Farida should have been running for class president, not me. She would have totally rocked it. She's got more courage in her little finger than I have in my entire body. If it hadn't been for Mayor Abbott running for governor, she would have been the one doing it. No wonder she's angry.

She looks me in the eye. "So are you quitting the race?" she asks.

"No. I'm going to be part of the fight. But, for the record, you're right—it should have been you running."

"Well, buckle up. It's going to be a bumpy ride."

"Will you still ride shotgun?" I ask. "Look, I know I can be totally clueless, and I keep making stupid mistakes and getting things wrong, and I'm sorry, but you're my best friend and I wouldn't even be doing this without your encouragement. I want us to be in this together."

It seems like forever before Farida shrugs and half smiles. "Yeah, I guess. Who else is going to tell you when you need to check your privilege?"

Exhaling a sigh of relief, I link my arm through hers.

"Hopefully, you won't need to do it as often," I say. "And now to face Chris. This should be a blast."

"Chin up, and don't let him see you're afraid," Farida says.

We still have a lot of stuff to work through, but we walk into the classroom together. And all through class, I think about what I can do to try to make it right.

After dinner that night, I'm in my room, reporting more horrible comments on the Tigris Facebook page, when Mom comes in.

"I'm sorry about this morning, Stella," she says. "It's true that your dad and I have been very focused on Rob and . . . well, it's like they say about the squeaky wheel. You always seem to be doing so well that I guess it's easy for us to forget that you need attention, too."

Wait, what?

"So . . . are you saying that I need to mess up more to get you to notice me?"

"No!" Mom says, throwing her hands up in mock despair. "That isn't at all what I'm saying!"

"What *are* you saying, exactly?"

"I'm saying I'm sorry. And I'm going to make more of an effort—that Dad and I *both* are going to make more of an effort—to give you the attention you need and deserve."

"And can you tell me when things are happening instead of pretending that everything's fine when it's totally obvious that it isn't?" I ask. "Because that just makes it worse."

Mom sighs. "We thought we were protecting you. We didn't want you to be stressed out, especially when we didn't have a diagnosis yet."

"But you ended up making me more stressed out," I say. "I have eyes and ears and a brain. I see what's going on. I'm trying to figure it all out, and knowing that my parents are hiding stuff from me just makes it all scarier."

"I'm sorry, Stella. All I can say is that Dad and I are human. We do the best we can to get it right, but we make mistakes." She reaches over and hugs me. "Hopefully, we'll learn from them."

I want proof that things are going to be different, that she's not just saying this, but I still hug her back. And as I do, I realize that this is how Farida must feel over and over about me. I have to do something. I have to act.

"I've been reporting as many of these hateful comments on Facebook as I can. Mom, I'm really worried about what's going to happen to Tigris because of us. Some of these comments are calling for a boycott." I gesture to my laptop. "What can we do? The El-Rahims didn't do anything wrong and this could ruin them."

"I know. It makes me furious." She shakes her head. "I spoke with Layla this morning to see how they were holding up. She's worried that things could escalate from online unpleasantness into real-life violence."

Then, seeing the look of panic on my face, she adds, "They've talked to the police, and a squad car is going to make more frequent patrols by the restaurant."

"But is that enough?" I ask.

"I don't know. I invited them to stay here for a few days, but Layla said that would probably just fan the conspiracy theorists." Mom sighs. "We live in a crazy world."

"But what can we do?" I say, the urgency making my chest feel tight. "There has to be *something*."

Mom stares at the posts on my computer screen. "What if we countered these hateful posts with good reviews?"

"Yes . . ." I say. Then I get another idea. "And what if we encourage everyone in Argleton to either go to dinner or order out from Tigris to show our support?"

"Good thinking," Mom says.

"I'll start a secret group and invite you, and then you can share the link."

"It's a start!" Mom says, getting up. She ruffles my hair and kisses me. "I'm proud of you, Stella."

I smile up at her and the vise that's been constricting my chest loosens a little, because now there's something practical I can do instead of just feeling angry and helpless.

It goes without saying that a politician who's running for governor is well-connected. You don't scale the political heights without knowing people who know people who know people who know people.

But the thing I've learned in the last week is that even though my family isn't famous, or the mayor, or in positions that other people might consider "important," we know people, too. It turns out the people we know also know people, and those people know people. Like Mr. McNeill, one of the veterans at the American Legion post, also belongs to the Rotary Club and knows Ms. Stephanie Nagy, the anchor for one of our local news stations.

After Mr. McNeill called Ms. Nagy and explained the situation, and she and her team did some further research, she agreed to do a special-interest piece about Rob and the problems vets have when they transition home from active duty. An in-depth investigation showing that Rob is more than an angry veteran who broke a teenager's nose at the mall for no apparent reason. A piece that will provide context about what happened and hopefully deal with the half-truths being spread by Mayor Abbott's campaign.

"Now, as for any dealings with journalists, you never know exactly how it's going to come out till it airs," Mr. McNeill tells Rob while we're waiting for the TV crew to arrive at the house. "It's up to them how they frame and edit the story. But from my dealings with Stephanie Nagy in the past, I'm confident that she'll treat you fairly."

Rob shrugs. "It's not like she can make me look much worse, right?"

After making the mistake of reading some of the online comments on the America News Channel story, I'm not so sure. I'm beginning to think that things can always get worse, depending on what part of the story is presented and what people are willing to believe.

But I know to keep that thought to myself. It's hard enough for my brother right now. At least he's had a haircut and is freshly shaved, dressed in nice jeans and a button-down shirt. He looks clean-cut and normal. When I told Rob that, he said, "So did Ted Bundy, and he was a serial killer." I guess he has a point.

"We really appreciate you setting this up, Joe," Mom tells Mr. McNeill, giving Rob a *mind your manners* look.

"Yeah, thank you," Rob says. "I'm really grateful to you for doing this."

"Don't you even think about it," Mr. McNeill says. "I'm happy to help."

He takes a sip of coffee and then sighs. "What I still don't understand is why we don't learn. We're one of the greatest countries in the world, and we keep sending young folks off to war, but we don't remember the lessons about the problems they face when they come home, from one war to the next."

"Institutional amnesia," Mom says with a sigh.

"That's right," Mr. McNeill says. "So we waste a lot of time reinventing the wheel, and meanwhile our soldiers and their families suffer."

"Why do we spend so much money to go to war and then cheap out on looking after the people who fight it?" I ask. "Aren't the people more important?"

"You'd think, wouldn't you?" my dad says. "But we're just the grunts, Stella. We go where we're told and do what our country asks. We don't have any more say in the matter than you do."

"But pretty much every politician says they support the troops," I say. "The troops are people. So why don't they actually fund the support?"

Dad says, "Sometimes you find that they have different *priorities*."

"So . . . weapons and war matter more than people?" I ask, feeling myself getting angrier by the minute.

"I wouldn't put it like that, exactly," Mom says.

"More like some people matter more than others to the folks who make decisions," Dad says.

"And us grunts aren't the ones that matter," Rob says. "Especially not once we're broken. It's like Spock said: 'This troubled planet is a place of the most violent contrasts. Those who receive the rewards are totally separated from those who shoulder the burdens.'"

"You're not broken, Rob," Mr. McNeill says. "I know you're hurting, but don't you ever think you're broken."

I want to ask more questions, but just then the doorbell rings. The truck from the TV station is here, and so is Stephanie Nagy. It's just a sign of how weird our lives have become lately that we have a celebrity in our living room. Us, the extremely ordinary Walker family.

Who am I kidding? Nothing's been ordinary since Rob came home. And that's what this is all about.

Ms. Nagy sits with us for a few minutes, asking questions as the video crew sets up lighting and figures out the best seating and camera positions. One of the crew puts mics on Rob and my parents.

I'm not going to be part of the news story, even though I was there when it happened, and the ripples from it affect my life every day. The producers are trying to keep the segment focused on Iraq and Afghanistan veterans and their difficulty getting treatment for PTSD as much as possible. But since Mayor Abbott dragged the El-Rahims into Rob's situation for no good reason, Ms. Nagy is also going to Tigris to interview them about how their lives have been affected by everything.

I spend the time trying to learn by observing. Watching how the news stories we see are put together, because I'm in the middle of creating a story of my own for Argleton High, and I have decisions to make, choices about what I include and what I don't.

What I've learned is that the decisions I make might affect what people will think is the truth—or even whose stories get told in the first place. That seems like it should be a big responsibility, one that should be taken with a lot of care and thought. Did Mayor Abbott and the network that showed the clip of Rob hitting Wade without any context of what came before think about that when they started dragging my brother's name through the mud because it helped Mayor Abbott score a political point? Did they think about the effect it would have on Farida and her family when they pulled her into the story, just because she happened to be both my friend and Muslim? Did they have any twinge of conscience about grabbing at those tenuous straws and twisting them so they'd fit with what Mayor Abbott had been saying?

I want to win the election. It's important to win. We're told that constantly. But is how you go about winning important, too? No one ever seems to talk to us about that.

Sometimes I wonder if I'll ever find the answers. Or even if there are any. But I can't stop asking the questions. If I've learned anything from all this, it's that's who I am.

Hey, Roadrunner—

Who would've thought this guy would be the star of local news? Specialist ThunderGeek, TV celebrity. Of all the people in our squad, I'd be the last one anyone would suspect, right? It should have been Reyes. Or you, before Reyes died and you started blaming yourself for it.

Out of all of us, I was the quiet one. Mr. One-Liner, you called me once. "You sit there all stealth-like, and then you lob a one-liner that kills, like a grenade."

I thought that was the funniest thing, until I actually killed someone.

It's what I was supposed to do, right?

I'm a marine, that's what I signed up for.

But death isn't like it is in the movies or in video games.

I don't regret for a second that it was him and not me. But I still see his face. He looked confused as it happened.

Confused, like it wasn't supposed to end this way.

None of it was supposed to end this way.

Huh, so that was interesting. Stella just came into my room and asked me for advice. Me, the one who has managed to mess up my own life and done a pretty good job of screwing things up for my entire family, too. And let's not forget Stella's friend. Why would she want MY advice? Me, of all people?

This is what she asked me: Is it more important to do the right thing or is it more important to win?

When did the cute little kid who followed me around like a puppy get so deep?

And more to the point—how was I supposed to answer that?

Should I have told her the answer I learned at church? The one I think Mom and Dad would tell her? That would be "do the right thing."

But she didn't ask Mom and Dad. She asked me.

Why?

Maybe she knows what Mom and Dad would tell her.

Maybe she trusts me to tell her the truth about the world. What happens in the REAL WORLD, not in fantasy land.

Is combat the real world? In some ways it felt like the most real of worlds. When the adrenaline was pumping and time slowed down and every decision and movement could make the difference between life or death.

Do I tell her what war taught me? Win at all costs. Because otherwise you come home in a flag-draped casket.

But war isn't the world I want to be real for Stella. We fight different battles now that we're back home.

What would you have said?

I don't know if I did the right thing. I'm not a parent or even a guy who has his head on straight, but I told her that there are going to be people who do both, and only she can decide which one of them she wants to be. She just has to remember that no matter what she chooses, she'll have to live with the consequences. Maybe she'll win, maybe she'll lose.

As long as she can live with who she sees when she looks in the mirror.

Because that's the problem with winning at all costs.

Somehow, you have to figure out how to live with yourself afterward.

You didn't.

Me? I'm still trying.

ThunderGeek out.

CHAPTER ELEVEN

My lungs feel like they are about to explode, my breathing sounds like I'm an antique steam locomotive, and I'm regretting the day I thought Adam Swann was cute.

"Are . . . you . . . trying . . . to . . . give . . . me . . . a . . . heart . . . attack?" I say, wheezing, to his flannel-covered back.

He stops and turns, smiling at me, but I'm too out of breath to even enjoy the sight of his single dimple. "We're almost there. I promise. Just a little bit longer."

"You . . . said . . . that . . . before, you . . . liar."

Adam laughs. "But this time I really mean it." He reaches out his hand and takes mine. "You can do it, Stella. How about you take the lead?" He grins and winks at me. "Then I can push you if you need it."

"Ha-ha," I pant. "But . . . what . . . if . . . there's a s-snake?"

"Stella, it's in the forties, and most snakes are brumating."

"Which means?"

"They're chilling at their snake pads, rather than lying in wait to freak you out," he says, kissing me lightly on the forehead. Then he touches his lips to mine. It leaves me even more breathless, and I lay my head on his chest.

"Is it really only a little bit longer?" I mumble into his jacket. "No lie?"

"No lie," he says. "And I promise, it'll be worth it."

"Okay," I say, pulling away. "But next time I get to pick the activity, and it's going to involve a couch, an old movie, and no strenuous activity or potentially poisonous animals."

"You've got yourself a deal," he says.

I set off slowly, focusing on the ground in front of me rather than ahead on the trail because I'm not sure I entirely buy the snakes-are-chilling-at-their-snake-pads story. I'm so focused on just putting one foot in front of the other I don't even notice that we've made it to the summit.

"We're there," Adam says.

I look up to a beautiful vista of the Blue Ridge Mountains and the lake in the valley below where we started our hike. "Wow. You weren't kidding. It *is* worth it."

He stands behind me and puts his arms around me, and I lean back against him. "I wouldn't lie to you, Stella."

I've been wrestling with the idea of truth and understanding how much of our perception of it can depend on who tells the story and how it's told. I'm starting to realize how much of what I've taken for granted as true about life and my country is because of who got to tell the story.

I've also been figuring out who my true friends are, and what it means to be a friend. Realizing how important it is to speak out, but also how important it is to listen.

We walk over to a large boulder and sit. I snuggle into the warmth of Adam's arm and pull a bag of trail mix out of my pocket. We munch in silence, enjoying each other's company and the beauty of the day.

When we finish the trail mix, Adam takes my hand and strokes my knuckles with his thumb.

"Now that we're here, can I confess something?" he says.

"Wait . . . did you lie to me about the snakes brumating? I knew it! Tell me there are no poisonous snakes around here!"

He laughs. "No, that's the truth! Relax and enjoy the view."

I pull away from his arm and face him.

"I guess the view isn't so bad," I say, smiling.

He smiles back, revealing that dangerous dimple. He's still holding my hand, and he reaches to take the other one.

"This isn't about snakes. It's not really about us. Well, not exactly. It's just that I want to be honest with you. Really honest."

"O-kay," I say, wondering what's coming. "This sounds kind of ominous."

"It's not. At least I don't think it is. It's just . . . well, my dad's the best in a lot of ways, and I'm grateful that he's taught me so much about survivalist techniques and all, because I love the outdoors, and if the zombie apocalypse ever happens, you totally want me by your side because I know exactly how to keep us both alive but . . ."

He stops and looks away out over the horizon.

"But what?"

"I feel guilty for saying this, because he's my dad, and I love him, but I don't want to live my life the way he does, thinking the worst of everyone and everything, and always waiting for horrible things to happen," Adam says, turning back and leaning his forehead against mine. "I'd rather spend *my* life fighting to *prevent* the worst things from happening. Even though I'm just one person, and who knows if I can really make a difference."

"It's like Farida said, we have to keep on fighting, because we have no other choice."

He squeezes my fingers gently. "Stella, if I tell you something, will you promise you won't hate me?"

"You've had plenty of reasons to hate me and you've managed not to, so it's the least I can do," I say.

"Good point. But this is a big one." he says. "See, my dad's a big fan of Mayor Abbott."

He looks in my eyes searchingly, as if to gauge my reaction before he goes on. It's hard to hide the fact that I'm a little rattled by this news, but I squeeze his hand to encourage him to continue.

"I can never bring you guys to my house. I've tried talking sense to him, but we just end up having huge fights. He believes what he believes and that's the end of it."

So *that's* why I've never been to Adam's house or met his dad. I thought maybe he was too embarrassed because of all the stuff with my family, but I didn't realize it was about *his* dad, too.

"Wow," I say. "That must be hard. Especially if that's not how you feel."

"Stella, you know that's not how I feel," he says. "Since my mom died—well, my dad's just gotten angrier at the world, and he's taken to blaming all his problems on everyone else."

He looks away and takes a deep breath before continuing.

"One night I got so upset I told him I was sick of listening to him and stormed out of the house. I went for a long walk in the woods and didn't get back till almost midnight. Saw a great horned owl out hunting, which was pretty cool, but what I realized by the time I got back was that my dad was kind of a hypocrite."

"How's that?" I ask.

"After my mom died, he made his entire life—and did his best to make mine—about being self-sufficient, but meanwhile he's blaming everyone else for his problems instead of looking in the mirror and facing them," Adam says. "My dad's got a lot of good qualities, but I don't want to be him. Is that terrible?"

"No," I say. "At least I hope not. I don't want to be my parents, either. I mean, I hope I can take on their good traits, but I don't want to be *exactly* like them. I want to be my own person. Example A: The military was the right decision for them, but I'm not sure if it's the right choice for me."

"I can see that," he says.

"But then I worry if it's because I've always felt like a coward in my family—a coward and a loser. Everyone else has served in the military. I've had it drilled into my head that we're supposed to serve. Walkers are patriots. That's what we do," I explain. "And then when the graffiti happened and people started calling Rob a traitor, it made me wonder about what it means to serve, and what it means to be a patriot."

Adam nods.

"And I wondered—do I have to be in the military to serve my country? Is that the only way to be a patriot? Can't I serve in other ways?"

"Well, there's the Peace Corps, AmeriCorps . . ."

"Yeah, but I'm thinking something else," I say. "Journalism. Asking hard questions. Looking at how stories are told. At *what* stories are told. I'm going to take a journalism class and join the school paper. Try to report the things that happen at school besides just sports. See if this is the path for me instead of boot camp."

"Sounds like a plan," Adam says.

"You think? You don't think it's a cop-out? That I'm letting down my family?"

"It's not a cop-out. What if you have other skills? Or if you just want to go in another direction? Is there some law that says we have to do exactly what our parents do and think exactly the same way they think?" Adam says. "I mean, we're being encouraged to use critical-thinking skills, right? And doesn't that mean that maybe, sometimes, we might come up with different answers?"

"Good point," I say, so relieved I feel like I could float off this cliff and soar hawk-like down to the lake below. But instead, I lean over and give Adam a kiss.

"Did I ever tell you how awesome you are?"

"You might have," he says. "But it's something that can never be said enough as far as I'm concerned."

"You're awesome," I repeat, curling into his side and looking up at the clear blue sky, decorated with a few puffy cumulus clouds.

I close my eyes, enjoying the feeling that for at least this moment, everything feels right in the world. I know that there are more battles to fight, that beyond this valley, this day, this moment, there are bad things we have to deal with. But for right now, I'm going to enjoy this time, this place, and being with this boy, because it will help to give me the strength for whatever lies ahead.

———————————

More of my election posters have been ripped down on Monday. Others have *Traitor* written across them in black marker. I take them to the office to show Principal Hart.

"It's bad enough I've had to take my social media accounts private because of what's going on with my brother," I complain. "But now I can't even have posters up around school without them being torn down or defaced?"

"I hear you, Stella. But unfortunately, the divisiveness of the state elections is trickling down to our school," Principal Hart says. "Some parents and, I hate to say, even some of the faculty have suggested suspending elections in favor of having administration appoint class officers."

"Suspend elections?" I exclaim. "But that's . . . that's *so wrong*! We're allowed to elect our own officers!" I point to my posters. "Anyway, it's too late. The 'divisiveness' is already here."

"Exactly. That's why I refused to entertain the notion, even though there was significant pressure from certain quarters," he says. "Not only that, I still believe it's our job to prepare you for citizenship, not just employment. If I gave in to pressure to suspend elections, what message would I be sending about the importance of democracy and using your vote when you graduate from high school?"

"Thanks for not doing that," I say. "But what can I do about my posters? It takes time and money to make them, and if they keep being destroyed . . ."

"I'll make an announcement later today," Principal Hart says. "And it'll be clear what the consequences are for tampering with election posters."

"Thanks, Principal Hart," I say. "It's hard enough running right now as it is."

"I know. I'm going to be taking flak from the school board for this decision. But 'right is right and politics is politics,' as my grandma used to say."

I think about that saying for the rest of the day. Do the two have to be mutually exclusive?

We prepare dinner on trays that evening so we can watch Stephanie Nagy's special report together.

My brother's super quiet, sitting on the corner of the sofa with Peggy by his side, his knee bouncing constantly under his dinner tray so that I'm afraid his meat casserole is going to end up on the carpet.

I'm beginning to suspect Peggy isn't just sitting by his side for supportive purposes; this time I think she might have an ulterior motive.

"Are you scared this is going to make it worse?" I ask Rob.

"I'd be crazy not to," he says. "It's hard to know who to trust anymore." He gives a short, bitter laugh. "Heck, I thought I could trust the nation I served to have my back and look how well *that* worked out."

I feel like I should remind him that there are people in the nation who still have his back—look at how the people from the Legion came over and helped to clean the graffiti off the house. But I get what he's talking about. It's the system. How long it's taking Rob to get his appointment. It's how the Powers That Be had no problems writing the checks to go to war, but suddenly there's not enough money now that the soldiers who fought it need care.

But there are still individuals like Mayor Abbott. And Chris. And Wade and Jed. Not to mention all the people who believe Mayor Abbott. People who think my brother is some kind of violent person, even though they don't know all the facts. They're individuals, not "the system."

So I just lay my head on his shoulder and say, "We've always got your back. Don't ever forget that."

"Yeah. I know," he says. "Thanks."

I think we're having a moment, and I smile.

Then Rob says, "Now can you get your greasy head off my shoulder?"

World's Shortest Moment Ever.

"I washed my hair this morning, loser!" I retort.

"Quiet, you two! The news is starting," Mom says.

Dad turns up the volume.

Mayor Abbott's face flashes on the screen as they cover his latest campaign event. Dad starts booing and the rest of us join him.

"I know I'm setting a bad example for you kids," Dad says, "but after what that man's done to Rob . . ."

"Stella, I'm sure I don't have to tell you that you shouldn't act like Dad when Chris speaks at your school assembly," Mom says, giving Dad warning look. "Don't visit the sins of the father on the child."

I refrain from rolling my eyes. "No, you don't need to tell me," I say.

But what I'm thinking is: *Like he and his friends aren't 'visiting the sins' of my brother on me? Or even worse, on Farida and her family?*

Finally, the anchor says, "And now it's time for Special Report with Stephanie Nagy. Tonight she reports on the plight of American veterans—and how lack of resources at the Department of Veterans Affairs has affected one local vet's life in a very dramatic way . . ."

Stephanie starts off outside the local VA hospital, talking about problems with the VA system and long delays for people getting appointments, particularly for mental health care. She tells us that thirty veterans die by suicide out of 100,000 in their population compared to fourteen people out of 100,000 in the civilian population. Then she's sitting in our living room, the one we're all gathered in now, watching her, talking to Rob and my parents about the challenges we've faced as a family since he got back.

The cameraman zooms into a close-up on Rob's face when she asks him what happened at the mall. He starts talking about Jason and then covers his face. Then they cut to an interview with Ashar and his parents. He talks about how Wade and Jed were harassing him, and repeats the awful things they were saying. "What country am I supposed to go back to? I was born right here in Virginia. I'm just as American as they are!" he says. "It's gets real old real fast having to explain my skin color and my religion all the time. Why do some people think they're more American than I am just because their skin is lighter than mine?"

Then it cuts to an exterior shot of Tigris, and Ms. Nagy talks about the cable news piece where Wade made what she calls a "spurious link" to a local Iraqi American family, proprietors of a successful restaurant in Argleton, because of Farida's friendship with me. She interviews Mr. and Mrs. El-Rahim, and she looks as horrified as I felt when they show her some of the terrible comments on Yelp and Facebook.

Finally, there are short clips of Mr. Neustadt and Mr. McNeill from the American Legion talking about how disgusted they were when our house was covered in graffiti calling Rob a traitor, and why they came to help clean it off.

Then it cuts back to Rob. "I take the Marine Corps values seriously. Things like integrity, respecting human dignity, adhering to a higher standard of personal conduct, and leading by example. I thought that by intervening in the situation I was living up to those values. But I failed when I allowed myself to be provoked into losing control. I failed to maintain personal discipline. In my defense, I recognized I was struggling since I got back from my last deployment, and I was trying to get help before the incident happened. The problem for me, and so many vets like me, is that the wait to get an appointment for evaluation at the VA hospital is way too long. I'm still waiting for mine. The appointment didn't come soon enough for my friend Jason, and as you can see, the delay has affected my life. Not just mine. I regret that I've let down the corps. I regret that I've let down my family and that a totally innocent family, our friends the El-Rahims, have been drawn into this, just because of their faith. That a kid just trying to earn some money at a part-time job was treated the way he was. That doesn't seem to reflect the American values I put on a uniform for and risked my life to defend." The last shot is of Mom and Dad sitting on either side of Rob. Dad says, "We raised our son to stand up for others. Why is this country breaking its promise to stand up for him?"

Rob exhales loudly as Ms. Nagy concludes with, "This is Stephanie Nagy for Channel Seven News," like he'd been holding his breath the entire time.

Dad turns off the TV.

"She did a great job," he says. "That should help turn things around."

"I sure hope so," Mom says.

"If people watched it," Rob mutters.

"We'll encourage them to watch it," Mom says. "I'm going to send out the link to everyone I know and tell them to send it to everyone they know."

"Your mother and her networks are on the case," Dad says. "Mayor Abbott is going to learn he should never have messed with the Fightin' Walkers."

"I'm going to take Peggy out for a walk," Rob says suddenly, getting up off the sofa. "I need some fresh air."

Mom casts him a worried glance.

"I feel like some fresh air, too," Dad says, catching Mom's glance and acting like he really does need fresh air.

I'm pretty sure Rob sees through the charade, but he doesn't say anything.

"I'll get the leash," he says.

I wait till I hear the front door close behind them before asking Mom the burning question. "Do you think it's going to be enough to change peoples' minds about Rob?"

She takes long enough to answer that I feel panic struggle to take flight in my stomach.

"There's no way we can change everyone's mind, Stella," Mom says, speaking in the soft voice she always used when I was a kid and had a bad dream and she was trying to tell me it wasn't real. Except that this one is real. "But I do think this'll help Rob in the court of public opinion. It was smart of Ms. Nagy to interview Ashar. He made Wade and Jed look like ignorant, badly behaved teens, parroting the words of their elders—and he provided context for that video clip Mayor Abbott used to make Rob look like he was being violent out of nowhere."

"But will it be *enough*?" I ask. "Do you think the prosecutor is still going to press for prison?"

"Who knows if what we do is ever enough?" Mom says. "We have to stay true to ourselves and do the best we can. Sometimes the most we can do is make people think."

The next day it seems like at least some kids saw the piece, whether on TV or online.

Haley and I haven't spoken since the day after the mall incident when she took Wade's word over mine. But she comes up to me at my locker first thing in the morning.

"Hey, Stella," she says.

"Hey."

"I . . . well, I saw your brother on the news in the piece about veterans last night," she says.

I don't say anything. I'm waiting to hear where she's going with this.

"I just want to say . . . I'm sorry. I shouldn't have just assumed Wade and Jed were telling the truth. I guess I . . . well, I'm sorry."

"It was easier to go along with the crowd and believe them than to believe me, who you've known since kindergarten?"

"I wouldn't have done that if Rob hadn't acted so weird at the convenience store," Haley protests. "I didn't realize it might be PTSD or whatever. It just seemed so out there."

I guess I can see where she's coming from. But it still hurts.

"Anyway, I'm sorry," she says. "I feel bad. I hope he feels better soon."

"You and me both," I say. "But thanks."

I don't know where this leaves our friendship. But her saying sorry is a step in the right direction. After all, Farida has forgiven me for making mistakes more times than I can count.

Tom Zweibel, who made the stupid crack about Rob when I was interviewing him for the election video, stops me in the hall.

"Hey, Stella. I saw that thing about your brother and, um . . . I just want to say he's all right," he says.

Am I supposed to thank him for that?

"I knew he was all right all along," I tell Tom. "I'm glad you finally realized it."

Tom flushes. "Yeah, well . . . That's all I wanted to say."

"Okay. Noted."

As I walk to class, I wonder if it would have killed him to say "I'm sorry." Two little words, which when said with sincerity, go a long way. If he'd said "I'm sorry," maybe I'd have been less snarky in return.

I see Charity Hernandez and Sierra Foster outside the door to my class.

"Hey! When's the first basketball game of the season?" I ask before I go in. "I want to make sure I come."

"The Monday after Thanksgiving," Sierra says. "Awesome that you remembered."

"Yeah. Oh, hey, I saw that thing about your brother," Charity adds. "He's good people."

"Thanks," I say. "I like him."

"What Mayor Abbott is saying about him is just wrong," Sierra says.

"Ugh. I know," I say. "It wasn't anything like Mayor Abbott tells it."

"How can he get away with saying all that fake stuff on the news?" Charity asks. "There should be a law or something."

"There is a law," I say. "It's called the First Amendment. It means he gets to say whatever he wants, even if it's not true."

"Yeah, but on the *news*?" Charity says. "Aren't they supposed to say if it's true or not?"

"Exactly," Sierra chimes in. "You know, isn't that their job? To fact-check or whatever?"

"Right?" I say.

"And it was so unreal that Farida got dragged into it," Sierra says.

"I know—have you posted a good review on the Tigris Facebook and Yelp pages yet?" I ask. "I'm trying to get people to do that to drown out all the awful stuff."

"I saw that," Charity says. "My mom ordered takeout from there for dinner yesterday."

"I wrote a good review on Facebook and Yelp, and I sent the link to all my friends," Sierra says.

"Great, thanks."

But as I walk away, I feel kind of hypocritical because I still haven't decided what I'm going to do about the video for my election speech. It's not that I'm planning to totally lie about things, but like the America News Channel, I've been playing around with selective editing.

"You wouldn't know anything about some secret Facebook group that's encouraging people to eat at Tigris and leave positive reviews, would you?" Farida asks me at lunch.

"Facebook group? What? Me?" I say, attempting to deny all knowledge.

"Don't ever try out for drama," Ken says. "You're a terrible actress."

I make an exaggerated pouty face.

"I'm actually going to agree with Kenny on this," Farida says. "Stop the press!" She hugs me. "But thanks. It's still pretty stressful at home, but Dad says there's already been a pickup in takeout orders. And the Yelp reviews are more positive than negative again."

"I told you I'd try harder," I say.

"When the phone started ringing so much more all of a sudden, we couldn't figure out if it was a sudden rush because people saw Mom and Dad interviewed on Stephanie Nagy's special report. Business had been slow since the thing on the America News Channel," Farida says. "My parents have been pretty worried. Then Jenny Moss's family came in for dinner and she told me about the secret group."

"Which is apparently no longer a secret," Adam says. "By the way, how's the video coming along?"

I hesitate, because even though my gut's been telling me one thing, I still don't know if I should do the opposite to give me a better chance of winning.

"Okay," I say. "It's a ton of work to edit. Thankfully, I have the amazing and talented Ken to help."

"It'll be worth it when you win," Farida says.

"Well, actually . . . I want to ask your opinion about something."

Ken flashes me a warning look. I know he doesn't want to share the rough version of the Win at All Costs video we've created with Farida or anyone else just yet, but I'm done with keeping stuff from my best friend.

"It's just . . . well, the whole situation with Rob made me think about how the way things are presented can change what we think about them. So Ken and I started experimenting with different ways of editing the interviews we did, and . . . okay, let me just show you."

I've copied the two draft versions onto my phone—the WaAC (Win at All Costs) version and the TILII (Tell It Like It Is) version.

I don't give any explanation. I just play them both.

"See how number one is much more positive?" Ken says.

"No way," Farida says. "It's totally manipulative. I mean, you cut out all the things we agreed should be included. I thought the whole point was that you understood people want to be heard. It's denying our voice. We're supposed to be representing all students, not just pretending everything is perfect."

This is exactly what I was afraid of.

"Number one is more upbeat and persuasive," Ken argues. "It'll appeal to more people. We want to win, don't we?"

"It'll appeal to more of the same people who would vote for Chris is what you're saying without actually using the words," Farida says, her words clipped with anger.

Ken stills, looking stunned. "Wait. What are you saying? You're not calling me a racist, are you?"

Farida is quiet for just one second too long for him before she says, "No, I'm—"

"Seriously, Farida?" Ken explodes. "We're friends. How can you think that?"

"That's not what I'm saying," she says. "It's just that—"

But he doesn't let her finish.

"Forget it. You can be campaign manager on your own. I'm outta here," he says, getting up and storming out of the cafeteria.

Farida turns to Adam and me, with wide, stricken eyes.

"I was just trying to think of the best words to tell him how I felt," she said. "It's always hard to have these conversations."

"I totally get that," I say. And it sucks that Farida is always put in the position of having to explain it. "Can you tell me? I honestly want to know."

"Are you sure?" Farida asks. "One-hundred-percent sure?"

"Yes. That's why I asked."

She glances over at Adam, who nods, as if confirming that he's witness to my answer before she speaks.

"Stella, obviously I want you to win. I was the one who encouraged you to run in the first place."

"I know," I say.

"But that first video is dishonest," she says. "And that hurts. Especially after everything that's happened in the last few weeks. It's portraying things to make it seem like we all think everything's great here. You cut out all the parts where we talked about the real problems we experience every day at Argleton High."

I nod. "But that's the way it works in the real world. I mean, look at Rob. Even at school, people just believed Jed's story. So I thought—isn't it better to play the game the way it's done and win, so we can actually get things accomplished?"

"But don't you see," she says. "You've just bought into the same system that's excluded and ignored our voices in the first place."

"I know, but once I'm elected, I'll—"

"Yeah, that's what they all say," Farida says. "Do you even hear yourself? Did you even listen the other day when I tried to explain about all the everyday crap I put up with that you don't even notice? That you've been able to ignore for all the years we've been friends? Didn't you hear what Ashar said on TV?"

She picks up her tray with the remains of her lunch and gets up.

"Wait, Farida, don't go, I—"

"I thought you were finally starting to get it, like *actually* get it. But maybe you just won't. Ever." She grips the edges of her tray and a look of defeat crosses her face. "I've lost my appetite," she says, and walks away.

I've lost mine, too, knowing that my best friend thinks I'm part of the problem, and realizing that no matter how good my intentions are, it looks like she's right.

"Great," I say to Adam. "I've gone from two campaign managers to zero in one lunch period."

He doesn't say anything but just looks at me, and I don't feel good about what I see in his eyes.

"You're mad at me, too."

"Not mad, exactly," he says quietly. "More . . . disappointed."

"I'm disappointing everyone right now," I say with a sigh. "And the election hasn't even happened yet."

"Let me ask you a question," Adam says. "Why do you think I like you? I mean, *like* like you."

Talk about an awkward question. I'm not sure how to answer, so I fall back on humor. "My good looks and sharp wit?"

"There is that," he allows, a hint of a smile tugging at the corner of his mouth. "But dig a little deeper."

"I can't read your mind. And clearly I'm not even that good at hearing when people tell me things," I say. "But maybe you can try?"

He takes my hand under the table, and despite being miserable in the crowded cafeteria, it reminds me of being on the cliff with the valley below, when everything still seemed possible.

"Most people look at me and see a freak," he says. "I'm the kid of the weird survivalist guy who lives in the woods and believes in every conspiracy theory out there."

I look down at our clasped hands, feeling guilty. I don't know if I would have gone so far as *freak*, but it's fair to say that I always assumed Adam was a little weird, like his dad. It didn't help that he was so quiet. It's only been this year that I've gotten to know him better and realized he's so much more than that.

"It's okay," he says, squeezing my hand. "I know you probably thought that, too. But you looked beyond it to the real me, something most people don't bother to do."

"So I'm not a total disappointment to you?" I ask.

"The reason why I *like* you is because you want to change things. And because you're smart and funny, and you're not afraid to say what you think," Adam says. "One of my favorite things in the world is watching you put Chris in his place."

I smile. "True confession: I kind of enjoy doing that."

"So why are you trying to play it safe all of a sudden with that video? I don't get it."

Sometimes you don't need to be told the answer. You just need someone to ask you the right question.

What *has* trying to play it safe done for me? It's upset my best friend, making her feel like I haven't been listening, and made me feel bad about myself because I wasn't listening to what I knew was right.

"I don't know," I tell him. "But I definitely know what I've got to do now. It's going to be a long night."

Hey, Roadrunner—

So it looks like Operation Make Rob Look More Respectable has been a moderate success. When I went to campus for class the next day a few people said they'd seen the thing. Two younger guys, Cody and Kyle, hadn't realized I'd served and they wanted to know combat details. The stuff that I don't want to talk about because that's what we glorify without talking about the rest of it. They've watched the hero movies, played Halo, Gears of War, or Call of Duty, but that never tells you what it's really like.

They don't know the guilt. The randomness. The what-ifs? The death and destruction.

And there's so much more.

I said I had a class to get to and walked away. Went and sat in the john, just so I didn't have to talk to anyone. Portrait of courage, right?

But after my next class, I had a break and I was hungry, so I went to the cafeteria for a snack and some coffee, found a table in the corner, and got out a textbook, hoping that no one else would talk to me.

Head down, trying to focus on my work, minding my own business.

"Mind if sit here?"

I looked up ready to say yes, ready to say I'm studying and I need to be alone. But then I saw her smile and the words stuck in my throat. I know, I sound like a lovesick moron, right? I can hear you and the rest of the guys ragging on me.

245

But I played it a little cool at least. Said, "Sure, suit yourself,"

and then pretended I was reading my textbook, but my palms

were sweating and I was aware of every move she made as she sat

down with her Diet Coke and package of mini Oreos.

"I'm Caitlin Stuart," she said. "And aren't you Rob Walker?"

My heart sank. If she knew who I was, then there was no way

I had a chance. So I just laid it out there straight on the table.

"Yeah, the violent veteran. As seen on TV."

She shook her head no, and I got this waft of shampoo smell

from her hair. Something flowery and clean.

"No, that's not what I meant. I mean, I knew who you are from

seeing you around campus, and then I saw you on TV but . . ." She

reached out and touched my hand. "I don't think you're violent or

disturbed or whatever."

I'd forgotten what it felt like to feel hopeful about anything

until that moment.

We ended up talking all the way through my next class. Both

her sister and her cousin served in Iraq. She's studying to be a

social worker. I asked her, "Doesn't that get depressing?"

"Doesn't war get depressing?" she asked with a smile.

"Touché," I admitted.

"But there are still things about it that my sister and

cousin miss," she continued. "I try hard to understand, but I

can't, because the thought of being in a war zone and seeing all

that freaks me out."

I wanted to tell her it freaked us out, too. That I'm still working on trying to get over how much it freaked me out, and I wonder if I ever will. That you decided you couldn't get over it.

But I didn't want to scare her off with too much honesty. Because I like this girl Caitlin. Yes, you heard it here first. I haven't told anyone else, not my parents or Stella. Only Peggy, because she's real good at keeping my secrets.

Caitlin told me which days she has classes. And then she gave me her phone number. Should I text her?

Or maybe I should just forget I ever met her, because I need to get my head straight before risking getting involved with anyone. Especially someone as cool as she is.

The last thing she needs is to be involved with someone like me.

What would you do, Jason?

No. I'm not going to do that, now that I have this phone number. Even if I never text her, just having it, just the thought that someday I might call, is enough.

I think I've rediscovered something.

That thing called possibility.

ThunderGeek out.

CHAPTER TWELVE

Late that night, I'm still editing the video, based on what Farida, Rob, and Adam said. At midnight, Mom and Dad come into my room.

"Bedtime," Dad says. "We know this is important, but so is getting enough sleep."

"But the class election speeches are tomorrow! I have to finish!"

"Stella, you've been working on this for weeks," Mom says. "I know you. You're a perfectionist. It can be ninety-nine-point seven percent perfect instead of one hundred, and that is still okay."

"Would you say that about a surgery?" I ask, rubbing my eyes, which are strained from being glued to the screen for so long. "Would you sew up a patient without doing one hundred percent of the job just because you were tired?"

Dad tries to cover up a snort but fails, as Mom looks at him helplessly.

"She's definitely my daughter, isn't she?" Mom sighs.

"Was that ever in doubt?" I ask.

"Okay, enough snarking at your mother," Dad says. "Go to bed now and get some sleep. I'll wake you up at zero dark thirty, and you can finish in the morning."

Reluctantly, I close my laptop, tell my parents good night, and turn off the light. But as soon as I hear them go into their room and close the door, I get out of bed, snag my laptop from the desk, and burrow under the covers with it. Because everything that's happened has convinced me I should listen to my heart and my gut, not to mention my best friend, who has told me why I need to have courage instead of being a coward—even if it means I don't win. I want to be class president, but I also have to be true to who I am.

In my bedcover blue-lit editing cave, I keep working to create a video that shows our school as it really is, in the voices of its students, so I can talk about my ideas for moving us toward where we want it to be. Maybe if we hear ourselves articulating the vision, one day we'll get there.

When Dad comes to wake me up at five thirty in the morning to work on my video, he finds me under the covers with my head on the keyboard.

"You might be facing time in the stockade for insubordination, young lady," he says. "But first—I'll go put on the coffee. Looks to me like you're going to need a few cups of battery acid to get you through the day at school."

"Thanks, Dad," I groan. I can barely crack my eyelids open, but I finished. I have no idea what time it was, but when I watched the final edit under the covers last night, I was proud of the interviews my friends and I had done. It made all the hours I'd spent editing them worth it.

The other night I asked Rob what I should do, because I trusted him to give me a practical answer. He's close enough to having graduated high school that he still remembers how it is.

He told me that whatever choice I make, I have to be prepared to live with the consequences—like if I win or if I lose—but most important, that I have to feel okay about it when I look myself in the mirror. With this video, I can. I feel better than okay.

I don't know if all the hard work we've done will be enough to change people's minds. I don't know if it will be enough to help me win the election for junior class president. But one thing I'm sure of—it'll make people think. Like Mom said, in the end, maybe that's the best we can do.

Rob gives me a ride to school.

"You look nice," he says when I get in the car. "What's the occasion?"

"Wow, I bet you do really well with girls," I say. I love my brother, but he can be a real dork sometimes.

He laughs, but I notice that he's blushing, which is weird.

"Sorry. That didn't come out the way I meant it."

"Duh, I hope not."

"I'll have to Google some 'how to give compliments to girls' videos to brush up on my technique," he says.

"That could get weird really fast," I warn him. "I'll give you advice for free. Just leave off the 'what's the occasion' part, which makes it sound like I don't usually look nice."

"That's not how I meant it, but anyway . . . why *are* you so dressed up?"

"Junior class assembly. I have to make a speech before the election."

"Ah . . . so did you come to a decision on what we talked about?"

"Yeah. Once I did, I couldn't believe I ever had to ask myself the question."

"And survey says . . . ?"

"I edited it as honestly as I could, showing as many voices as possible," I explain. "Which means it's not as guaranteed a vote getter as promising soft toilet paper and ice cream on Fridays, or as vague as saying I'm going to 'Make Argleton High Awesome' without saying how, exactly."

I look over at him. "Whatever happens, I'm sure I've made the right decision. Or at least as sure as I can be."

Rob just keeps driving, his leg bouncing up and down.

"Listen, you don't have to say it out loud for me to know that the real reason you're afraid of losing is because of me," he says.

He's not wrong. But still . . .

"Whether I win or lose, I've learned something just by running," I tell him. "And maybe one of the most important things I learned is from you—that I can't be afraid to step up and fight for what is right. Although I'll definitely stop short of breaking noses to convince people to vote for me."

Rob laughs. "A very wise decision," he says. "Learn from my mistakes."

We lapse into silence. The lack of sound makes my brain train stop at all the stations of worry.

What if I lose? What if the video doesn't work? What if I sound like an idiot?

At the next red light, Rob turns to me.

"I hope your classmates are smart enough to see that they'd be lucky to have someone like you at their six," he says. "I know I am."

Maybe my brother isn't so awful at compliments after all, because that makes me feel so good it puts the brakes on the anxiety train for a little while.

Luckily, the assembly is first thing in the morning, which means I don't have to stress about it all day. I don't know if it's because of Dad's superstrong coffee or nerves, but my stomach feels like it's being nibbled away by an army of ants as I sit on stage with Chris Abbott and Amy Sarducci and all the candidates for the other offices, watching the junior class file into the auditorium. I haven't had a chance to show the final edit to Farida, Ken, and Adam. None of them know what I've done. We've been a team, but yesterday that team fractured and now I'm sitting up here hoping that no one can tell how nervous I am, and that I won't let everyone down after the hard work they've put in. Most of all, I hope my indecision yesterday hasn't broken our friendship.

I sneak out my phone to text Farida.

ME: I'm really sorry about yesterday. I messed up. AGAIN.
ME: Please. Trust me. I listened. I couldn't have done this without you.

She doesn't reply. More than anyone, her opinion on this matters. I'm as tired of letting her down as she's tired of me letting her down. I want to get it right from now on.

Then I text Ken.

ME: I'm really sorry about yesterday. I hope you like the final video, which I finished at some ungodly hour. I couldn't have done any of this without you.

He doesn't reply, either.

Finally, I text Adam.

ME: Do you think anyone will vote for me if I throw up onstage?
ADAM: It depends on how theatrically you do it.
ADAM: Maybe if you throw up ON Principal Hart? 🤮
ME: OMG can you imagine how the news would spin that? "Terrorist-loving femme fatale spews plutonium puke on principal!"
ADAM: LOL, okay, no vomit. Just be you.

ME: Have you seen Farida or Ken?

ADAM: Saw Ken earlier—haven't seen Farida yet.

ME: Tell them to trust me.

ADAM: ? Okay.

Principal Hart tells us that the candidates for class president will speak after all the other class officer candidates, and that we'll speak by alphabetical order within each office, which means that I am going to be the last one to give a speech. Pros: I get to listen to what Chris and Amy say and adapt the brief remarks I plan to make after showing the video to rebut them if necessary. Cons: There's more time for the ant army to eat away at my stomach.

Most of the speeches for vice president, secretary, and treasurer are a series of jokes with a moment or two of seriousness about the job. The ants gnaw harder. Maybe I've gone about this wrong. Maybe I've taken the whole thing too seriously. Maybe instead of gathering so many interviews of people to get their thoughts about the school and spending so many hours editing the video, I should have been practicing stand-up comedy to make myself more likable. I knew this was a popularity contest, but I let myself get carried away thinking it really could be about the issues.

Who was I kidding?

I've worked myself into a vortex of self-doubt by the time we get to the class president candidates. I search for my friends in the audience, but I can't find them, and that makes me feel even more uncertain.

Chris "A is for Abbott" steps up to the podium. He's wearing a blue blazer with an American flag tie and a flag pin, just like the one his dad wears on TV. When he's introduced, loud cheers erupt from some sections of the auditorium and polite clapping from the rest of it. The ants nibble faster as I wonder how the applause-o-meter translates into election votes. Will all our work be for nothing if I lose? Or even if the video makes just one person in this auditorium feel heard, should that be enough?

The thought of coming in third after toilet paper and ice cream that has no realistic chance of happening kills me.

Chris's speech is remarkably similar in theme to the Win at All Costs video. Argleton High School is generally awesome, except for the losers who don't go to games to support the teams because they lack sufficient school spirit.

"All of us Argleton Astros should come together to support the blue and white," Chris concludes. "And if you elect me as junior class president, I promise to work to Make Argleton High Awesome."

The applause is louder and more uniform after his speech. I scribble a sentence onto my notes and hope that I can read what I wrote when it's my turn to speak.

There's no doubt who registers highest in popularity according to the applause-o-meter when Amy is introduced. She's got the double advantage of being well liked socially and running on a platform everyone loves, even if it has zero possibility of happening.

But if running for class president has taught me anything, it's that reality and logic don't seem to matter the way I was brought up to think they did. Amy Sarducci has the entire auditorium eating out of her hand.

"Softer toilet paper is something we can all get behind," she says, with emphasis on the word *behind*.

Everyone cracks up. *Need. More. Jokes. Quick, Stella, think of something funny!*

My mind is a humor blank.

Amy, however is on a roll. *A toilet roll. HA, HA, HA, HA.* Maybe I can be funny after all.

"Junior year is totally stressful. We're starting to think about graduation and what we're going to do next. There are all these tests to take. So we deserve to chill out"—she winks as she says this—"with ice cream once a week, don't you agree?"

Who wouldn't agree with that? Her question is answered by wild cheering from the entire auditorium.

I am definitely going to come in last.

When Principal Hart calls my name, I'm so nervous that my ears can't register the applause to judge how it stacks up.

I hold on to the podium to still my trembling fingers and center myself.

"When I decided to run for class president, I asked members of different school clubs to go out and talk to you guys about what you thought makes someone a good member of the

Argleton High community," I say. "Here's a short video of your answers."

I press PLAY on the computer, and Ricky up in the AV booth dims the lights.

I've included short clips of the difficult questions raised in our interviews. Instead of creatively editing the problems people raised, the video highlights them, and it ends with *JUSTICE ISN'T FOR JUST US!—Vote STELLA WALKER—the Smart Solution for Junior Class President.*

I debated leaving off Walker, because even though I love my family and I'm proud to be a Walker, our name's been all over the news. But I realized I can't run from who I am, and I don't want to. I'm proud that my brother was willing to stand up for another person. He shouldn't have punched Wade. He shouldn't have broken his nose. But he was right to intervene. I'm not ashamed of him for doing that. It was the right thing to do.

Apparently, my name wasn't a problem, because even though there are a few boos, there's a lot of cheering going on in this auditorium right now, much to my dazed, overtired, amazement.

Ricky turns up the lights and I go back to the mic.

"Thank you. I want to add a few quick things to think about when you're casting your vote. The first is that as much as I would love softer toilet paper, when our teachers have to go on DonorsChoose to get classroom supplies, let's face it, anyone promising you're going to get that is selling you a bum deal. And as much as I, too, would love to chill out with ice cream every week, same deal."

What had been cheering and applause after the video turns into groaning and even some booing, until Principal Hart reminds everyone that they are supposed to be civil. One thing is for sure—telling people the boring, undeniable truth doesn't go down nearly as well as telling them a complete fiction that they want to hear.

"I'll finish by saying that Argleton High is already pretty awesome, but there's always room for improvement, right? Together we can make it awesome for everyone. If you vote for me, I'll do my best to make that happen. Thank you."

Pretty good applause, I think. At least they weren't groaning, and now that the speech is over, the ants have stopped feasting on my insides. I look for Farida's face in the crowd. When I finally spot her, to my relief, she gives me a small smile.

"Nice job, everyone," Principal Hart says. "Good luck with tomorrow's vote. May the best candidate win."

Ken texts me. I still think the other one would have clinched it, but you done good.

ME: Thanks. ☺

Then I get a text from Farida to meet her in the girls' bathroom nearest the auditorium. She's there before me, sitting on the radiator.

"So . . . what did you think?" I ask.

"You were right. I should have trusted you," she says.

"Well, you were right, too," I tell her. "Because I was tempted to use the other version so I'd have a better chance of winning. Even though I knew deep down it was the wrong thing to do."

"So why didn't you?" she asks, meeting my gaze in the mirror.

"Because I'm lucky enough to have a best friend who isn't afraid to tell me when I'm about to do something really stupid," I say as I hop up next to her on the radiator.

"I'm lucky to have a bestie who isn't afraid to listen to me when she's about to do something really stupid," she says.

We laugh, and I lean into her.

"It was scary getting up there and speaking," I say.

"You didn't look scared," she says.

"Well, I was. A great big mass of quivering scaredy-catness." I look down at our dangling feet, my black boots next to her identical ones, and get warm fuzzies realizing that she wore her BFF boots today, too, even though we hadn't talked about it and she was mad at me. "Do you think I've got the slightest chance at all of pulling this off? Honestly?"

"I do," she says, swinging her feet, heels thumping gently against the radiator. "I mean, the stuff with your brother has definitely complicated things, but I think you've got a chance."

"We'll know soon enough," I say.

"Yup," she replies. "By the end of school tomorrow. Come on, we're going to be late for class."

She hops off the radiator, pulling me along with her.

When we meet to go to lunch, things are still kind of awkward between Ken and Farida.

"I've been hearing great comments about the video," Ken says.

"See, it was right not to use the other one," Farida says.

"Yeah," Ken says. "If Stella wins, that is."

I can see another fight brewing and I want to try to end it before it starts.

"'You can't fight in here! This is the War Room!'" I say, deploying one of my favorite lines from *Dr. Strangelove or: How I Learned to Stop Worrying and Love the Bomb.*

Ken and Farida look at me and then at each other.

"Ouch. She Strangeloved us," Ken says. "She's using the heavy artillery."

"I know," Farida says. "But I guess it's fair. We should call a truce. I mean, Stella had to speak in front of the entire junior class this morning."

"And she did a good job," Ken says.

"Um, hello? Could you stop talking about me like I'm not here?" I suggest.

Adam finds all this highly amusing.

"See, being a coach potato and watching old movies comes in

handy," I tell him. "You can't learn useful quotes from brumating snakes. Or even worse, from *not* brumating snakes."

"So I'm discovering," he says, smiling.

That dimple should come with a hazard warning. It's way too cute for safety.

As we head to the cafeteria, people keep stopping us in the hall to say how much they liked the video. By the time we get there, I'm starting to wonder if maybe, just maybe, there's a chance I won't come in last place. Farida and Adam are even more optimistic.

"I think you could win," Adam says. "I wasn't sure before, but now I think you've got a fighting chance."

"You know what I think," Farida says. "You definitely have a chance. That video slayed."

Wade, who has been walking behind us, starts laughing.

I stop and turn to look at him, trying to avoid staring at his nose, which has healed crookedly. Rumor is that he's going to have to have a nose job but has to wait six months before they can do it.

"You think she can win? Dream on."

"We don't have to dream," Farida replies, lifting her chin. "We can just vote tomorrow."

"Yeah," Ken says.

"Chris's dad is right," Jed says, looking straight at Farida. "We should send you people back to where you came from."

"*You people?* What does that even mean?" I say, glaring. "Farida *is* American."

"You're just an American by accident of birth," she adds. "My parents *chose* to become US citizens."

Chris walks up to where we're standing, and I say this for his benefit as much as I do Wade's and Jed's.

"Jed, do you really think about the things you say, or do you just repeat whatever you hear on TV?"

"Says the sister of a psycho traitor," Jed says, and in that instant, even though I'll never be able to prove it, I'm certain that he was one of the people who spray-painted our house.

"Yo, Jed, chill," Chris says.

"What do you mean, chill?" Jed asks, turning to him, even though the meaning seems pretty obvious to me.

"I mean, just shut it." Chris takes a step forward and stands between his friends and us. "Leave them alone."

"What's the matter with you, Abbott?" Wade asks.

Chris just stares at him. "Nothing is the matter with me. But you? You're being a tool, dude." He turns on his heel and storms down the hall, away from the cafeteria.

Jed shrugs. "What got into him?"

"No idea," Wade says. "But I'm hungry and I'm tired of talking to these losers."

"Yeah," Jed says, and they head into the caf.

Farida, Ken, Adam, and I stand there, stunned, watching Chris stalk off.

"That was weird," Ken says in a low voice.

"Extremely strange," Farida agrees.

It was something more, too, and I need to understand it.

"I'll be back in a minute," I tell them, and start to follow Chris down the hall, ignoring the "What?" "Where are you going?" questions called out in my wake.

I call after Chris to wait. To my surprise, he does.

When I catch up to him, he stands with his arms crossed across his chest, leaning against the lockers.

"What do you want, Walker?"

"I was wondering if we could talk," I say.

"Isn't that what we're doing now?"

I glance up at the clock and see that the bell is going to ring in forty-five seconds.

"I mean talk for real. For more than a minute. Not in school."

His eyes search my face. I can tell he's not sure what to make of this. So I risk saying one thing.

"Thanks for doing that."

Something flickers in his eyes.

"After school. Three o'clock. I'll meet you by the band shell."

"Okay. See you then," I tell him.

Without another word, he turns and walks away, and I head to the cafeteria to have lunch with my friends.

When I get to the Argleton band shell after school, Chris isn't there, and I wonder if he's decided to blow me off. It's at the end of the town green. My family has gone here every year to see the fireworks on the Fourth of July, with a local band playing patriotic songs. It's something Rob's not sure he'll ever be able to enjoy again, and I frown thinking about how it's another small way his life has been changed by war.

"You look sad."

I turn around and Chris is standing there, his hands jammed in his jacket pockets.

"I was thinking about my brother."

Chris shifts from foot to foot. "So, uh, you wanted to talk?"

"Yeah. I guess I just wanted to thank you. For what you did today."

He kicks a pebble and then glances at me briefly. "It was no big deal."

"It kind of was, coming from you. It took me by surprise," I tell him. "What made you do it, when you haven't before?"

"I don't know . . . I guess I've learned something lately. It's like . . ." He looks up at the sky, where the sun is trying to peak out from behind a massive puff of clouds. "Well . . . imagine if all your life the person you admire and look up to the most in the world told you the sky was green." His eyes meet mine. "Then one day you looked up and you saw that it was really blue. What would you do then?"

He's opened a door. I don't want it to slam shut in my face by saying the wrong thing.

"Could you talk to that person you admire?" I ask, because even though I can't imagine having conversations with Mayor

Abbott like I do with my dad, he's not my father. Maybe he and Chris are really tight. "Could you tell him that you see the color of the sky differently?"

"Yeah. Tried that," Chris says with a wry grin. "The fireworks display on July Fourth was nothing compared to the argument that started."

"I'm sorry. Maybe . . . maybe it'll just take time."

"Dad running for governor doesn't help," Chris says. "It means I can't disagree with him publicly. You know, because"—he rolls his eyes—"it's important that we're all on the same page."

His shoulders slump. "It doesn't seem to matter to him that I might want to turn the page. That I might have developed different opinions on things."

"I get that you can't make a big public speech or anything. But . . . didn't speaking up today feel big?"

He shrugs. "I don't know. They were being idiots. I just told them to stop. It wasn't such a big deal."

"It's not the first time your friends have given Farida a hard time. Not just her. Other kids, too," I point out. "What made you say something today?"

Chris's eyes widen. "You never let it go, do you, Walker?"

I shrug. "I'm curious. It's a problem I have."

"So was the cat. And look how that turned out," Chris says.

I laugh. "I'll take my chances," I tell him. "So . . . why did you?"

"Well . . . I guess I never really thought about any of it before all the stuff happened with your brother. My dad's a politician; he has a lot of opinions about a lot of things. He can be pretty convincing and you just learn to go with it at my house. But then I kept hearing and reading things that made me think, and I started wondering if what I believed was right after all."

"Is that bad, though?" I ask him. "I mean, isn't that what we're supposed to be doing? Learning to figure out what color the sky is for ourselves? Because it's not just blue. Sometimes it's gray, and at sunset it's orange, red, and purple, even."

"I guess," he mutters. "But it's making things really hard at home. And with my friends."

"If it were easy to be courageous, they wouldn't give medals for bravery."

"I don't want a medal. I just want to eat dinner without getting into a shouting match with my dad and listening to my mom sigh because the two of us are fighting again. And then being reminded, yet again, that I better keep my thoughts to myself because of the campaign. Like voters really care what I think."

"That must be really hard."

He shrugs. "You know, you really pissed me off when you made such a big deal about my campaign posters. Dad said it was 'typical ugly feminists trying to ruin everything.' And as mad as I was at you and Farida about it, I thought, wait, they're not ugly. Why does he automatically assume they're ugly?"

He starts flushing. "I can't even repeat some of the other stuff he said. So I went to talk to Mom after dinner. Turns out that she thought the posters were wrong, too. But she won't say so in front of Dad."

He falls silent and I don't really know what to say. I guess while I was navigating my version of this mess, so was Chris. We just sort of stand there in the breeze, not talking for a minute. He jams his hands back in his jacket pockets, as if he's suddenly aware of how much of himself he's revealed and he's beginning to regret it.

"Stella . . . you can't tell anyone about this. What it's like for me with my dad. If it gets out, I'm toast," Chris says quietly.

I don't answer his unasked question. Instead, I ask one of my own. "I know today was hard for you, but I'm really glad you did it. It matters. Will you keep doing it?"

"What do you mean?" he asks.

"I mean you have power. You're popular. People look up to you. If you just stand there when your friends do crappy things, you're as good as saying it's okay."

"I don't always agree with them—"

"Doesn't matter. You might as well be doing it yourself if you don't say anything and just let it happen."

I see the look in his eye that he gets when we're taking opposing sides in a debate.

"But what about their right to free speech?" he says. "Aren't they entitled to express their opinions? Or does everywhere have to be a 'safe space'?"

He does air quotes with his fingers to make his point.

"Is that really about a 'safe space'"—I air-quote back at him—"or is it actually, to use the words of a certain Chris Abbott, about not 'being a tool'?"

Chris opens his mouth to speak and then closes it. He gives me a rueful look and shakes his head.

"You're a pain in the butt, Walker, but you make me think."

"I'll take that as a compliment," I say with a grin.

"I'm sorry. For what happened with your brother, and how my dad used it. And that Farida and her family got dragged into it."

He says it so quietly that at first I think I've misheard him.

Then he half smiles, gives me a thumbs-up, and we both head our separate ways.

I'm not naive enough to imagine that this is a happily ever after, or that Chris and I are suddenly going to be BFFs. But hey, we have to start somewhere.

Maybe talking and starting to understand each other a little is that first step. Even if we don't agree on everything, or really hardly anything, maybe we can find common ground on the important things—like at least showing respect for each other.

Roadrunner—

Last night I entered Caitlin's number into my phone. I started to text her twenty-nine times. You know me, ThunderGeek, I had to count.

Ha! I can hear you guys now, calling me a wimp and things that are a lot worse.

But it's not that. Well, maybe a small fraction was the usual "What if I ask her out and she says no?" Still, if it were only that, I'd have texted her after the first false start. Because that's one thing that I learned from Afghanistan—hesitation can be just as fatal as rushing in blindly.

I lay awake until the small hours trying to figure out why I couldn't pull the trigger.

Oh crap. Sorry, buddy. Lack of sleep is making me stupid.

What I meant to say is that I was trying to figure out why I couldn't press "send." The fact is, I'm afraid that she'll realize how messed up I am. Right now, she liked me enough to give me her number. She thinks I'm okay. But if she gets to know me any more, she'll find out that I'm not.

She'll find out about the nightmares, the little things that send me back there in an instant without any warning.

She'll find out that I still can't make sense of it all no matter how much I try, and I don't know if I ever will. I don't know if it's possible, even.

How do I make peace with that?

What if she finds out that my biggest fear is that I really am what they're trying to make me out to be?

That's why I decided to go to the counseling office at the community college today. It's taking forever to get an appointment at the VA. Maybe this way I can talk to someone sooner.

Before I lose the chance to imagine someone else with me on a picnic. Before I lose a chance to hope.

ThunderGeek out.

CHAPTER THIRTEEN

It's sunny and unseasonably warm on class election day, which means I have to rethink my outfit at the last minute and I'm running late for school. Farida had a meeting with Mr. Walsh, so she had to go without me. Now Rob's honking the horn in the driveway and Mom's shoving a granola bar in my hand to eat on the way.

"Good luck!" she says, giving me a quick kiss on the cheek. "Remember, you're a winner with me no matter what the final tally says."

"You have to say that, you're my mom," I point out.

"Doesn't mean it isn't true," she says.

I concede the point because I'm late.

"Dinner at Tigris in your honor tonight, either way," my mom calls after me.

I throw her a thumbs-up as I dash out the door.

Rob is drumming his fingers on the steering wheel as I slide into the passenger seat.

"What, you want to be fashionably late to cast your vote?" he says. "Emphasis on fashionably."

"Wait a minute . . . is that . . . a stealth compliment?"

"Might be."

"Not that one can really trust the judgment of a guy who thinks cargo shorts are the height of fashion, but thanks!"

"Anytime," he says. "So what are the odds of me greeting Madam President at dinner tonight?"

"Your guess is as good as mine," I reply. "I guess I'm a teensy bit more confident than I was yesterday? But I could still lose to the false promise of softer toilet paper."

"You wouldn't be the first person who lost an election to someone who makes completely unrealistic promises," Rob points out. "Nor the last."

"I know. It just seems ridiculous that people aren't clued up enough to see through all that crap."

"Frank Meyers says democracy is messy but it's better than all the other options," Rob says. "Doesn't matter if it's American-style democracy or a different kind. As long as the people have a voice."

"People are messy and complex, and so is life," I say.

"Some lives are messier and more complex than others. Like mine, for example."

I reach over and pat his shoulder awkwardly.

"Everything's going to be okay," I tell him.

He half smiles. "Yeah. It'll all be okay."

We're both smart enough to realize that there's no way of knowing if that's true, but that's all right, because we're lying to make each other feel better.

Rob wishes me good luck when he drops me off at school. "Vote early and often!"

"Are you encouraging me to engage in voter fraud? Shame on you!" I scold him, laughing, as I wave good-bye.

We have from the beginning of the day through sixth period to vote online by logging in using our student ID numbers. It's strange to mark the ballot next to my own name. I realize it's the biggest expression of confidence I've ever given myself.

Now to wait until seventh period, when the election results will be announced.

***

"It's going to be a long day," Farida says to me in AP Gov.

"Tell me about it." I sigh. "I don't know how I'm going to make it till the end of the day."

"How are you holding up?" Adam asks, giving my shoulder a comforting squeeze.

"I'm not sure if I'll feel better or worse when the results come out, but at least it'll be over," I tell him. "So there's that."

"Here's something to keep you going," he says, and he hands me some Hershey's Dark Chocolate Kisses.

"You sure know the way to my heart," I say, unwrapping one.

"That's kind of what I was hoping," he replies with an adorable grin.

His smile fades as Chris walks over.

"May the best person win," Chris says, sticking out his hand to shake.

I laugh at the formality but shake his hand. "Or the one who made the best promises, even if they can't be kept," I say. "'Cause I mean, let's face it, we both have a good chance of losing to Amy."

"Yeah. If we both lose to ice cream and toilet paper, then there's something wrong," Chris says. "I just wish my dad's election would be over by the end of today."

Farida shoots me a quick glance, like she's wondering if I'm going to tell him how much I wish his dad's election would be over, too, and that his dad loses big time.

But there's no point in me saying those words out loud. He already knows that's what I want, and not just because of his political views.

If Mayor Abbott loses, it's more likely that Rob will get to make a plea bargain and we can avoid a trial. Then Rob will know where he stands, and we can focus on getting him treatment. Life can move forward.

Instead, I just say, "Yeah, I'll bet. But not long now."

"It still feels like a million years," he says.

Kind of like waiting for the announcement of the election results during seventh period.

When Principal Hart finally does come over the loudspeaker to announce the election results, my mouth becomes cotton dry and my hands clench into fists beneath the desk.

The freshman and sophomore class officers come first before he says, "The results of the junior class elections are as follows," and then he goes to list the secretary, the treasurer, and the vice president. Then, at last, he announces the results for president: "In third place, Amy Sarducci with one hundred and thirteen votes; second place, Stella Walker with one hundred and ninety votes; and your new Junior Class President is Chris Abbott with two hundred and six votes. Congratulations, Chris!"

Well, that's it. I lost. It was close, closer than I thought it would ever be when I decided to run, but I still lost. I lost to Chris, who was the whole reason that Farida wanted me to run in the first place. I failed. All that work for nothing. I feel the weight of it, of knowing that I've let my friends down. Disappointment worms its way into my stomach.

"Hey, sorry you didn't win," Tanzie tells me. "The video you did was lit."

"Seriously," Mary Maddox agrees.

"Yeah, I was going to vote for Amy, but that made me change my mind," Jenny Bradford says. "'Cause it was real, you know? But my boyfriend voted for Chris."

I wonder how many other people's boyfriends voted for Chris. But whatever. It's over. I lost.

When I see Farida in the hall, she doesn't say anything. She just envelopes me in a big bear hug.

"I'm sorry," I say, swallowing hard. "I failed you. I failed everyone."

"Sheesh, Stella, who do you think you are, Atlas? Stop taking the whole world on your shoulders," she says. "It was close. Closer than we thought it would be, especially with all the other crap going on. And people are talking about the video." She pulls away and gives me an encouraging little shake. "You're allowed a short SulkFest, but then it's on to the next fight, okay?"

The thought of another fight right now is exhausting, but I nod.

"Can you come over and sulk with me? Sulking alone is no fun. We can eat ice cream and watch *Gentlemen Prefer Blondes*. Then we can talk about all the ways the title alone is wrong."

"I can't—I have to work a shift at the restaurant this afternoon. We've been slammed lately," she says with a smile on her face.

"What? That's awesome!" I say.

"I think your not-so-secret Facebook group has started to go viral. There were all those terrible comments everywhere and then suddenly, other people start posting about how amazing the food was and that it was worth the trip, and it just spread. People have been coming from all over the area. It's kind of incredible. We've never been this busy."

I squeal and give Farida a giant hug, and I feel a small weight lift from my chest. I've felt so guilty about Farida's family and Tigris getting dragged into the mess that is my life, but I feel a tiny bit better hearing that sometimes you can drown out the hate.

She hugs me back. "So I can't hang out this afternoon, but I can give you a ride home."

I make an exaggerated sad face at her but say, "I'll take it! And my mom said we're going to dinner at Tigris tonight, so I'll guess I'll see you there. If we can get a table . . ."

She laughs. "You can be such a dork sometimes."

"Just sometimes?"

When we're in the car, I've recovered enough to come to a realization. "I don't know why I'm so upset. I never really thought I had a chance to win, especially after what happened with Rob, and I just hoped the video was enough to make people think."

"The vote was close," Farida says. "*And* you beat Amy and her never-gonna-happen platform into third place."

"A lot closer than Ken thought it would ever be. Especially after we went against his advice with the video."

And it made Chris speak up in a way he'd never done before. Maybe he'll do it again, the next time his friends are being idiots. Maybe for now, that has to be the victory.

"Since I'm not going to be class president, I'm going to have some spare time. So I'm going to talk to Ms. Elias about joining the school paper. I think it's early enough in the year that I can," I tell Farida.

"That's cool," she says. "Maybe you can get them to write about some of the less-covered activities at school."

"My thoughts exactly."

"Great minds and all that," Farida says as she pulls up in front of the house. "Go sulk for a while, but remember, giving up isn't an option. Okay?"

I give her a solidarity fist. "Right on. Sulk first, but keep fighting."

"I think you finally got it," she says, giving me a hug before she drives off to work.

I'm sitting on the sofa, eating ice cream out of the container with Peggy curled up next to me, watching *Gentleman Prefer Blondes* so I don't have to risk a news story with Mayor Abbott's face. The self-pity is flowing strong. Even ice cream straight from the container isn't putting a dent in it.

"Peggy, I'm a LOSER. Do you hear me? I LOST," I proclaim to the dog. She ignores me, keeping her eyes on the ice cream container.

The doorbell rings, startling both of us. Peggy barks and jumps off the sofa. It's not like I invited anyone besides Farida to my SulkFest. This is supposed to be an exclusive fest.

Adam is standing on the doorstep with a bag of chocolate chip cookies.

"These are for you," he says. "Because you're a winner as far as I'm concerned."

"Thank you," I say.

"And also, because rumor has it there's a SulkFest going on here. I was hoping you'd let me join it."

"Welllllll . . . it was supposed to be a party for one—okay, two if you count Peggy—but it looks like you know the secret password," I say, nodding to the bag of cookies. "Come on in."

"What would you like to drink? Milk, soda?" I ask Adam, who has trailed behind Peggy into the kitchen. "Although you look waaaaaay too cheerful to be sulking, if you ask me."

He quickly puts on a laughably exaggerated pout. "Milk is the only acceptable drink with chocolate chip cookies. Unless that would be too joyful, and in which case I'll take a glass of hemlock."

"Um . . . just want to point out that this is a SulkFest, not a Socratic Execution."

Adam smiles, and his single dimple appears. I can't help but give a small grin back.

I pour us both glasses of milk. We go back into the living room and sit on the sofa to indulge in movies, cookies, milk, and all the sulks. Peggy stands guard by Adam, looking up at him hopefully with big brown puppy eyes.

"She's sussed you out as the weakest link," I tell him. "That didn't take long."

"What? No way! I'm like . . . titanium alloy. I'm superstrong. I will not bend."

Then Peg puts her chin on his knee, and he looks at me with a sheepish and completely adorable smile. "Uh, is it okay if I give her a little bit of cookie?"

"What was that about being super strong and unbendable?" I say.

He flashes me an okay-you-got-me smile and gives her a cookie crumb, making sure there's no chocolate.

"You've got a friend for life now," I tell him. "Peggy is easily bought."

"How are you holding up?" he asks. "I mean, I'm glad Peggy is my BFF and all, but it's you I really came here to hang with."

"I'm okay," I say, because that's what everyone expects. But Adam isn't just anyone, so I decide to be honest. "Well, no. I'm not. I'm sad. I'm disappointed. I guess I was dumb enough that I still wanted to believe, deep down, if you do the right thing in life, everything turns out okay. But it doesn't. I should have known better. I lost, and it feels horrible and it stinks."

He takes my hand. As our fingers twine together, I feel a small pulse beat between us. "Yeah, it does stink. Big time," he says, running his thumb over my knuckles in that way he does. Tingles spread all the way to my toes. "And it's not being dumb. The fact that you hold on to ideals is one of the things I like about you. It's like the opposite of my dad, who calls himself a realist, but is really just a complete pessimist. He wouldn't see the glass half full even if it were overflowing onto his lap."

I look at him, surprised. "I was expecting a pep talk."

"Is that what you want? I thought this was a SulkFest."

"No!" I exclaim. "At least . . . not yet. Right now, I want some time to feel sorry for myself. *Then* I want the pep talk."

"Noted," he says with a grin. "Do you have a specific timetable set out yet, or are we going with the flow?"

"If I'm still in self-pity mode tomorrow morning, then hit me with a Grade-A Pep Talk."

"It's a deal," he says. "Now, how about another cookie?"

He hands me the bag and we each take one. "To Stella," Adam says, touching his cookie to mine. "Who was by far the best candidate as far as I'm concerned."

"Thanks. Even if that wasn't good enough to win."

We both take a bite of cookie and munch. When Adam has swallowed, he takes a drink of milk and then says, "Here's sulking at you, kid!" riffing off Humphrey Bogart's line in *Casablanca*.

I laugh. "Hey, I'm still allowed a few more hours!"

He gently turns my face toward him. "I know," he says softly. "Feel as bad as you want."

And he leans forward and touches his lips to mine, which doesn't feel bad at all.

"Was that okay?" he asks. "I was hoping that might aid the cheering-up process."

"I think that actually helped," I whisper, snaking an arm around his neck and pulling him closer. "But I only have one data point. We need to do further experimentation just to be sure."

"I love a girl who feels strongly about the need for scientific inquiry," he says. And then he kisses me again. I'm glad he is so obliging with research data.

After several more data points, I tell him, "This might be better than chocolate chip cookies. At least that's my current hypothesis."

Adam bursts out laughing. "Now, that's what I call a compliment."

He puts his arm around me and I curl into him. We sit in silence for a minute or two, which isn't at all awkward. We're just enjoying the quiet of the moment.

"So this isn't a pep talk," Adam starts. "No way do I want to deny you any all-important feel-the-feels time. But . . . I just want to say . . . even though you lost the election to Chris, it's not like you didn't achieve anything. You helped change the conversation. Where you won is that you made Chris think enough to act differently from how he normally would. That's making a difference."

"*We* made him think. It wasn't just me. It was definitely a team effort," I say, thinking how I couldn't have done this without Farida, and how hard *she* works every day to change the conversation. Even when I mess up, she hasn't given up on me yet. I feel a rush of gratitude for my best friend. She pulled us all together: Ken, Adam, everyone we interviewed.

"Permission to say one more mildly pep-talky thing?" Adam says.

"Permission granted," I say. "But keep it short."

"I was thinking that even though your campaign is over, there's another pretty important campaign that's happening right this minute. I mean, I don't want to infringe on your sulk time but . . ." He hesitates.

"It's cool. Since I'm not going to be class president, I was thinking I might talk to Ms. Elias about joining the school paper. But what did you have in mind for my post-SulkFest time?"

"Nice! Well, what if we volunteer for Jack Witham's campaign? You know, the guy running against Mayor Abbott?" Adam suggests. "I've looked into his position on the important issues, and I think he's seems to support the right policies. No matter what, he's better than the alternative."

"That doesn't take much, given what Mayor Abbott's been doing," I say. "What would we do as volunteers?"

"I don't know. Probably get out the vote calls?"

I realize that as bummed as I am about losing the election, the thought of being able to do something that might help defeat Mayor Abbott makes me feel better.

Action is better than inaction.

"I like that idea and I'll look into his positions," I say. "Thanks to you, I think I can safely say the sulking phase of these proceedings is now over." Smiling at him, I add, "Let's move on to strategy."

Adam's smile is huge—and adorable. Strategizing might have to wait a few minutes.

Roadrunner, man—

I did it. When I say "it," I kind of mean two "its." The first "it"—I went to the counseling office at the college.

Ms. Rosner, the counselor, said that I shouldn't feel alone. That there are other people coming in feeling like I do. In fact, there are enough other vets here at the community college that she reached out to a local nonprofit to organize a specific group just for veterans.

At first I was like, "Nah, not my thing," when she talked about the group. The thought of having to let it all hang out in front of people I don't know just seemed a bit too out there.

But then I realized that I write to a dead friend. (No offense, dude, but that's a fact we both have to face.) Why was I being such a wuss that I can't talk to people who are alive?

Then I remembered the day I got the Dear John letter from Sandra. I thought she was going to wait for me to get back and instead it was "Dear Rob, this is the hardest letter I've ever had to write. I wish I could tell you this face-to-face, but I can't. So I'm just going to say it. I've met someone else." And just like that, the vision I'd had of the world I would be coming home to, the dreams that kept me going, were gone. Poof. Hardest letter she had to write? Wasn't so fun to read, either.

You remember that day? Each of you helped me in your own unique ways. Garcia kept telling jokes until I was laughing so hard that I cried. And it didn't matter if I cried a little over Sandra then, because I was laughing at the same time. Miller started composing me a profile for some dating website, making me sound way more interesting and funny than I actually am. When I asked him what the point of that was because it wasn't like I could actually go on a date with anyone while I was deployed, he said some cryptic pseudo-Yoda garbage like "Wide the sea is, fish many are in it, fishing never stop one must."

I think I threw a flip-flop at him, missed, and hit Robinson by accident. Of course, then Robinson and I had to wrestle, which helped me work off some of the anger about the letter.

I realized maybe that was like group therapy in a way.

Kayla had already sent you your Dear Jason letter, so you knew what I was going through.

So I told Ms. Rosner I'd go to the veterans' group.

I walked out of there feeling like I'd taken a step toward something. I wasn't sure toward what. But somehow, strange as it might sound, I felt a little lighter than I had going in.

I had a little time before my next class, so I went to the cafeteria to get a cup of coffee.

Guess who was sitting there, all alone at a table?

I bet you're wondering if it took me twenty-nine attempts to NOT go talk to her.

My first thought was to pretend I didn't see her and go sit at the opposite end of the cafeteria. Because what if she figures out all the bad things about me?

But then I decided to be brave and let hope happen. Why does that feel just as scary as going outside the wire? It never used to. Did the war change that?

So I went over with my coffee and asked, "Is this seat taken?"

And she smiled that smile, man, and said, "I've been saving it for you."

I can almost imagine going on a picnic again. Not to the beach yet—the mountains, maybe. And at least now I can imagine someone there with me. Someone with a really amazing smile.

Who knows, maybe someday it might happen.

If I don't end up in jail first.

ThunderGeek out.

CHAPTER FOURTEEN

Rob's lawyer debates if they should push his court date until the Monday after the election.

"Then if Abbott loses, it might be easier to get a plea deal," Rob says. "But if he wins, it might be harder.

"Is it worth taking the risk?" I ask.

"That's what we're paying Ms. Tilley the big bucks for," Dad says. "To give us advice and to deal with those contingencies."

"We decided to push it," Rob says.

I want Mayor Abbott to lose for many good policy reasons, but now it's even more personal.

"I'm volunteering for Jack Witham's campaign," I tell them. "We start tomorrow after school."

"You never told us that," Mom says.

"That's because I only decided to do it yesterday."

"That's my girl," Dad says. "Gets knocked down but gets right back up again."

"Unlike your son," Rob mutters.

He might as well have shouted through a megaphone for the effect it has on my parents, especially Dad, who looks like my brother just sucker punched him.

"Why would you say such a thing?" Dad asks in a quiet, even voice.

"Seriously? Like you haven't made it clear I'm pathetic for not being able to get my act together?"

"Rob, that's not fair," Mom says. "Your father—"

"No, Val, let him talk," Dad says. "Better we get this out in the open."

I sit, shocked and silent, wanting to be anywhere but this dinner table at this particular moment. But then I remember Rob saying: *I hope your classmates are smart enough to see that they'd be lucky to have someone like you at their six. I know I am,* and I feel ashamed. Because now that he and Dad are about to go head-to-head, I want to turn tail and run like the coward I am. I'm the worst six-haver ever.

"You met Mom with your guts hanging out. But you came back and got on with your life, so why can't I?" Rob says. "It's not like I've got any scars to show for my tours, right?"

"It's not about physical scars—"

"Val, I said let Rob speak," Dad cuts Mom off.

Mom flashes Dad an angry look, but she stays quiet—at least for now. I put down my knife and fork, because I can't eat another bite while this drama plays out in front of me.

"You were saying?" my father says to Rob.

But Rob's clammed up now. He pushes his food around his plate with his fork. The silence is suffocating. I might choke from it.

"Come on, Rob, what's on your mind?" Dad says. "Let's clear the air."

My brother just keeps pushing food around and avoiding my dad's gaze. I want to kick him under the table and tell him to spit it out. Anything to break the tension.

Instead, I sit there, listening to his fork scraping and my dad's breaths getting louder and slower as he waits and my mom's getting quicker as she becomes more anxious and Peggy gets up and starts pacing around the table because she can sense our heightened emotions and it's freaking her out, too.

"Spit it out, Rob. If you've got something to say, look me in the eye and say it."

Still no words. This is SO AWKWARD.

"You want to know what's on my mind? FINE!" Rob explodes, flinging his fork down on his plate so hard that food spatters onto the table. He pushes his chair back and stands up. "You never let me forget that you made it through your war without losing it. That you're a *real* man. Heck, Mom's more of a man than I am, right, Dad? And Stella—she gets knocked down, but she's just like you! She gets right back up again. NO BIG DEAL!"

My fists clench under the table. How can Rob say it's *no big deal* for me to get up and keep moving forward when bad things happen? He has *no idea*.

"Well, I'm sorry that I'm such a disappointment to you, Dad. Maybe I should have just bought it instead of coming home."

There are words you should never say to the family who was

worried about you dying every day during each of your twelve-month deployments.

My brother just said them, and I'm done.

"How can you say that to us?" I yell at him. "Can you even IMAGINE what it was like while you were away?"

I've been so quiet that my outburst takes everyone by surprise, especially Rob, whose mouth falls open in shock.

"Stella—" Dad says.

"No! I'm not going to shut up and let Rob speak, Dad. Not after that." I stare down Rob. "If you think my life is so easy, think again. We've all got stuff to deal with. You've had to deal with a lot more, I get it. But we're all part of it. So stop acting like it's only happening to you."

I don't wait around for his response. I'm so angry that we're doing everything we can think of to try to help him and then him throwing something like that in our face that I can't even stand to be in the same room as him right now, so I storm upstairs to my room and slam the door.

OMG, my brother makes me so MAD!!!!!!! ☹ I text Farida.

As they do. ☺ she texts back.

She has a point.

But this anger is bigger than the usual brother/sister stuff. This anger has my heart beating faster and my hands shaking, and I feel so much that my body doesn't feel big enough to contain it. My room doesn't feel big enough. I'm a ticking time bomb that will explode this house if I go off.

Then it hits me.

Is this Rob at the mall?

Is this Rob punching Wade?

Is that why he couldn't stop?

Is this how Farida feels every day?

When people tell her to go back to where she came from?

When even her best friend doesn't get it?

This anger at injustice that feels too big for the world?

ME: How do you cope?

FARIDA: Yusef's annoying at times, but he's not THAT BAD.

ME: Ha! Sorry, unidentified change of subject. I mean with unfairness. With anger. With so much crazy stuff going on in the world that makes no sense. With a best friend who never seems to get what the reality of your life is like.

FARIDA: Oh, THAT kind of mad.

ME: Yeah.

ME: Seriously . . . how do you keep going when you have to deal with so much? I know I sound super white-girl right now, but I feel like I'm going to explode.

FARIDA: Ha, you do sound super white-girl. You keep going because I mean, what else can I do? Give up? Not an option. Sit around and feel sorry for myself? Yeah, sometimes I do that, but where does that get me? Even more depressed about it all. So I just keep on going.

ME: I guess I've always felt like I had a choice. That's what my white girl status gave me. But now I don't feel like there's a choice anymore.

FARIDA: Welcome to my world!

ME: So what helps when you get to the feel-like-you're-about-to-explode stage?

FARIDA: Different things. Sometimes I play music really loud. I recommend Oversized Aviators or Barbie and the Bats. Sometimes I go for a run. Sometimes I eat too much baklava. Believe it or not, when you're not the one who's making me want to explode, you help, too!

ME: Good to know! I hope that the ratio of helping vs making you want to explode improves. I know I keep saying I get it and then I don't, but I *think* I get it more now. Not that I probably won't screw up again but . . .

FARIDA: And not that I won't tell you when you screw up again. But I'd rather not spend all my time with you doing that. There are so many more fun things to do. Like watch movies and argue about which band is better or check out new shoes. Or running lines for the musical auditions! Even if you sometimes sound like a croaky frog. 😄

ME: LOL. All of the above is true. Especially the croaky frog part. 🐸

There's a knock on my door.

"Stella—it's me. Can I come in?"

I thumb a quick text to Farida. Thanks sorry GTG. Brother at the door.

Good luck xo, she replies.

I tell Rob he can come in, and he does, followed by a tail-between-the-legs, head-down Peggy. Nobody is happy in this house—man, woman, or canine.

My brother sits on the end of my bed, and Peggy jumps up and lies between us, like a furry demilitarized zone.

I stroke her head while I wait for Rob to say something. He takes his time, opening his mouth and closing it, twice, before finally saying, "Stella, I'm sorry."

He doesn't say what, exactly, he's sorry for, but it doesn't matter right now. Just hearing him say the words is enough that the room slowly shrinks to the right size again, and the fuse inside me flickers and slowly fades. He's my brother, and even though he makes my life difficult at times, I still love him.

"We were so scared all the time that something would happen to you," I say. "And now . . . I'm scared you'll . . ."

I don't even want to say the words in case. I guess I inherited Mom's superstition.

He nods, like he knows what I mean.

"Are you? Going to? I mean, do you ever think about it?"

He hesitates a moment too long, so even if he says no, I know it will be a lie.

"Yeah, I have. In my worst moments," he admits. "But I'm not going to."

"But if you've thought about it, how can we be sure? You have to get help!"

"You think I'm not trying?" Rob says. "I did my part. I went to fight when and where I was told. I did the things my country asked me to do. And now that I'm back here and I need help, my country is taking its sweet time on that."

He sounds bitter and I can't blame him for it.

"It's not fair," I say.

"Nothing's fair," Rob says. "If things were fair, then Guillermo Reyes would be home getting drooled on by his baby girl and loving every minute of it. The only thing that baby girl is going to know about her dad is from pictures and the stories people tell. How is that fair?"

I feel so helpless, for my brother and for Jason and for Reyes and his daughter. For the graffiti on our house calling Rob a traitor, and the fact that he has to wait so long to get help from the government he served. I feel helpless because that help came too late for Jason, and now he's gone. And I don't know how I'm supposed to help Rob.

"Hey, come on now," Rob says, and he reaches across the Demilitarized Dog and puts his arm around me. "It's gonna be okay."

"How do you know?" I ask. "It wasn't for Jason."

"I won't do that, okay?"

"You better not. If you do, I'll kill you."

Rob's shoulder heaves with laughter under my head.

"Logic isn't your strong point," he says.

I realize my error and laugh with him. "You know what I mean."

"Yeah, I do. And I mean it, Stel. I'm really trying."

"Dad's proud of you. I don't know why you think he isn't," I tell him.

"Yeah, he and Mom just had that conversation with me."

"Seems like I'm not the only one having logic fails here."

"Who said I was thinking logically? Isn't that why I'm waiting for a shrink appointment at the VA?"

I hope this won't end up being like *Catch-22*—that Rob can't get help because he admitted he needs it. "When do they think you'll get one?"

He laughs bitterly. "Hopefully before I'm on Social Security."

Rob gets up off the bed and Peggy jumps down, ever his shadow.

"Mom wants to know if you're hungry. You stormed out before you finished dinner."

"Tell her I'm good," I say. "I need time to think."

He salutes and shuts the door behind him.

I turn on music and think about all the people like Rob and Jason who did what they were asked and then came home and haven't been looked after. It's easy to put a yellow ribbon magnet on your car or wear a flag pin or wave the Stars and Stripes at a parade or a football game. But what about the hard stuff like paying for care? Everyone's super patriotic when it's time to go to war, but what about when our veterans need something in return?

I still don't understand what patriotism means, what it really means to love our country and how to show it. But it has to be about more than just a symbol. Right?

Hey, Roadrunner—

I confronted something the other night—what Stella called my logic fail. I don't know what the shrink would call it because still no appointment with the VA.

I've been convinced that Dad thought I was weak. That I was less than him because I couldn't just come home and move on back into civilian life without batting an eye. That I could just "suck it up" and "be a man," whatever that means.

Especially since I don't even have any major scars to show for my tours like he does. Not on the outside, anyway.

Dad admitted that he had a real hard time with it, especially at first. But he also told me that it's not just about me and my stuff. He said that my behavior brought back memories of HIS father when he came back from Vietnam—and those weren't good memories. It messed him up and made him angry with me, until he finally talked that all through with Mom. But get this: He confessed that he even thought about going to see a shrink himself recently, because he wanted to work through it so he could help me get better.

Words I never thought I'd hear come out of Dad's mouth in my lifetime.

It made me feel like less of a failure.

But I still wonder: Why did Grandpa Harry and I come back messed up and Dad and Mom didn't?

Frank Meyers and I went fishing again the other day. Didn't catch much, but it was good to be out on the lake. I think he's been taking me under his wing because we've both had problems dealing with life post combat.

I asked him if he had any idea why my parents handled war better than we did.

He sat for a while, looking out over the lake with the thousand-yard stare.

I wondered if he'd answer, or if he'd gone to that dark 'Nam place he doesn't like to talk about. But finally he said, "The thing is, Rob, the war your parents fought had a beginning, a middle, and an end. There were clear objectives. Get the Iraqis out of Kuwait."

"And they did that and went home," I said.

"Right. Even though Bill got himself a nasty injury, he knew what he was there for. And they accomplished the mission. Whereas you and me . . . well, things weren't quite so clear, were they?"

And as much as I wanted to argue with him that what we were doing in Afghanistan was nothing like the mess of Vietnam, I couldn't. Because even though we succeeded in individual missions, I still can't tell you the long-term plan, if there is one at all. I mean, I know we're just the grunts who fight the thing—they don't need us to see the big picture.

But it would make it a lot easier to live with the crap that keeps me up at night if I knew that there was an actual endgame.

If I knew then what I know now, would I still have enlisted? Even though I feel like the country broke its promise to you, and me, and so many thousands of others?

The answer is still always yes. Yeah, I'm bitter, yeah, I'm angry, yeah, I feel betrayed and messed up, but I can't imagine not having done it.

I just wish everyone could share some of the garbage that we have to carry around with us because we did their dirty work for them.

I guess I do have "anger issues." But can you blame me?

Well, now for some good news. The vets' group started. Mrs. Cook, a counselor from an outside nonprofit, comes to the college once a week. Five of us meet with her in a room about the size of a broom closet and talk about stuff that's come up.

It doesn't sound like much, but it's helped me feel like I'm not alone. The other thing it's helped me realize is that even though I'm hurting, it doesn't mean I'm permanently broken.

Or you can look at it this way—it makes me unlucky like most of the other guys in the group, because our wounds from the war don't show on the outside. When you've lost a limb, people understand why you need disability or why you're angry or if you're having a bad day. You also get treatment faster.

When you look the same on the outside? Not so much.

Employers are afraid to hire you in case you lose it. Thanks to the video of me punching Wade Boles in the face, I'm the poster child for that now.

But one thing the group helped me understand was that I was a poster child for something else, too. I was on a roll, getting down on myself for living up to the stereotype of the angry vet who loses it. Remember how you said sometimes you thought the enemy was yourself? It's true—we do end up being our own worst enemy a lot of the time. But then Tony, one of the other guys in the group, said, "But you were putting yourself on the line to defend someone. That's what we do."

And other guy in the group, Jack, said, "Yeah, just because we take off the uniform, it doesn't mean we lose that commitment."

I'd been so busy hearing everybody else's voice in my head that I'd forgotten my own truth.

"I miss having a common purpose," I confessed. "I don't remember if it was like this before, but it seems like since I got out, everyone is out for themselves. I miss being part of a team. Something bigger."

Nods of agreement and "right ons" from the other guys.

"Have any of you experienced that sense of being part of something bigger since you've been out of the military?" Mrs. Cook asked.

Silence.

We were all looking at our hands and our feet, at anything but her or each other. Then I looked up and spoke, because I remembered that morning.

"The time when we'd woken up to find graffiti all over our house, calling me a traitor and a terrorist lover. When the folks from the American Legion came over and helped us clean it off," I told them. "At first I was . . . well, embarrassed, if you want to know the truth."

"Why?" Tony asked.

"Because they saw the graffiti. They saw the embarrassment I'd brought on my family," I confessed. *"And because I was going to need help cleaning up this mess. I'm used to being able to clean up after myself."*

"But isn't being part of a team that you can count on others to have your six?" Jack said.

And I thought . . . Duh. Yeah.

That's when Mrs. Cook said how we have to remember that it's okay to ask for help and to accept it when people offer it. That it's not weakness and there's no reason to feel shame.

Easier said than done.

But I guess you have to hear the message before you can start living it.

ThunderGeek out.

CHAPTER FIFTEEN

The day before the governor election, Ken, Farida, Adam, and I head to the local field office of Jack Witham after school to make get out the vote calls, like we've been doing a few afternoons a week. Between that, debate, working on *AstroNews*, and school, I haven't had any time to chill and watch movies or really to even chill, period.

"We'll have time to do that after the election," I reminded Ken when he started complaining about missing our Keeping It Reel sessions. "Priorities, dude. Right now the priority is making sure that we have a good governor."

"All work and no play makes Stella a dull girl. All work and no play makes Stella a dull girl. All work and no play makes Stella a dull girl," he says, quoting from *The Shining* movie.

Laughing, I remind him that the latest Marvel movie is coming out the week of the election. "We can go see it for our victory party!"

"Or to commiserate if Witham loses," he said.

"Don't even joke," I told him. It was bad enough losing the school election to Chris. Jack Witham *has* to win. The consequences of him losing are *way* bigger.

One thing I've learned volunteering is that making phone calls isn't my favorite thing to do. I don't like talking on the phone at the best of times, and it's worse calling someone I don't know, who might get angry and hang up on me as soon as they hear what I'm calling about.

But, although I'm getting used to being hung up on, when I get through and talk to someone who confirms they're going to vote for Jack Witham, it makes me sit up straight and dial again, because that's one more voter to help defeat Mayor Abbott.

And volunteering is something I can do that might help my brother and all of the people who the mayor has been targeting in his speeches.

It doesn't hurt that they have good snacks here, too.

"Ugh, I just got an Abbott's-right-about-immigrants! guy," Farida says. "Quick, hand me a gummy bear to take the bad taste out of my mouth."

I pass her the bowl.

"I just had this really supercool older lady who said she'd love to go door to door with me, but her walker would probably slow me down," Adam says. "I asked her if she needed a ride to go vote tomorrow and she said she voted absentee in case she died between now and then. She said if she goes, she wants voting to be the last thing she does."

"She's my hero," I say. "I want to be like her when I grow up."

"Do they still count her vote if she dies between now and then?" Farida asks.

"Good question," I say. "I hope so."

My next call picks up. According to the call sheet, he's a twenty-eight-year-old man who has only voted once. He says he's not going to vote because he doesn't like either of the candidates. "I hate politicians," he says. "You can't trust any of them. What's the point?"

"The point is that they make the policies that affect your life," I tell him. "Don't you want a say in that?"

"Yeah, like my one vote is going to make a difference." He laughs.

"All those one votes add up!" I say, but I'm speaking to myself. He's already hung up on me.

"Democracy is really hard work," I complain.

"No one ever said it was easy," Farida says.

"A lot of people I spoke to aren't paying attention," Adam says. "They don't even know what each of the candidates stands for. Or if they are paying attention, they think their vote doesn't matter."

"Well, it's definitely not going to matter if they don't bother to vote," I say. "I get that, and I'm not even old enough to do it yet!"

My frustration with voters is still hanging over me at dinner.

"What if people don't vote?" I ask.

"We just have to hope that more of Mayor Abbott's people don't vote than Jack Witham's," Dad says. "It's always a numbers game."

"But it's not a *game!*" I say. "It's important. It affects people's lives. Rob's life. Farida's life. The lives of so many people in our state."

"It *is* important," Mom says. "That's why it's great that you're volunteering."

"That's right," Dad says. "Democracy doesn't work well if we don't participate."

"Or if there's voter suppression," Rob adds.

"But what about 'liberty and justice for all'?" I say. "Are those just words? We say them all the time when we pledge allegiance to the flag."

"That's the ideal," Dad says. "It's been over two centuries, but we still have to keep fighting to make it happen."

I wonder if the work is ever done, or if our country will always be a work in progress, waiting for each generation to do its part. Will we ever get to just kick back and chill and say, "Yay! We did it!" Will it happen in our lifetime? In my kids' lifetime? In my grandkids'? Ugh, I don't want to have to think about that. It's hard enough to have to think ahead to senior year knowing that everything in the world isn't right.

Rob drops me off at Farida's at ten, after Tigris has closed. We don't have school on Election Day because Argleton High is a polling place, so Farida invited me for a sleepover and then in the morning we're meeting Adam and Ken back at the Witham for Governor office to make some more get out the calls.

"My feet," Farida moans, lounging on the bed when we're both in our pajamas. "Just looking at these supercute 'Shoes You Want in Your Closet for the Holidays' in *Teen Vogue* makes them hurt more."

"That's so wrong," I say. "If just *looking* at awesome shoes can make your feet hurt, then where is the joy in life?"

"I need a new jooooooy!" Farida exclaims. She puts down her phone. "And talk about irony . . . because of all this awful stuff I just might get one."

"What do you mean?"

"So business at the restaurant went down right after the America News Channel broadcast. But then the Stephanie Nagy report and the whole secret Facebook thing happened, and started going viral, and now it's even better than it was before, because people who'd never been to the restaurant ended up coming to support us and they liked the food."

"That's fantastic," I say.

"Well, obviously I'm happy about it except it's meant I've had to work lots of extra shifts and I've had hardly any time for myself. And I finally told my parents that I'm trying out for the winter musical."

"You didn't tell them till now? What did they say?"

"They said yes! They said that since business has picked up so much they could afford to hire a part-time server and won't need me as often. So musical tryouts, here I come!"

"That's amazing! You'll totally kill the audition. But are you and Ken going to be able to work on the musical together without arguing constantly?"

"He's backstage, and hopefully I'm going to be front and center. If this week's auditions go the way I want. I've decided to use 'Popular' for my solo audition, and the opening from *Rebecca* for my monologue. Anyway, Ken and I managed to survive your campaign, right?"

"True!" I say. "Barely."

"We've talked it through. I think he's starting to get it. At least he's starting to listen more, instead of automatically getting all defensive if I say something."

"We all have to start somewhere. It took me a while to learn how to do that. Longer than it should have, I know."

"It's just frustrating when you're the one who is suffering from injustice. You want it fixed today," Farida says. "Well, yesterday would be better. But then you're told: *Stop being so angry, you alienate people.* Or, *Rome wasn't built in a day.* And then I just want to say to them: *You realize that slaves built Rome, right? So what's your point exactly?*"

"Maybe you should say that," I tell her.

"Maybe one day I'll be fed up enough to do it," she says.

"I hope I'm there to see it when you do," I say. "Have things been any better at school?"

"Amazingly, yes," she says. "You know what's weird? Chris has been a better class president than I thought he'd be—at least so far. He's stepped up a few times when he's seen racist stuff going on. I never in a million years thought that would happen."

"People can change," I say slowly. "If they want to and they're open to it."

"I know. But I never thought he would."

She rolls onto her stomach, facing me. "But enough about Chris. I want to hear all about what's going on with Mountain Man. Do your parents like him?"

"My parents haven't met him. They . . . don't know I'm seeing him."

Farida's eyes widen in shock. "For real? But—"

"Things have just been so crazy at home what with waiting for Rob's trial and everything—I just didn't want to add that to the mix."

"Well, at least I feel better that I'm not the only one you keep secrets from," Farida says.

"I haven't met Adam's dad, either," I say, wondering if telling Farida this is the right thing to do. "Apparently he's . . . well, he's a big Mayor Abbott supporter, so . . ."

"Oh."

It feels like the temperature in the room just dropped by ten degrees.

"But Adam's not like that. He hates that his dad thinks that way. He was the one who suggested working on the Jack Witham campaign."

"I know," Farida says slowly. "It's just . . . it's creepy. Adam's a friend and then I find out his dad doesn't want my family here without even knowing us."

"Yeah. It makes you wonder how many people in Argleton think that way."

"We already knew there were enough to elect Chris's dad as mayor," Farida says.

"True. But you wonder how many aren't as vocal as Mayor Abbott," I say. "They just say that stuff in private like Adam's dad. Or pretend not to notice when Wade says something racist to another person."

"I really want Jack Witham to win tomorrow," Farida says. "It's bad enough that Chris's dad is mayor, but to have him as governor? Ugh."

"That's nothing more we can do tonight," I point out.

"True," Farida says. "How about watching *Fried Green Tomatoes*? I suggested it for Keeping It Reel, but Ken said it's 'too much of chick flick.'"

"The struggle is real and it never ends," I say, sighing. "Even with our friends."

"Tell me about it," she says, raising her eyebrow meaningfully.

"Okay, point taken," I say. "So what about some popcorn to go with our fried green tomatoes?"

"Now you're talking," she says, grabbing my hand and yanking me off the bed.

Normally, I'd just enjoy having Election Day off to do something fun with my friends, but this time it's different. I'm still hanging out with my friends, but instead of hanging out at someone's house or going to a movie, we're back at the Witham for Governor campaign office making more get out the vote calls.

"Talk about a hot date," Adam says to me between calls. "You take me to all the best places."

I smile, blow him a kiss, and dial the next number.

He winks and grins, showing off his single dimple, which my research tells me is a manifestation of a genetic defect caused by shortened facial muscles, and is rare when a person only has one.

When I told Adam this, he a) laughed and told me that it was my adorkable brain that attracted him to me in the first place—aside from my obvious adorableness, of course—and b) said that clearly he was rare and special and I should ensure that I treat him accordingly.

I may or may not have laughed.

If I'm honest, I can't say that making these phone calls is that much easier than it was when I started. It's still not something that comes naturally to me. But at least I'm more used to doing it, and I understand why it's so important. It matters if people don't vote.

By the time Farida drops me at home, my voice is hoarse from talking to people all day.

I lean over and hug her.

"I hope he wins," she says. "I wish I were old enough to vote."

"I know, me too," I say. "But at least we've done what we can to help him win."

I just hope it's enough.

The polls close at eight. My parents, Rob, and I are sitting in the living room, watching the results come in. It's even more nerve-racking than waiting for the results of the student government election. I just hope that this time, an Abbott isn't the winner.

There's no clear winner at eleven, with sixty percent of the votes counted.

"Stella, you have school tomorrow," Mom says. "You should think about getting to bed."

"*Mom!* How can I got to bed without knowing who won? There's no way I'll be able to sleep."

"Come on, Mom, let her stay up," Rob says. "She's been working on the campaign. She's invested in this."

I throw him a grateful glance.

"Okay. But I don't want any complaints about being tired tomorrow morning," Mom says.

"I'll be sure to prime the coffeemaker," Dad says. "That way you'll be fueled up and ready to go bright and early."

"Thanks, Dad," I say, nervously stroking Peggy's ears.

It's too close. Mayor Abbott could win. There's one district where Witham is only up by four votes, which means that Abbott could appeal for a recount. I want to go back in time and tell that to the guy who said that his vote wouldn't make a difference. It's probably not his district, but still. What if it is?

"How can you be so calm?" I ask Rob. "This affects you most of all."

He shrugs. "Yeah, it affects me, but what can I do?" he says. "I voted first thing this morning. Witham's either going to win or he isn't."

"Since when did you become so chill about life?" I ask.

"Maybe the group is helping," he says.

"What group?" Mom asks.

"The one for vets that the counselor at school set up," Rob says.

Dad mutes the volume on the TV.

"How come we didn't hear about this till now?" he asks.

"I'm an adult. I'm allowed to keep some things to myself," Rob points out.

"You're an adult living under our roof. Whose legal bills we're helping to fund," Dad says. "Don't you think that gives us some right to be kept informed?"

"Bill." Mom gives Dad a warning look, then asks, "So you're finding this group helpful?"

Rob nods.

"I've only been going for three weeks, but yeah, so far so good. It's keeping me going until the VA appointment comes through."

Mom's about to ask him another question when I notice the headline on the TV.

"Look! Jack Witham's declared victory!"

Dad fumbles for the remote for what seems like *forever* and finally turns the sound back on, just in time for us to hear Mayor Abbott making his concession speech. Chris is onstage with him, looking somber and uncomfortable in his blue blazer and khakis.

I lean over and hug my brother. "Maybe this is a sign that things are starting to turn around."

Peggy's tail thumps against the floor as she wags it in sleepy agreement.

"I feel a little better about the court date now," Rob says. "Still not looking forward to it."

"I think this calls for a celebration," Mom says. "Cookies, anyone?"

My cell is buzzing with texts. I'm elated but suddenly exhausted, too.

"I probably should get to bed," I say. "I have school tomorrow."

"Are you sure you're feeling okay?" Rob asks, feeling my forehead. "You never turn down a cookie."

I punch his arm.

"I'll be fine when I get a good night's sleep," I tell him. "That's if your face doesn't give me nightmares."

Sibling love.

Roadrunner, buddy—

Good news! Mayor Abbott lost the election!

Sometimes the good guys win. Maybe the tide is turning. Oh! And I finally got an appointment with the VA for an evaluation— for three weeks from now.

Luckily, in the meantime, I've got the group at college. Not sure how I'd be doing without that, if you want to know the truth.

What's that you're saying? "DUDE, you're burying the lede! What's up with Caitlin?"

Well, funnily enough, I talked about her with the group on Monday. I told them that we've been hanging out a lot at school and texting all the time when we're not at school, and I want to ask her out. I think she might want that, too, but I don't know if it's fair to get involved with her when my life is up in the air with the charges against me.

And most of the guys were like, "Yeah, that's a big thing to have hanging over you."

Then Mrs. Cook asked, "It seems like you have a real connection. Have you discussed your concerns with Caitlin?"

It was one of those look-at-the-floor-because-you-don't-want-to-admit-that-you-haven't-done-that-and-now-that-you-mention-it-it-seems-so-obvious moments.

When it was clear to everyone that I hadn't done it, we got onto this whole discussion about why we don't talk about the things that are most important.

"Don't you trust Caitlin to make the right choice for herself?" Mrs. C asked. "By not even discussing it, aren't you cheating both of you of the chance to see where this goes?"

That hit me straight in the gut. Because I imagined the riot act Mom would read me for thinking I knew better than Caitlin about what was best for her. I mean, forget Mom—Stella would probably give me the biggest dressing down of all. Nothing like a sister when you need someone to hold up a mirror to your flaws, right?

The bottom line is that I was scared. We survived combat by cutting off feelings. How else do you function day to day?

Group forces us to face those feelings. Because we've all been there, I'm not as afraid of being judged. The guys are honest, and they call me on my crap, but I don't feel as criticized as I do when my family does it, 'cause I know the next time it could be one of them in the hot seat.

Still, it's one thing to start "letting it all hang out" with the group. It's another to do it with a girl I really like.

The next time I saw Caitlin in the cafeteria, I asked her if we could talk. She smiled (that smile!) and said, "Haven't we been doing that?" But then she said, "Uh . . . sure, okay. Let's talk." She looked a little weirded out, like she didn't know where I was going with this, but she relaxed when I told her that I liked her and laid out, as best I could, all the bumps in my road.

I sat back and waited for her to tell me that it was going to be too complicated. That she had enough going on.

But instead she said, "You think you're the only one with potholes and bumps in the road? Isn't it easier to travel if we help each other spot them?"

Made sense to me.

It's still a long road ahead. I've got my court date next week, and I could end up in jail for all I know, putting an abrupt end to this—whatever "this" is. Being put behind bars might be a big enough pothole to break the axle.

Well, at least I can daydream about her smile when I'm stuck in my jail cell.

ThunderGeek out.

CHAPTER SIXTEEN

The morning of Rob's court appearance, I knock on his door before I have to leave for school.

"Are you wearing pants?" I ask. "Is it safe to come in?"

"What day of the week is it?" Rob asks.

"Monday," I say.

"Oh, okay. Not a no-pants day. You're safe."

When I go in, he's dressed in a dark suit, and he's shaved and looks like he could be going to a job interview—or a funeral.

"Looking good," I tell him.

"Do I look like someone you'd want to cut a plea deal with?"

"Definitely. But I'm kind of biased."

"I just hope the prosecutor isn't," Rob says.

"You've got character references from half of the Argleton American Legion post and your commanding officer. That's got to count for something, right?"

"Let's hope."

I take a few steps and throw my arms around him. "Good luck," I say. "And if you end up behind bars, I promise to bake you a cake with a file in it."

"Can you make that a cell phone and some wire cutters instead?" he jokes. "Files are so last century."

"Deal," I say.

"Anyway, this is just a hearing. If they won't agree to a plea bargain, it'll be a while till the trial, which means this will all just be hanging over my head for even longer."

"Fingers, toes, and everything else I can think of crossed for you," I tell him as I head out the door.

I keep looking at the clock during English, wondering how things are going at the courthouse. Mom promised to text me as soon as there was any news, but when I've checked my phone between classes there's been nothing.

"Stella, are you with us?" Ms. Elias asks. "I asked you for your thoughts on the essay."

"Oh, I'm sorry."

I make a major effort to stay focused till the bell rings. But my mind is down at the courthouse with Rob and my parents. Rob needs to move forward. We all do.

When the bell finally rings, Ms. Elias says, "Stella, can I speak with you for a moment?"

I'm dying to check my cell, but I can't exactly say no.

"Are you okay?" she asks. "You seemed very distracted in class."

"I know. I'm sorry," I tell her. "It's just . . . my brother's court hearing is today, and I've been really stressed waiting to hear what's happened."

"Have you heard anything?" she asks.

"I was just going to check," I say.

"Go right ahead," she tells me.

I pull my phone out of my backpack. There's a text from Mom.

MOM: Plea Deal. Pay for Boles medical expenses, $1500 fine, accepted group at college in lieu of anger management classes.

"Plea deal," I tell Ms. Elias with a grin.

ME: So definitely no jail?

MOM: One year probation.

"My mom says Rob's going to be on probation for a year, but otherwise no jail," I tell Ms. Elias.

"I'm glad to hear it," Ms. Elias says. "I taught your brother. Mayor Abbott had no business blowing that incident out of proportion and dragging his name and especially Farida's through the dirt for political gain." She sighs. "Politics can be a nasty business."

"Tell me about it," I say. "I just ran for junior class president."

She laughs. "So you did. And I hope you'll stay involved, because even though it's a messy process, it doesn't mean we can turn our backs on it."

"That's something I'm learning more each day," I say.

"Glad to hear it," Ms. Elias says. "Give your brother my best. And I'm looking forward to your piece on the Robotics Club for the *AstroNews*."

"I will," I promise, and head out of the classroom.

Mom's texted me again. Inviting a few people tonight to celebrate.

ME: Is Rob okay with that?
MOM: He says he is. He's going to invite a few friends from the college. (!!)
ME: Can I invite a few friends? Like three maybe?
MOM: Why not?

Rob's not going to jail, and we're having a party tonight.

Life is looking up by the minute.

I start to text Mom back, but I'm so busy looking at my phone that I walk straight into Chris and end up dropping my phone and my books with a spectacular crash.

"My apologies, Mr. President," I say, bending down to check that the good luck is continuing and my phone screen hasn't shattered. Thankfully, it hasn't.

Chris laughs and squats down to help retrieve my stuff.

"Good thing my Secret Service detail wasn't around to witness that." He hands me my books.

"Thanks. And . . . well, I can't honestly say I'm sorry your dad lost because I really wanted his opponent to win, but . . . I am honestly sorry if it was hard for you."

He smiles. "I wouldn't have believed you anyway if you'd said you were sorry my dad lost," he says. "But I can believe you're sorry that it's hard for me. Because you care about how people feel—which is pretty cool." Then, lowering his voice, he admits, "Between you and me, it's a relief. I wasn't looking forward to having to go everywhere with a security detail. And I would have had to change schools, because we'd have had to move into the governor's mansion."

"Just when you won the election here."

"Yeah," Chris says. "But I can't say that at home. Dad hasn't taken losing well, and . . . let's just say there's not a lot of room for talking about anything else. At least he's still serving out the rest of his term as mayor."

I roll my eyes at that.

He shrugs, as if he wants to shake off whatever feelings talking about this are giving him. "Whatever. Gotta go."

As we head in opposite directions down the hallway, I wonder why Chris can tell me that he's relieved his dad lost, but not his own family. Is that why Rob needs his veterans' group? Maybe there are things he can tell them that he doesn't feel he can talk to us about.

Do they understand him better? Or does he think our feelings about him are so big that we don't leave him room to have his own?

I still feel guilty that my attempt to help Rob went so spectacularly wrong and almost landed my brother in jail. Maybe he needs more than what we can give him. Maybe he needs the professional care, and to talk about things to people who really understand what he went through. Mom and Dad are vets, too, but somehow they came out okay. Mr. Meyers on the other hand— he had a hard time, too.

Why Rob? Why Jason? Why Frank Meyers?

But then why did some people in Rob's squad die or get injured, and Rob come back alive and physically uninjured?

I want to think everything is logical and that there's a purpose and a plan to life, but it seems like sometimes bad things just happen, even to people who don't deserve it. What do you do then?

I guess it's kind of like what Ms. Elias said about politics being messy. Life gets really messy, too, but we can't just turn our backs on the world when that happens, no matter how difficult and painful it gets. We have to stay involved. In fact, that's when we have to work even harder to make things better. It's the only way change ever happens.

When I get home, Mom tells me to hurry up and do my homework so I can help get ready for the party. But first, I go to find Rob, who is helping Dad set up folding chairs that they borrowed from the Legion hall in the living room so we have more seating.

"Congratulations," I say, high-fiving him. "Good to know that I won't have to smuggle contraband in a cake to you."

"Feel free to bake me a cake anyway," he says. "There can never be enough cake."

"Mom has the cake covered for tonight," Dad says.

"That's good, because I've got homework to do before this shindig starts."

I race upstairs to get my work done, trying to ignore all the party preparations going on below.

The scent of Dad's special chili wafts up from the kitchen, making my stomach growl, and then I smell the sweeter aroma of corn bread and cake.

Peggy wanders in to check on me.

"What's up, Peg? Is the smell driving you crazy, too?"

She wags her tail, brushes her body against my leg, and then walks out, her surveillance mission complete.

When I'm done, I go down to help—and steal a piece of corn bread, which earns me a scowl from Mom.

"Put it on the table and set out some butter on a plate. Then put the chips in a bowl. Guests will start arriving any minute."

When the doorbell rings, Rob comes bounding down the stairs, shouting, "I'll get it!"

He's freshly showered and dressed in jeans and a T-shirt that reads *Dune*, and—

"Are you wearing cologne?" I ask.

"Stella, do me a favor, and try really hard to act normal for a change," he says, glaring at me as he opens the door.

Since my brother appears to have been taken over by an alien, I stay to look at who is on the doorstep. It's a girl. Well, that explains it. Also, maybe why he is smiling more than I've seen him do in a long time, and giving her an awkward hug.

"Caitlin, this is my sister, Stella," Rob says. "Stella, this is Caitlin."

Caitlin has a really nice smile as she says hi to me. And from the way she and Rob smile at each other, I think they either are more than friends or want to be.

Rob really *has* been keeping secrets.

I hang back while he introduces her to Mom and Dad. Mom's voice gets slightly higher pitched like when she doesn't know someone and is really going all out to be friendly. Dad, on the other hand, gets super jovial. He could try out to be Santa Claus at the mall, he's so jolly. They just want to make a good impression because Rob has brought home a girl.

It's so awkward I think about uninviting Adam, but he's already texted me that he's on his way.

Fortunately for everyone involved in this excruciatingly embarrassing little scene, more guests arrive. Ken, a few of Rob's friends from school, Mr. Neustadt, Mr. Meyers, some of the other guys from the American Legion post. Lots of introductions for Caitlin. I feel sorry for her, but she handles it well. Farida arrives bearing trays of food from the restaurant and the awesome news that she landed the role of Glinda in *Wicked*. We jump up and down for, like, five minutes before Rob tells us to either take it outside or get a life.

"We've already got one," I tell him. "Farida's going to be Glinda in *Wicked*."

"Hey, that's great!" he says, high-fiving her.

For a Monday night impromptu celebration, this is turning out to be quite the party.

Luckily for me—and him—Adam arrives at the same time as Rob's friends from college, so he manages to slip in without getting the third degree.

"So this is what it's like to come to a non-SulkFest at your house," he says, giving me a very brief hug due to the presence of relatives.

"Yeah, it's better catered than the other kind. It's not just ice cream and cookies. Now there's chili and corn bread, amazing food from Tigris, and cake."

"Glad to hear it—otherwise I would have to leave right now."

Peggy comes straight up to Adam and licks his hand.

"Ah, Peggy," he says, "You've got a good memory for weak links, I gather."

"The best," I say. "She's your BFF now. Until another weak link comes along."

"Well, at least I know where I stand, which is a lot less confusing than it is with most girls," Adam says. Then, seeing the look on my face, he quickly adds, "Wait. That came out wrong. Totally wrong. I'm not comparing you to a dog. Or another girl. I mean—"

"How about we go get some food to put in your mouth instead of your foot?" I say.

"Great idea!" he says with a relieved smile.

The food is amazing. Dad's outdone himself with his chili, and the El-Rahims sent dolma stuffed with the most delicious spiced lamb, and chicken kebabs, as well as hummus, baba ganoush, and pita. There's enough food to feed a small army, let alone a celebrating group of friends and veterans.

As I sit eating with my friends, I keep looking over at my brother and this mystery girl. I know it's not just her, he's also relieved that he can put the threat of jail behind him, but he's more animated than I've seen him in months. I mean, he agreed to have this party, which is more than he did when he came home.

"We're out of ice," Ken says.

"I'll go get some," I say, getting up and taking the ice bucket from him.

I'm getting ice out of the freezer when one of Rob's friends from college comes in to get another beer out of the fridge.

"Hey, I'm Jack," he says. "Nice to meet you. I'm in the vets' group."

"I'm Stella, Rob's sister."

He pops the cap on his beer and leans back against the kitchen sink.

"Ah, so you're the famous Stella," he says.

Famous?

"Is being famous in your group a good thing or a bad thing?" I ask, wondering if this means I'm one of the major sources of Rob's problems. I imagine him telling them: "You think fighting a war was bad—now I have to be under the same roof as my obnoxious little sister."

"In your case, good. Your brother thinks you're pretty awesome."

"So . . . he doesn't blame me for almost getting him put in prison?"

Jack's sharp intake of breath tells me I've managed to shock him.

"Oh, kid—you've been carrying that weight around?"

I shrug, suddenly feeling awkward.

"Well, that and putting my best friend's family in danger and risking their restaurant."

"He's been too busy blaming himself for those same things, plus a whole lot more, for him to spare any blame for you," Jack says. "I'm just happy that the plea deal was accepted so he can move on."

I glance into the living room where Rob is sitting with Tony, another friend from group, and Farida. Caitlin is on the sofa next to him, and he has his arm around her.

"She's great," Jack says, following my gaze. "I'm glad Rob gave it a chance instead of backing off because he was afraid of going to jail."

I'm happy, too. Except . . . I live across the hall from my brother, and I just found out she existed today. But I guess I haven't exactly shared with him about Adam. I guess we're both in for surprises today.

"Yeah," I say, but apparently it's not convincing.

"Don't you like her?"

"I just met her. Rob's never even mentioned her name until she showed up for the party."

"Oh," he says.

"We used to talk," I tell him. "So yeah, I'm glad that he's happy, but I'm sad about the secrets. He was away for so long and now I'm afraid he's never really going to be back, even though he's here." I throw more ice into the bucket, then put it on the counter. "Do you think he'll ever talk to me about the important things in his life again?"

"Caitlin is different. And I can understand why that hurts, but . . . some things are just . . . hard to talk about to anyone who hasn't been there," Jack says. "Especially the people you love most."

He picks at the label of his beer bottle. "The group is helping me realize it's okay to feel. It's helping me to face some of the crap that gives me nightmares so I don't want to feel."

"Rob gets nightmares, too."

"Yeah. He said he told you about the kid."

I nod. "The night we went to the movies. I was trying to get him out of the house for a change, because he'd been in a serious funk and they were showing the director's cut of *Alien*." I sigh. "But it turned out to be a disaster because that's the night the thing happened with Wade Boles."

"He told you about it that same night?" Jack asks.

"Yeah. Right before we went into the mall. Because a dog ran in front of the car and we almost hit it. That really freaked him out. I guess it reminded him because . . . well . . . because."

"So his wires were already buzzing before he even went into the mall," Jack explains.

"His wires?"

"That's just how I describe it," Jack says. "Like your veins are wires and when something sets you off, they start buzzing with high-voltage electricity."

"That sounds . . . uncomfortable."

"Well, it explains why he'd get set off so easily," Jack says. "We're doing Mindfulness exercises in group. It's supposed to help cope with that. The counselor is trying to set up something at a yoga place for us."

I giggle, and Jack gives me a strange look.

"What's so funny?"

"Nothing—I'm just trying to picture Rob in yoga pants."

"We can wear shorts and T-shirts, so you'll have to figure out something else to tease him about."

"Tease Rob? Me? Never!"

He grins at me. "Riiiight."

Then, seeing that Mom's starting to cut the cake, he says, "I'm going to go help myself to some of that cake before the gang demolishes it."

I stand watching from the outside for a few moments before going in to join everyone, grateful to see Rob happy, and wondering if he'll let me be a part of his inner world again. I guess it's a two-way street, though. I have to let him back into mine, too.

Maybe we have to grow back into that. We have to relearn how to trust each other. I just hope he's not lost to me forever.

A warm arm comes around my shoulder. "You look wistful. Do I need to go out and get some ice cream?" Adam whispers in my ear.

I laugh. It's weird how well he gets me.

"A piece of cake will do."

He's about to take his arm away to get me a piece, but I grab his hand to keep it there.

"Or just staying here and chilling for a little while."

"I can manage that. What's on your mind?"

"Change. How it can be good and bad, but either way, it's not always easy."

"Oh, so just some light thoughts for a party, then," he says, chuckling.

I turn to him and smile ruefully. "I guess one thing is clear. I suck at parties, huh?"

"I don't know . . . I seem to recall enjoying your SulkFest a great deal."

He's smiling and his lips are close enough to kiss if I just lean forward. It's so tempting I forget, for a hot second of insanity, that my entire family is in the next room.

It feels so right, but it turns out to be a bad mistake.

"Ooooh! Stella's got *a boyfriend*!" Rob shouts.

Seriously?

I feel my face start to flush, and I can't even look at Adam.

"Wait, is this the brother who asked me to 'act normal for a change' before opening the door to *his girlfriend*?"

It gives me great satisfaction to see my brother's face turn as red as mine feels.

I can't tell whose friends are laughing harder—Rob's or mine.

"How old are our kids again?" Mom asks Dad.

"As you're so fond of reminding me, you should know, you were there," Dad says, putting his arm around her and kissing her.

Mom laughs and kisses him back.

It feels good to see my family laugh again—even if they are the most embarrassing people on the planet.

Maybe laughter is the first step to making us whole again.

Roadrunner—

Remember that time when things were really bad and I was trying to imagine what a picnic would look like and I couldn't? When things were so bad that I thought I'd always be alone, and I'd always feel messed up, and it was hard to feel hope?

How long ago was that?

Well, guess what I did today?

I went on a picnic—with Caitlin and some friends from group and their significant others. We went to the mountains for a hike and picnicked at the top of a peak. The view was amazing. It was like watching a commercial, except it was actually my life with the sun shining and people laughing and I was able to be there, in the moment, having a good time for hours. We raised a toast to absent friends—and I thought of you and Reyes. I've been keeping in touch with the other guys in the squad. Some are doing better than others. But I think that we'll all make it from here. Even when we feel like our country isn't stepping up for us, we're doing our best to be there for each other.

Our yoga teacher (don't laugh, it's really helped) told us something this spiritual guy Ram Dass said: "We're all just walking each other home." We went to war and saw things that I wish we'd never had to see. Heard things I wish we'd never had to hear. Now, those of us who returned, we're all helping to walk each other home.

I wish you'd waited for us on the road, buddy.

I wish that every single day.

ThunderGeek out.

CHAPTER SEVENTEEN

Rob comes into my room late on Saturday night while I'm reading before bed. As usual, Peggy follows at his heels like his not-so-little lamb.

"Wanna take a road trip tomorrow?"

"Where to?"

"DC."

"What for?"

"I want to go to the Vietnam Veterans Memorial. Since we don't have a memorial for our war yet, I want to leave something for Reyes and Jason."

"Yeah. Sure," I say. "But . . . why are you asking me to come and not Caitlin? Or Jack?"

Rob sits on the bed and picks up my stuffed unicorn, which is worn and faded from so much love, and has stitches from the time our old dog, Cosmo, kidnapped him and used him as a chew toy.

"I just thought it might be good to spend some time together," he says. "You know, when we're not driving to school or sitting around the house."

I almost fall off my chair from shock.

"Wait—are you saying you actually *want* to spend time with me?" I say, not sure if I actually buy it. While I've always looked up to Rob, to him I've always been the tagalong baby sister, the one he resented having to babysit. And since he got home, it's obvious that hasn't changed.

"Don't act so surprised. I mean, yeah, you were a total pain in the butt when you were younger, but you've actually turned out to be pretty interesting."

"Is that another one of your heavily disguised compliments?"

Rob laughs. "See, that's what I'm talking about." He pats the bed next to him and Peggy jumps up to sit by his side.

"So what do you say? Road trip with Robbie?"

"As long as you promise not to punch anyone," I tell him. "I want to see the sights, not the inside of a police station."

"Punch? Me, Mr. Zen Yoga Dude?" Rob says. "Puh-leeze!"

So that's how Rob and I end up in the car heading up to DC bright and early the next morning, singing at the top our lungs. One thing is for sure: We're not going to be joining a band or a choir anytime soon. But what we lack in tunefulness, we make up in enthusiasm.

"Has Caitlin heard you sing yet?" I ask.

"Yeah, why?"

"And she's still willing to date you?"

"She thinks it's cute," Rob says.

"Love is inexplicable," I say, shaking my head.

"It is," he agrees.

"For the record, I just want to say that I like her."

"Noted," he says. "And appreciated."

"What made you want to visit the memorial now?" I ask. "Is there a special reason or . . ."

"I don't know. I just need to do something to honor them and I can't afford to go out to California to visit Reyes's grave or Wisconsin to visit Jason's. So I figure The Wall is the next best thing."

He drums his fingers on the steering wheel.

"I've got the appointment with the VA next week. I'm not going to jail. I've met someone who gets me. It feels like my life is opening up again. And I should be happy. I am happy. But I also feel guilty. Why me? Why am I the one who's here and not Reyes. I don't have a wife and a kid."

"But you have me. You have Mom and Dad."

"I know. But that's different."

"It wouldn't have felt different to us," I say, unable to catch the bitterness before it seeps out.

"Hey, I'm here, okay. And I know, but it was just . . . different."

"I get it," I say, even though I know I don't fully understand his demons around dying. "Why can't you get it through your thick skull how important you are to us and how much our life would suck without you?"

He takes one hand off the wheel and strokes the back of my head like he does to Peggy when she's upset.

"Because of said thick skull. But I need you to keep telling me the truth enough times that it finally gets through," he says. "You're one of the people I trust to tell it to me, Stella."

Trust is something I've been struggling with, too, because of what happened. Trust in the government that sent Rob and his fellow vets to fight and didn't provide enough for their care when they came home; trust in what to believe when it comes to the news; trust in politicians like Mayor Abbott, who were willing to take a situation and exploit it in ways that hurt innocent people like Farida's family, just for political gain; trust in my country, which has failed to live up to its ideals; trust in my town, which has been so easily divided; trust in friends who were so quick to think the worst of my family and Farida's without knowing all the facts. I understand a little why Rob felt like withdrawing from the world for a while. I'm even beginning to understand why Adam's dad's gone the doomsday prepper route, even if I don't agree with it. It's hard to stay present in the world when you look all around and don't know who or what you can believe in.

"You know Adam's dad is one of those survivalist prepper dudes, right?" I say.

"Yeah—to be honest, Adam surprised me," Rob says. "He's different from how I would have expected, having been raised that way."

"He loves his dad, but he doesn't agree with everything he thinks," I say.

"It happens to the best of us," Rob says. "That's part of growing up. Figuring out how and what to think for ourselves."

"In some ways I understand why Mr. Swann doesn't trust anything," I say. "I've had to question so much recently, it would be easy to just think everything is hopeless and there's no way to fix it and it's all going to end in a terrible apocalypse so we better prepare for it. Or else just give up and say YOLO or whatever and be selfish."

"But you don't. And that's what makes you and your friends so cool. It's also what surprised me about your Adam. That he's charting his own course. That takes guts when you're a junior in high school. I wouldn't have been that brave."

"He's not *my Adam*. He's . . . Adam."

"Okay, fine. Adam."

"You say you wouldn't have been that brave, but you enlisted while we were at war and you served two tours," I say. "That's brave."

"When *haven't* we been at war since the day you were born, Stella?" he says. "You read Orwell's *1984*. It's just a matter if the current enemy is Eurasia or Eastasia. They send guys like me over to fight and die and then what?"

"But you signed up. You fought. You had to face things that messed up your head," I say. "And now you're having to re-face all those awful things to help you recover. That's brave. Can't you just give yourself a break?"

He turns up the music. "That's what this is supposed to be—a break. Come on, sing it, kid."

Subject closed, it appears.

We park a mile and a half away from the Vietnam Veterans Memorial, but I don't care, because I'm excited to be on the streets of the capital. You'd think we'd come here more given that we live in Virginia, but I haven't been since my eighth-grade class trip. I don't mind the brisk air or even the wind when it blows off the Potomac River. I feel like all the questions I've been asking myself come to life right here in this city, and now I'm here, too.

We approach the monument, a long wall of black granite, like a sunken scar cut into the landscape of the park. Even though it's a cold December day, there are clusters of people searching for names, touching the smooth stone with trembling fingers, leaving flowers, flags, and notes.

Rob's brought two patches from his regiment and two small American flags to leave by The Wall. He's written a note for Reyes and one for Jason.

We walk slowly along the memorial, looking at all the tributes people have left. Every day they're collected and cataloged by the National Park Service. The hope is to someday display them in an education center, once enough money is raised to pay for that.

We continue to walk along The Wall, me trailing behind Rob. I run my fingers over the smooth granite and the rough cuts where names have been engraved. I'm suddenly overwhelmed by all the names sprawling before us, each of them someone who was loved, someone who is missed. There are more than fifty-eight thousand names here. And this is just one war. Before I go any deeper, Rob interrupts my internal spiral.

"I'll know when I've found the right place to leave these," Rob says. "I'll just get a feeling."

I know he can't see me, but I nod anyway, because my throat feels too tight to get out any words.

"No way. Walker? Is that you?"

I glance back from The Wall and see a well-built guy with dark hair in a buzz cut wearing a camo jacket, looking at my brother, arms outstretched.

"Widerski? How are you here? And standing?" My brother embraces the guy and I think they're never going to let go of each other. "I thought you were still at Walter Reed."

"I'm sprung. Head back to Indiana tomorrow. Oh, and I'm standing on my bionic legs," he says.

I realize that this Widerski must be Rob's friend Travis, the one who lost both his legs when he stepped on an IED.

Sure enough, my brother introduces us.

"Travis, this is my sister, Stella."

I put out my hand, but Travis embraces me in a bear hug.

"Little sister Stella. I've heard so much about you."

"Only the good things are true," I tell him.

"I've only heard good things," he says. "Hey, let's pull up a park bench and I'll show off my prosthetics."

"Hey, not in front of the minor," Rob says.

"I'll keep it G-rated," Travis promises him.

We head to the nearest bench. I watch Travis as he walks and I'm amazed, because if I didn't know he'd been a double amputee, I'd never guess he was walking on prosthetic legs.

After he sits, Travis rolls up the legs of his cargo pants. "Check out these sweet pieces of technology, my friends."

Underneath his pants he's got two high-tech prosthetic legs.

"These things are amazing," he says. "Sure, I'd rather have the real thing, but since that's not an option, I'm lucky to have these."

"A few more limbs and you're in Terminator territory," Rob says.

"Rob!" I smack his arm in horror that he'd even joke.

"It's cool, Stella. Dark humor is what kept us going," Travis says. "But I plan to keep the rest of the limbs I've got, thanks. Rehab has been brutal. I mean, everyone was amazing there, but I'm glad to be sprung."

Rob's right. I don't think I'll ever understand the way Mr. Meyers, or Travis, or Jack or another vet will. Maybe my job is to listen and be there, to be the sister he can always trust to tell him the truth as I see it.

"Maybe I should have lost a limb instead of just coming back with a messed-up head," Rob says. "Seems like they'd treat that faster and better."

Travis punches him in the arm, hard.

"Dude, I'm just as mad as you about Jason, and your situation sucks, but as sweet as these things are, I'd still rather have my legs."

"Sorry, man. That was a really stupid thing to say."

"Look, I get it. What's stupid is that I can get help and you're left to rot. It's not like it's a big secret that soldiers come back from combat mentally messed up. It's always happened. Every single war. They just called it by different names—nostalgia, soldier's heart, shell shock, battle fatigue, combat stress reaction . . . So why aren't they prepared?"

"That's what I keep asking," I say. "And no one has answers."

"At least you're asking," Travis says as he rolls down his pant legs. "Keep on asking. Squeaky wheels and all that."

"Do you think they'll ever build a monument for our dead?" Rob says. "For all of the Never-Ending War operations?"

"Would they include Jason?" I ask. "They should. Because he was a casualty of the war, too, even if he wasn't killed in combat."

"Good question. The Vietnam Veterans Memorial doesn't. It just lists people who died in combat or went missing in action and are presumed dead."

"Maybe we should create a monument for all our brothers- and sisters-in-arms who died by suicide," Rob says. "Might clarify the thinking of the folks down there."

He gestures with his thumb toward the opposite end of the Mall. We can't see them from here, because the Washington Monument is in the way, but if we keep walking all the way down, the White House is off to the left and the dome of the Capitol building rises from the horizon at the other end.

"They'll probably need more of us to be casualties before they'll fork out for a memorial for our wars," Travis says. "Or maybe we'll have to wait as long as the Korean War vets, in which case our memorial will go up in, like, fifty years."

"What about the tributes for Reyes and Jason?" I ask. "Where are we going to put them in the meantime?"

"Tributes for Reyes and Traitt?" Travis asks.

"Yeah. I've brought these." Rob shows him the flags and patches and folded notes. He wouldn't let me see what he'd written, and it looks like he's not going to show Travis either.

"I've got a spot," Travis says. We get up and he leads us to the January 1968 panel where he points out a name: John Doneski.

"The great-uncle I never met because he died before I was born," he says. "On my mom's side. He's the reason I came today. My middle name is John, after him."

Travis takes a small flag out of his pocket and places it carefully at the bottom of The Wall under his great-uncle's name. Rob puts the patches, flags, and notes for Guillermo Reyes and Jason Traitt next to the flag for John Doneski, who was killed in another long, seemingly endless war a half century earlier.

"We will never stop honoring you," Travis says.

"We will never forget you," Rob says.

"And we'll always remember that you fought for us, even if you didn't always know what we were fighting for," I say.

"And we'll miss you," Rob says, his voice breaking. "Always."

"Always," Travis echoes.

He and I both put our arms around Rob and the three of us

stand, huddled in quiet community and contemplation and grief, me for people I didn't know, but feel like I did, through my brother.

Rob stands up straight finally, and says, "Ten-hut!"

He and Travis salute The Wall and the mementos left for their fallen friends.

And then my brother puts his hand on my shoulder. "Stella, how about we take Travis to lunch and then head home? We've got some living to do."

I smile, overwhelmed with gratitude and happiness, because here at this memorial to the war dead, I know he's making a promise to me that he'll remain among the living. That even though the road ahead might be challenging, we will walk it together.

War changed my brother in ways I can't ever really understand, but finally, he is really beginning to come home.

I'm making a promise to him, too. I'm going to keep working with my friends, even though it's hard and messy, to move the country he's come home to closer to that ideal he fought for, the one I believe in, of liberty and justice for all. Because it can't happen without us.

ACKNOWLEDGMENTS

The poet John Donne wrote, "No man is an island, entire of itself." No woman is either, and that's especially true of writers. We do spend a lot of time alone thinking, wasting time on the internet in the guise of "research," and eventually writing, but this book is the product of a community.

It wouldn't even be a novel at all if not for my brilliant editor, Jody Corbett, who kept pushing me to go deeper. I handed her a rickety scaffold of ideas and themes, and she helped me craft it into a book.

I am so fortunate to work with Team Scholastic: David Levithan, Nina Goffi, Tracy van Straaten, Lizette Serrano, Emily Heddleson, Nikki Mutch, Robin Bailey Hoffman, Ann Marie Wong, Anna Swenson, Mariclaire Jastremsky, Donalyn Miller, and too many others to mention, all of whom who are dedicated to promoting literacy and a genuine love of reading.

Jennifer Laughran is an agent extraordinaire. I'm a lucky author.

Thank you to Steve Gifford, former Captain, Armor, US Army; Steve Kennedy, former airborne infantryman and founder of Vets Space; and Samantha Torres for patiently answering my research questions. Thanks also to my cousins Helene and Dr. Christopher

Kain, former Lt Commander USNR, Medical Corps, for their insights and research help. Above all, thanks to Rob "Robbie Rocker" Jordan, CMSgt, USAF (retired), to whom this book is dedicated, for getting me so angry about the treatment of our veterans that I had to write a book, and then constantly posting jokes that kept me laughing while I was doing it.

Dr. Kareem Adeeb of the American Institute for Islamic and Arabic Studies said, "Justice isn't for just us," at an interfaith rally in Stamford, Connecticut, in support of the people of Charlottesville, Virginia, following the white supremacist violence there. It resonated so strongly that I borrowed that phrase for Stella to use in her speech.

I'm incredibly grateful to Neesha Meminger and Dahlia Petrus for their careful and insightful readings. Their feedback was invaluable and only helped make this story stronger.

Thank you to Tejas Bhatt, assistant public defender, and to Meghan Smith and the ACLU of Connecticut for helping with my legal queries, and to Greg Goldstein, Greenwich High School student body president, for sharing insights about high school politics.

A long-distance bear hug to Maura Keaney for her quick answers about political campaign issues in Virginia, but most of all for her wisdom and friendship.

Love and an upraised solidarity fist to the attendees of Kindling Words East 2017 and to the Shenanigals for reminding me that words don't just matter, they can change the world.

My beloved children, Josh and Amie, make me proud and give me hope for the future. My husband, Hank, is a rock of stability in a crazy world. My extended family provides a circle of love. Special thanks to Dylan Davis, for keeping Auntie Sarah up to date on gaming.

My parents, Susan and Stanley Darer, have passed, but I felt their presence strongly as I wrote this book. They instilled values of curiosity and empathy, of citizenship and service, and they impressed upon me that the United States exists as part of a wider world. Whatever I have achieved in life is built on absorbing their values, and those of my ancestors. In Hebrew we say: L'Dor v'dor—from generation to generation.

Last, and certainly not least, thank you, dear readers. As a political writer I've been bombarded by hate speech, which can make it hard to be brave. Your letters and emails give me the strength and courage to keep going. Stella is right: It can't happen without you.